Robert Etheridge, Charles E. De Rance

The Superficial Geology of the Country Adjoining the Coasts of Southwest Lancashire

comprised in sheet 90, quarter sheet 91 S. W., parts of 89 N. W. and S. W., 79 N. E.

and 91 S. E., of the 1 inch geological survey map of England and Wales

Robert Etheridge, Charles E. De Rance

The Superficial Geology of the Country Adjoining the Coasts of Southwest Lancashire
comprised in sheet 90, quarter sheet 91 S. W., parts of 89 N. W. and S. W., 79 N. E. and 91 S.
E., of the 1 inch geological survey map of England and Wales

ISBN/EAN: 9783337328818

Printed in Europe, USA, Canada, Australia, Japan

Cover: Foto ©Andreas Hilbeck / pixelio.de

More available books at **www.hansebooks.com**

MEMOIRS OF THE GEOLOGICAL SURVEY

OF

ENGLAND AND WALES.

THE

SUPERFICIAL GEOLOGY

OF THE

COUNTRY ADJOINING THE COASTS OF SOUTH-WEST LANCASHIRE,

COMPRISED IN SHEET 90, QUARTER SHEET 91 S.W., PARTS OF 89 N.W. AND S.W., 79 N.E., AND 91 S.E., OF THE 1-INCH GEOLOGICAL SURVEY MAP OF ENGLAND AND WALES.

BY

C. E. DE RANCE, F.G.S.

THE LISTS OF FOSSILS REVISED BY R. ETHERIDGE, F.R.S.

PUBLISHED BY ORDER OF THE LORDS COMMISSIONERS OF HER MAJESTY'S TREASURY.

LONDON:
PRINTED FOR HER MAJESTY'S STATIONERY OFFICE.

PUBLISHED BY

LONGMANS & Co.

AND BY

EDWARD STANFORD, CHARING CROSS, S.W.

1877.

THE GEOLOGICAL MAPS OF ENGLAND AND WALES.

On the scale of one inch to a mile.

(With explanatory Horizontal and Vertical Sections, and Memoirs.)

COMPLETED COUNTIES.

For further particulars see the detailed List of the separate Sheets in the Survey Catalogue.

The sheets marked * have Descriptive Memoirs.
Those marked † are illustrated by general Memoirs.

ANGLESEY,—sheets 77 (N), 78. Horizontal Sections, sheet 40.
BEDFORDSHIRE,—sheets 46 (NW, NE, SW†, & SE†), 52 (NW, NE, SW, & SE).
BERKSHIRE,—sheets 7*, 8†, 12*, 13*, 34*, 45 (SW*). Horizontal sections, sheets 59, 71, 72, 80.
BRECKNOCKSHIRE,—sheets 36, 41, 42, 56 (NW & SW), 67 (NE & SE). Horizontal Sections, sheets 4, 5, 6, 11; and Vertical Sections, sheets 4 and 10.
BUCKINGHAMSHIRE,—7*, 13*, 45* (NE, SE), 46 (NW, SW†), 52 (SW). Horizontal Sections 74, 79.
CARMARTHENSHIRE,—37, 38, 40, 41, 42 (NW & SW), 56 (SW), 57 (SW & SE). Horizontal Sections 2, 3, 4, 7, 8, 9; and Vertical Sections 3, 4, 5, 6, 13, 14.
CAERNARVONSHIRE,—74 (NW), 75, 76, 77 (N), 78, 79 (NW & SW). Horizontal Sections 28, 31, 40.
CARDIGANSHIRE,—40, 41, 56 (NW), 57, 58, 59 (SE), 60 (SW). Horizontal Sections 4, 5, 6.
CHESHIRE,—73 (NE & NW), 79 (NE & SE), 80, 81 (NW* & SW*), 88 (SW). Horizontal Sections 18, 43, 44, 60, 64, 65, 67, 70.
CORNWALL,—24†, 25†, 26†, 29†, 30†, 31†, 32†, & 33†.
DENBIGH,—73 (NW), 74, 75 (NE), 78 (NE & SE), 79 (NW, SW, & SE), 80 (SW). Horizontal Sections 31, 35, 38, 39, 43, 44; and Vertical Sections, sheet 24.
DERBYSHIRE,—62 (NE), 63 (NW), 71 (NW, SW, & SE), 72 (NE, SE), 81, 82, 88 (SW, SE). Horizontal Sections 18, 46, 60, 61, 69, 70.
DEVONSHIRE,—20†, 21†, 22†, 23†, 24†, 25†, 26†, & 27†. Horizontal Sections, sheet 19.
  † The Geology of the Counties of Cornwall and Devon is fully illustrated by Sir H. De la Beche's "Report." 8vo. 14s.
DORSETSHIRE,—15, 16, 17, 18, 21, 22. Horizontal Sections, sheets 19, 20, 21, 22, 56; Vertical Sections, sheet 22.
FLINTSHIRE,—74 (NE), 79. Horizontal Sections, sheet 43.
GLAMORGANSHIRE,—20, 36, 37, 41 & 42 (SE & SW). Horizontal Sections, sheets 7, 8, 9, 10, 11; and Vertical Sections, sheets 2, 4, 5, 6, 7, 9, 10, 47.
GLOUCESTERSHIRE,—19, 34*, 35, 43 (NE, SW, & SE), 44*. Horizontal Sections 12, 13, 14, 15, 59; and Vertical Sections 7, 11, 15, 46, 47, 48, 49, 50, 51.
HAMPSHIRE,—8†, 9, 10*, 11, 12*, 14, 15, 16. Horizontal Section, sheet 80.
HEREFORDSHIRE,—42 (NE & SE), 43, 55, 56 (NE & SE). Horizontal Sections 5, 13, 27, 30, 34; and Vertical Sections, sheet 15.
KENT,—1† (SW & SE), 2†, 3†, 4*, 5, 6†. Horizontal Sections, sheets 77 and 78.
MERIONETHSHIRE,—59 (NE & SE), 60 (NW), 74, 75 (NE & SE). Horizontal Sections, sheets 26, 28, 29, 31, 32, 35, 37, 38, 39.
MIDDLESEX,—1† (NW & SW), 7*, 8†. Horizontal Sections, sheet 79.
MONMOUTHSHIRE,—35, 36, 42 (SE & NE), 43 (SW). Horizontal Sections, sheets 5 and 12; and Vertical Sections, sheets 8, 9, 10, 12.
MONTGOMERYSHIRE,—56 (NW), 59 (NE & SE), 60, 74 (SW & SE). Horizontal Sections, sheets 26, 27, 29, 30, 32, 34, 35, 36, 38, 107.
NORTHAMPTONSHIRE, 64, 45 (NW and NE), 46 (NW), 52 (NW, NE, & SW), 63 (NE, SW, & SE), 63 (SE), 64.
OXFORDSHIRE,—7*, 13*, 34* 44*, 45*, 53 (SE*, SW*). Horizontal Sections, sheets 71, 72, 81, 82.
PEMBROKESHIRE,—38, 39, 40, 41, 58. Horizontal Sections, sheets 1 and 2; and Vertical Sections, sheets 12 and 13.
RADNORSHIRE,—42 (NW & NE), 56, 60 (SW & SE). Horizontal Sections, sheets 5, 6, 27.
RUTLANDSHIRE,—this county is included in sheet 64.
SHROPSHIRE,—55 (NW, NE), 56 (NE), 60 (NW, SE), 61, 62 (NW), 73, 74, (NE, SE). Horizontal Sections, sheets 24, 25, 30, 33, 34, 36, 41, 44, 45, 53, 54, 56; and Vertical Sections, sheets 23, 24.
SOMERSETSHIRE,—18, 19, 20, 21, 27, 35. Horizontal Sections, sheets 15, 16, 17, 20, 21, 22, 103, 104, & 105; and Vertical Sections, sheets 12, 46, 47, 48, 49, 50, & 51.
STAFFORDSHIRE,—54 (NW), 55 (NE), 61 (NE, SE), 62, 63 (NW), 71 (SW), 72, 73 (NE, SE), 81 (SE, SW). Horizontal Sections 18, 23, 24, 25, 41, 42, 45, 49, 54, 57, 58, 60; and Vertical Sections 16, 17, 18, 19, 20, 21, 23, 26.
SURREY,—1 (SW†), 6†, 7*, 8†, 9. Horizontal Sections, sheets 74, 75, 76, & 79.
SUSSEX,—4*, 5, 6, 8, 9, 11. Horizontal Sections, sheets 73, 75, 76, 77, 78.
WARWICKSHIRE,—44*, 45 (NW), 53*, 54, 62 (NE, SW, & SE), 63 (NW, SW, & SE). Horizontal Sections, sheets 23, 48, 49, 50, 51, 82, 83; and Vertical Sections, sheet 21.
WILTSHIRE,—12*, 13*, 14, 15, 18, 19, 34*, & 35. Horizontal Sections, sheets 15 & 59.
WORCESTERSHIRE,—43 (NE), 44*, 54, 55, 62 (SW & SE), 61 (SE). Horizontal Sections 13, 23, 25, 56, & 59; and Vertical Section 15.

FRONTISPIECE.

Fig. 18.

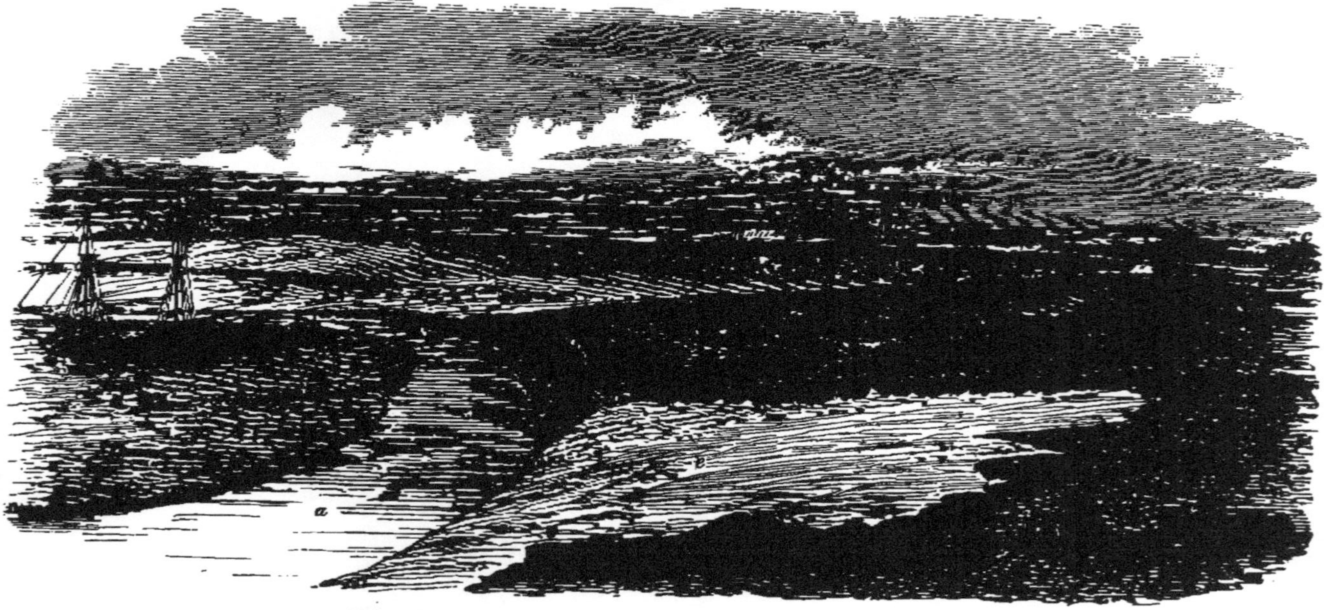

Submerged Forest, at the Mouth of the River Alt (*see* p. 64).

a. River Alt. *b.* Old Light-house. *c.* Sand Dunes. *d.* Peat with trunks of trees. *e.* Grey clay.

MEMOIRS OF THE GEOLOGICAL SURVEY

OF

ENGLAND AND WALES.

THE

SUPERFICIAL GEOLOGY

OF THE

COUNTRY ADJOINING THE COASTS OF SOUTH-WEST LANCASHIRE,

COMPRISED IN SHEET 90, QUARTER SHEET 91 S.W., PARTS OF 89 N.W. AND S.W., 79 N.E., AND 91 S.E., OF THE 1-INCH GEOLOGICAL SURVEY MAP OF ENGLAND AND WALES.

BY

C. E. DE RANCE, F.G.S.

THE LISTS OF FOSSILS REVISED BY R. ETHERIDGE, F.R.S.

PUBLISHED BY ORDER OF THE LORDS COMMISSIONERS OF HER MAJESTY'S TREASURY.

LONDON:
PRINTED FOR HER MAJESTY'S STATIONERY OFFICE.

PUBLISHED BY

LONGMANS & Co.

AND BY

EDWARD STANFORD, CHARING CROSS, S.W.

1877.

[*Price Seventeen Shillings.*]

Reduced to 10/6.

CONTENTS.

THE following Memoir by Mr. C. E. De Rance is specially devoted to the Superficial Deposits of that part of Lancashire that lies between the Mersey and the Ribble, though in the introductory chapter some useful notices are introduced of adjoining districts as far north as the country east and north of Morecambe Bay, and as far south as the estuary of the Dee.

In the two first chapters the various members of the Glacial Deposits are described, and the remainder of the Memoir is chiefly devoted to the description of the Post-Glacial Deposits.

Availing himself of the work of preceding writers, in addition to his own minute knowledge of the country, the Author has been able to produce a more complete account of its Superficial Geology than has heretofore been given in any single Memoir. The list of fossils at the end forms a valuable table of reference, all the more so that at a glance the reader can see where and in what divisions of the Glacial Deposits the species have been found.

ANDREW C. RAMSAY,

8th September 1876.   Director General.

34644.   Wt. 4387.   A 3

NOTICE.

THE Drift shown on the maps to which this Memoir refers was surveyed by Mr. C. E. De Rance, with the exception of parts of 89 N.W., which were mapped by Messrs. Tiddeman and Shelswell.

The Memoir has been written by Mr. De Rance to supply a fuller and more detailed description of the Superficial or Drift Deposits of South-western Lancashire, than that contained in the short account of them which has been already given in the published Explanation of maps 90 S.E. and N.E., and 91 S.W.

The drift-covered area of the country immediately to the east, in parts of maps 89 N.W. and S.W., and 91 S.E., is so intimately connected with that lying nearer the coast, that it has been considered necessary to describe both those areas together.

The Memoir, to a certain extent, shows the connection between the Drift Deposits of the country around Manchester, (which is comprised in quarter-sheets 81 N.W., 88 S.W., and 89 S.E., mapped by Professor E. Hull,) and those on the sea-coast (in maps 91 S.W., 90 N.E., and 90 S.E.): thus describing all the Superficial Deposits between the Mersey and the Ribble.

In order to make this Memoir more useful, short abstracts are given of the more important papers on the Superficial Geology of the district (including those describing the Drift Deposits around Manchester) that have been published in the Transactions of various societies.

The lists of fossils have been revised by Mr. Etheridge, F.R.S.

H. W. BRISTOW,

Senior Director.

Geological Survey Office,
   28, Jermyn Street, London, S.W.,
      30th June 1876.

SUPERFICIAL GEOLOGY OF SOUTH-WEST LANCASHIRE.

CHAPTER I.

PHYSICAL GEOGRAPHY OF THE DISTRICT, AND FORM OF THE GROUND BENEATH THE GLACIAL DEPOSITS.

THE area described in this Memoir embraces the low-lying drift-covered plains lying between the estuaries of the Mersey and the Lune, bounded westward by the sea, and eastward by the hills or "Fells," which, rising abruptly above the plains, cut off to a great extent the easterly extension of both glacial and post-glacial drift deposits. These however, in the southern portion of the area described, are deflected eastward, following the lines of the valley of the river Mersey and its tributaries to their sources amongst the Fells of the Pennine dividing ridge, where an extent of country above the 500 feet contour line of the Ordnance Survey occurs in the basins of the rivers Mersey and Ribble of not less than 500 square miles.

The Mersey has a drainage area of 885 square miles ; the rainfall at Manchester being 42·5 inches, at Rochdale 40·8, and at Bolton 43·4.

The Weaver and estuary of the Mersey have an area of 711 square miles, with a rainfall at Runcorn Gap of 29·1 inches.

The Alt drains 126 square miles, with a rainfall of 27·4.

Small streams and artificial drains at Southport take off the rainfall of 55 square miles, which amounts to 20·7 inches.

The Douglas, 168 miles, with a rainfall at Ormskirk of 30·4 inches.

The Ribble drains 585 square miles; the rainfall at Preston being 34·2, at Ribchester 36·1, on the Hodder 47·0 inches.

The Wyre takes off the drainage of 208 square miles, with a rainfall in its upper reaches of 44·6; only 31·0 falling at Blackpool, which may be considered as occupying a small drainage area of its own, about 2 square miles in extent ; while the rain which falls between Lytham and Southshore drains into the Ribble, and that falling at Poulton-le-Fylde into the Wyre.

Between the mouths of the Wyre and Lune several small streams, of a more or less artificial character, take off the drainage of the low-lying peat tracts of Pilling and Rawcliffe Moss.

There is an entire absence of cliffs of rock in the coast line of the peninsula of Wirral, with the one exception of the Red Noses, where red beds of the Upper Mottled Sandstone, slightly capped by Boulder Clay, abruptly dip towards the Mersey. The bottom of much of that river probably consists of Boulder Clay resting on the rock, as the base of the boulder beds at Codling Gap, near Egremont, are not seen at low water ; and Boulder

Clay is also seen on the Liverpool side of the Mersey, dipping down in pre-glacial hollows in the rock below the level of the tides.

Northward from Liverpool, the older rocks never appear on the coast until the estuary of the Lune is reached, where a low cliff of Permian Red Sandstone, capped by Upper Boulder Clay, forms a small promontory jutting into the sea, on which stand the ruins of Cockerham Abbey, and some shattered tombstones of Knights of the Temple. Large boulders of Volcanic Breccia and Trap, derived from the Lake District, resting directly on the rock, lie scattered between the tide marks, attesting the former seaward extension of the cliff, which has evidently been much denuded since the erection of the Abbey, some of the remaining walls projecting over the edge and crumbling daily into the sea. At Heysham, a few miles north of the Lune and of the area described in this Memoir, glacial striæ occur beneath a Boulder Clay, which, I think, is higher than the Sand and Shingle of Carnforth.

In the centre of the area occupied by the Garstang sheet (91 S.E.), Grit hills from 200 to 600 feet in height occupy a zone of country intervening between the Plain of Glacial Drift and the High Fells, rising to more than 1,700 feet ; while on either side of the Ribble valley to the south these Fells rise at once abruptly from the drift-covered rock-plane below, which occupies even a lower level relatively to the sea than it does further north. This intermediate range of low flanking hills, from thus occupying the space where the Boulder Drift should have been, causes the Glacial Deposits to be sparsely represented in this portion of the district (the hills being barely covered), and the drift plain to terminate at 180 feet above the sea, instead of at nearly 600. This is more and more the case in advancing to the north, the hills gradually approaching the existing coast line, until at Hest Bank the Drift Plain commences at the sea, and ends within a mile against the hills ; and at Warton Crag, beyond Carnforth, it has disappeared altogether. Glacial Drift, to the north and west, nearly surrounds the hills and fills up the valleys, the tops of the hills and mountains being bare of drift, as in the country around Ormskirk and Wigan to the *south* of the plain ; while, in the great drift plain extending from north of Ormskirk to south of Lancaster, the crests of the hills are the exact points where the drift is thickest.

Form of the Ground beneath the Glacial Deposits. — It is probable that the drift only exhibits the phenomenon of a smooth inclined plain dipping towards the sea, where it rests upon a similar plane of rock beneath; and that where the original "rock-surface" was undulating, the drift has merely filled in the hollows, most of which have been in great measure re-excavated by modern stream action. Examples of this are seen in the spur of the Penine chain, called by Professor Hull the Pendle range, part of which runs along the south-eastern edge of the area now under review. The inclined plain of Glacial Drift probably owes its origin to being deposited during subsidence upon an old rock plain of marine denudation, the eastern limit of which forms a bay running from near Rufford, by Eccleston, Euxton, Bamber Bridge, Samelsbury, and the Ribble valley, in the direction of Ribchester, and thence westward by

Broughton, Garstang, and Cockerham to the sea ; westward of which line the rock surface is either little above, at, and often below the existing sea-level, in which, from the superposition of Glacial Drifts, the surface of the country is often 170 feet above it.

Through extensive denudation, in comparatively recent times, the glacial beds form a great terrace around the high grounds of North Wales, East and North Lancashire, and running up the great valleys. The great denudation that produced the low-lying plains, at or beneath high-water mark, must have come into operation before the deposition of the earliest glacial deposits, as the rocks are scratched and covered with the drift-beds known in Lancashire as the Lower Boulder Clay, and Middle Sands.

In the north of the Hundred of Wirral, the southern limit of the low-lying plain of Birket is formed by an abrupt cliff cutting off all those numerous longitudinal valleys which run with the strike of the New Red rocks; of which latter tract the district ca led Wallasey is a portion, separated from the rest by the transverse valley, at the bottom of which flows Wallasey Pool.

In this low-lying plain, the base of the Boulder Clay is not seen at the lowest low-water mark, from the rock surface beneath the glacial deposits being below low-water mark. The denudation that removed the longitudinal ridge and valleys was evidently pre-glacial, as Boulder Clay lies on the plain and partially fills up the valleys. Traces of one of these old denuded ridges remain in its submarine ridge of rocks, culminating in Hilbre Island in the Dee.

In the valley of the Ribble above Preston none of the deep brook "cloughs" or dales of the district are as yet cut sufficiently deep to expose any section of the Pebble Beds, except in Bezza Brook, east of Samelsbury Hall, in the immediate neighbourhood of the Ribble plain, which, as well as that of its tributary the Darwen, is cut down as low as high-water mark near the junction of the two rivers. The rock forms a flat uniform surface, extending under the drift plains as well as under the alluvial flat, as shown in the following diagram.

Fig. 1.

S.W.

West of Penwortham
House.

R. Ribble.

N.E.

Preston
South Meadow Lane.

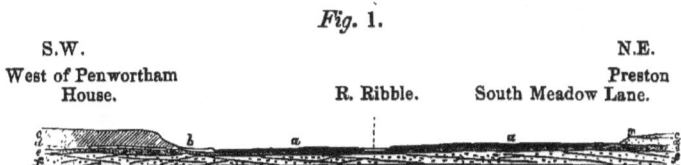

Section across the Plain of the Ribble.

a. a. Alluvium.	*b.* Old Alluvial Terrace.
c. c. Upper Boulder Clay.	*d. d.* Middle Sand.
e. e. Lower Boulder Clay.	*f. f.* Pebble Beds (Bunter).

From the above it will be seen that it is in the drift deposits only that the river Ribble at Preston has excavated its valley; a channel being cut in the rock to a slight depth, only at a few points, where the original surface of the rock rose above the level of the inclined plane, representing the lowest possible " gradient of fall " attainable by the river so long as the sea retains its present level,—a gradient which it has already reached, its denuding powers being confined to lateral denudation of the banks bounding the river, and to the wearing back here and there of the bluffs forming the limits of the valley. The rock-surface slopes from the land towards the sea, but the gradient of its fall being rather steeper than that of the river bed, causes the rock to be more and more exposed in the river banks in advancing inland from Preston.

Seawards and westwards the river bed is nearly level and tidal, while the slope of the rock-surface continues, never permitting the base of the Glacial Drifts to be seen in the coast lines of the area lying between the Mersey and the Wyre, the rock-surface being 50 or 60 feet beneath high-water mark.

In October 1836 a series of borings* and other observations were carried out by the late Mr. P. Park, of Preston, and Messrs. R. Stephenson and Son, for " the Ribble Navigation Company," the results of which are given in abstract in the following tables, the observations being recorded on a continuous levelled section from the sea at Lytham up to Brockholes Bridge, above Preston ; the high-water line being taken from the actual rise of the tide opposite the striped buoy at Lytham, on the 20th September, at Lytham being 19·1 feet, and at Ashton Wharf, Preston, 6 feet. These borings, made every 100 yards apart from Penwortham Bridge to the sea, prove the rock-surface of the Ribble bed under the shingle and alluvial loam, though never rising above a gradual sloping plain from the sea towards the land, to be extremely unequal, worn, and rugged beneath it, rising into banks or ridges, bare of shingle, or only covered with very thin deposits of sand and silt, and at other times sinking into hollows occupied by the three or four different alluvial beds, which cover patches of Lower Boulder Clay ; thus tending to prove that the worn appearance of this rock-floor of the river-bed is due to pre-glacial denudation.

	Feet above the base.
The level of the Ribble at Brockholes Bridge was	53¼
The level below the bridge at high tide - -	46
The level of the river below the bridge at low tide	44½
The level of the bed of the river at the same point - - - -	36
The level of a freshet at Walton Bridge -	58¾
The level of the bed of the river, junction of river Darwen - -	38
The level of high-water - -	46
The level of low-water - -	43
The level of Tramroad Bridge - -	55½
The level of high-water at Tramroad Bridge -	46
The level of low-water at Tramroad Bridge	43
The level of the bed of the river at this point -	41½
Low-water at Preston Wharf	39¾
The level of high-water at Penwortham Bridge -	46
The level of low-water at Penwortham Bridge -	42
The level of extremely high tide, Dec. 31st, 1833	55½
The level of Liverpool Road adjacent - -	50¾
Boring No. 1. was made in the river, rock being reached at 8 feet.	

* Kindly communicated to me by B. Sykes, Esq., of the firm of Messrs. Garlick, Park, and Sykes, C.E.

Miles from Brockholes Bridge, E. of Preston.	Number of Boring.	Level below Preston Low-water Mark.	Strata.	High-water Line.	Low-water Line.	Level of Land.	Remarks.
1	1	0	Gravel 5 feet, Rock 5 feet -	—	—	—	
2	2	2½	„ „ „ „ „ „ -	—	—	—	
3	3	„	„ „ „ „ „ „ - -	—	—	—	
4	4	„	„ 8 „ „ „ „ - -	—	—	—	
5	5	„	„ 3½ „ „ 8 „ - -	—	—	—	
—	6	„	„ 7 „ „ 3 „ -	—	—	—	
—	7	0	„ 8½ „ „ 2½ „ - -	—	—	—	
—	9-28	2½	„ 12½ „ „ not reached -	—	—	—	
—	29	1	Sand 5 feet, Gravel 6 feet - -	—	—	—	
—	30	3	„ 5 „ „ 4 „ - -	—	—	—	
—	31	„	Gravel 1 feet, Sand 4 feet, Gravel 3 ft.	—	—	—	
—	32	2½	„ 3 „ „ 3 „ „ 2 „	—	—	—	
—	33	2	„ 2½ „ „ 3 „ „ 3 „	—	—	—	
—	34	2	Sand 5½ feet, Gravel 5 feet, Rock 1 ft.	46	39½	—	
—	35	1	„ 4 „ „ 2½ „ „ 4½ „	—	—	—	
—	36	2	„ 2 „ „ 2 „ „ 6 „	—	—	—	
—	37	—	„ 8 „ „ 2 „ „ 5 „	—	—	—	
—	38	—	„ 0 „ „ 1½ „ „ 0 „	—	—	—	
—	39	2	„ 3½ „ „ 0 „ „ 0 „	—	—	—	
—	40	1	„ 5½ „ „ 0 „ „ 4 „	—	—	—	
—	42	2½	„ 7½ „ „ 0 „ „ 1 „	—	—	—	
—	43	3	„ 4½ „ „ 0 „ „ 3 „	—	—	—	Low water same as sea low-water.
—	44	4½	„ 0 „ „ 0 „ „ 9 „	46	—	—	At 45 bore-hole Dec. 18, 1833, high-water 55 feet at Preston Wharf.
at 47½	49	4½	„ 0½ „ „ 0 „ „ 9 „	—	—	—	
—	50	3	„ 4 „ „ 0 „ „ 5 „	—	—	—	
—	56	7½	„ 3½ „ „ 0 „ „ 4 „	—	—	—	Opposite lane to Pilkington's.
—	58	3	Gravel 2 feet, Sand 0 feet, Rock 6 ft.	—	—	—	
—	60	9	„ 1½ „ „ 2½ „ „ 2 „	—	—	—	
—	62	8½	„ 0½ „ „ 4½ „ „ 7 „	—	—	—	
—	64	1½	„ 9 „ „ 0 „ „ 3 „	—	—	—	
6	65	2½	„ 5 „ „ 9 „ „ 0 „	—	—	—	
—	68	4½	„ 0 „ „ 8 „ „ 0 „	—	—	—	Opposite Quarry.
—	70	2½	„ 0 „ „ 9 „ „ 0 „	—	—	—	
—	71	1½	„ 0 „ „ 6 „ Clay 7 „	—	—	—	
—	72	3½	Sand 1½ „ Gravel 5 „ Rock 5 „	—	—	—	
—	73	5½	„ 7½ „ „ 0 „ „ 2 „	—	—	—	
—	74	4	„ 3½ „ „ 2 „ „ 4 „	—	—	—	
—	75	3	„ 7½ „ „ 0 „ „ 5 „	—	—	—	
—	77	—	„ 15 „ „ 0 „ „ 0 „	—	—	—	
—	79	3	„ 0 „ „ 10 „ „ 0 „	—	—	—	Sands and Gravels.
½	82	—	„ 9 „ „ 8 „ „ 0 „	—	—	—	
—	86	2	Loam 1 foot, Sand 10 feet -	—	—	—	Boundary of Ashton and Lea.
—	87	3	Loamy Sand, 8 feet - - -	—	—	—	
—	88	1	„ 4 „ Gravel 5 feet -	—	—	—	Mound of Gravel.
—	90	1½	„ 10 „ „ 0 „ -	—	—	—	
—	91	3	„ 1 „ „ 10 „ -	—	—	—	
7	92½	6	„ 3 „ „ 3 „ -	—	—	—	Pot-hole.
—	93	—	———	—	—	—	Gravel thins out.
7½	101½	8	Sand 5 feet - -	46½	—	40	Lea and Clifton Savick Brook.
—	109½	8½	„ 6 „ - -	—	—	—	
8	110½	9½	„ 6 „ - - - -	—	—	—	
9	128	6	„ 11 „ - - - -	—	35½	—	
9½	137½	5½	„ 9 „ - - -	—	—	—	
—	138	—	„ 6 „ Clay 3 feet -	—	—	—	
—	142	6½	„ 1½ „ Gravel 7 „ - -	—	—	—	
—	143	6	„ 8½ „ „ 0 „ - -	—	35	—	
10	145½	7	„ 8 „ „ 0 „ - -	—	—	—	
10½	154	9	„ 8 „ „ 0 „ - -	—	33½	—	
11	163	8½	„ 9 „ „ 9 „ - -	—	32½	—	
—	169	9½	„ 0 „ „ 1 „ - -	—	—	—	
—	170	9	„ 0 „ 9 „ - -	—	—	—	
—	171	9½	„ 7 „ 2 „ -	—	—	—	
—	173	9½	„ 0½ „ 9 „ - -	—	—	—	
—	174	10	„ 4½ „ 4 „ - -	—	—	—	
12	180½	11	„ 4 „ 3 „ Clay 1 feet -	—	30½	—	Freckleton Pool.
—	185	10½	„ 2½ „ 0 „ „ 5 „	—	—	—	
—	197	12½	„ 7½ „ 0 „ „ 0½ „	—	—	—	
13	198	12½	„ 10 „ - - - -	46½	28½	—	
—	199	—	———	—	—	—	
—	202	13½	———	—	—	—	
—	203	—	———	—	—	—	Clay thins out.
13½	206½	—	„ 9 „ Sandy Gravel, 4 feet -	—	—	—	
—	208	—	„ 0 „ „ 9 „ -	—	—	—	
—	213	—	„ 0 „ „ 10 „ -	—	—	—	
—	214	—	„ 8½ „ „ 0½ „ -	—	—	—	

Miles from Brook-holes Bridge, R. of Preston.	Number of Boring.	Level below Preston Low-water Mark.	Strata.	High-water Line.	Low-water Line.	Level of Land.	Remarks.
14	215½	15	Sand 9 ft., Sandy Gravel 0 feet	—	27¾	—	
—	221	—	Gravel Mound	—	—	—	
—	224	—	„	—	—	—	
—	225	15	Sand 9 ft., Sandy Gravel 0 ft., Clay ½ ft.	—	—	—	
15	233	16	„ 0 „ „ 0 „ „ 12 „	—	25½	—	
—	241	17½	„ 1½ „ { Gravel 8 ft., Clay 1 ft. / Red Gravel 3 feet }	—	--	—	Bank of gravel against sand.
16	250	19	„ 0 „ -	—	22½	—	
—	256	17½	„ 0 „ Clay, 1 foot	—	—	—	
—	257	17	„ 4 „ „ 2½ „	—	—	—	
—		18½	„ 7 „ „ 2 „	—	—	—	
—		16	„ 11 „ „ 0 „	—	—	—	
16¼	—		Striped Buoy at Lytham	—	21·37	—	

Following the old pre-glacial coast line of Heysham and Bannister Hall, from Rufford by Scarisbrick, Formby, and Bootle to the Mersey, it is found to run up the valley of that river for a considerable distance, and does not appear to be connected with old lines of escarpment which form the southern limit of the Birket plain in the promontory of Wirral. The observations that have been taken from borings, made to great depths through the Glacial Drift between Birkenhead and Runcorn, prove that the bottom of the Mersey valley had a far greater depth than at present obtains, the trough being filled up with nearly 200 feet of Glacial Drift, the surface of which is but little above high-water mark.

Mr. M. Reade has shown, from the examination of a large number of journals of borings and wells made at various points along the banks of Mersey* between Warrington and New Brighton, that this river runs over an old pre-glacial valley, now filled up with Glacial Drift deposits ; that the centre of this old depression lay to north of the present river at Runcorn, so that the river ran through part of Widnes, on the Lancashire side, instead of through Runcorn Gap, as at present; the old bed of the river (?) being 115 feet below the Ordnance datum line, 87 at Warrington Bridge, and 100 feet below it at Sankey Bridge.

Westward of Widnes, at Hooton, the rock surface was reached at 65 feet below Ordnance datum line ; at Tranmere it was reached at 44 feet, Canada Dock 44·15, Garston Dock about 5 feet. Entrance of Wallasey Pool about west side of Pool 50 feet, Wallasey Water-works, 57 feet, Beaufort Street 69 feet, Livingston Street 115 feet, Leasowe Castle 180 feet.

From these borings it would appear that the surface of the rock valley is lower near Widnes than at Birkenhead nearer to the sea, and the existing bed of the stream opposite Princes Dock is slightly lower than the rock-bed beneath the glacial beds under Wallasey Pool, the latter sloping in both directions towards the Mersey and towards Leasowe.

---

* "Buried Valley of the Mersey ;" by T. Mellard Reade, C.E., F.G.S. Liverpool, Proc. Lit. Phil. Soc. 1872.

GLACIAL DRIFT DEPOSITS.

TILL AND LOWER BOULDER CLAY.

In that portion of the district lying at elevations of 200 feet and more above the sea the threefold division is maintained by the substitution of a bed of dark-grey clay, with sub-angular fragments of local rocks without sea-shells, for the ordinary marine Lower Boulder Clay.

A good section of this dark leaden-coloured clay, or Till, was exposed during the construction of the Chorley and Blackburn Railway at Brinscall in 1868. The included fragments of dark Carboniferous Limestone and other rocks would appear to have been transported from the Bolland district, through the Roddlesworth valley. Thirteen feet of the clay was exposed in the cutting beneath the Middle Sand and Shingle and the Upper Boulder Clay.

Fig. 2.

W.N.W.   E.S.E.

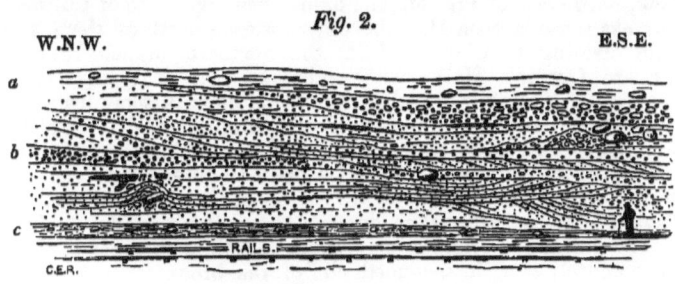

Section at Brinscall Railway Station.

a. Upper Boulder Clay.
b. Middle drift, sand, and large shingle.
c. Till.

I noticed a clay in 1870,* very similar in the manner of its occurrence to the above at the Little Ormes Head, Llandudno. It contained fragments of rocks derived from the valley of the Conway to the south, and its surface was mammillated and water-worn, and overlaid by Lower Boulder Clays and Middle Sands, with marine shells, capped with Upper Boulder Clay; so that it would appear that this Till with local fragments is of older date than the Marine Lower Boulder Clay.

LOWER BOULDER CLAY.—Between Liverpool and Ormskirk a considerable area of Boulder Clay occurs; but from the absence of the Middle Sand, it is difficult to identify its geological position; it most probably belongs to the Lower Boulder Clay.

Undoubted Lower Boulder Clay is well seen in a cutting near the Preston Waggon Works at Marsh End, where it underlies the Middle Sand and Upper Boulder Clay. It is of reddish-brown colour, and contains numerous stones and boulders, chiefly derived from the Lake district of Cumberland and Westmorland. One boulder†

---

* Geol. Mag., vol. viii. p. 41, 1871. Nature, vol. ii. p. 398, 1870.

† My suggestion to the Town Clerk of Preston, in 1872, that this fine boulder should be placed in one of the public parks, has, I understand, been at length carried out.

is of greyish-white granite, with large crystals of black mica, is 5 × 4 × 3 feet in size; it, as well as most of the smaller erratics, is scratched in more than one direction. The lower and upper clays precisely resemble each other in this section, the lower perhaps having the greater number of stones per cubic yard, and occasionally containing large boulders of volcanic altered breccias from the Lake District, more than a yard in length.

At the top of the cliff and bluff forming the southern limit of the plain of the Ribble at Penwortham, is built a church on the ruins of an old abbey, occupying the site of a still more ancient camp. Several sections of the Middle Sand and Lower Clay occur. The former is well seen in the lane leading from the churchyard down to the alluvial plain to the north. In this area the Glacial Drift is not less than 140 feet thick, and the rock nowhere appears.

On the 1-inch map 89 N.W. a brook is seen to bifurcate near Laurel Bank, north-west of Preston, one branch running south of Fulwood Barracks towards Sion Hill, the other passing north of them, and again dividing at Clayton Villa, the northern branch running N.E. to Gerard's Hall. All the brooks east of Withy Trees flow through flat alluvial plains, flanked by cliffs, in some instances smooth and rounded, resembling those bounding the Ribble plain, hereafter described as bluffs. These cliffs or bluffs exhibit fine sections of the Middle Drift and Upper Boulder Clay; and the former, on the south side of the brook from Gerard's Hall to Clayton Villa, is seen resting on the Lower Boulder Clay; which is here a dull red-coloured clay, well packed with stones. It is also obscurely seen in the north cliff of the brook from the latter villa to the "Hall;" also in the brook south of the Barracks, both on the north side below the word "Manor House," and on the south side of Holmes Slack.

The Lower Boulder Clay occurs at the base of the long winding bluff forming the northern limit of the Ribble plain from above Walton-le-Dale Bridge to Alston Hall; and beyond the margin of the map, at Red Scar, this bluff has been eaten by the river into a cliff, at the base of which the Lower Boulder Clay appears as a rather stiff clay, with a great number of scratched pebbles, the clay being of the usual red colour (Fig. 35.)

In the river bed near Ashton, westward of Preston the Lower Boulder Clay rests directly on the Red Sandstone of the Pebble Beds. The terrace walk between Marsh End and the Willows is situated on it, the slipping tendency of the ground being prevented by stone retaining walls. Its base resting on the sandstone is there about 5 feet above the river-level. It is well seen in several pits near New Lea Hall, in one of which the following section occurs: —

feet.

a. Upper Boulder Clay - - - - 10
b. Gravel, 2 ft.; sand, 1 ft.; gravel, 1 ft.; sand, 5 ft. 9
c. Lower Boulder Clay - - - - 2 (+)

The surface of c is about 28 feet above the mean sea-level. The spring, a few yards distant, called St. Catherine's well, appears to issue from the junction of the Upper Boulder Clay and the Middle Sand; a thin bed of impermeable silt, or consolidated gravel, probably occurring at the top of the gravel. Massive fragments, some 9 feet in length, of consolidated shingle, forming a conglomerate resembling some of the coarsest beds of the Kinderscout Millstone Grit, occur in a pit a little to the east, at the base of the Upper Boulder Clay, of which 30 feet is there seen.

In the cliffs of the sea-coast north of Blackpool, still further west, several good exposures of Lower Boulder Clay occur, rising in large mound-shaped masses, beneath the Middle Sands, which have been deposited against their sloping sides. The finest section in these cliffs, and probably in Lancashire, is that seen in Eagberg Brow, Norbreck, where a long dome-shaped mass of Lower Boulder Clay rises to a height of nearly 30 feet, and is overlaid by a pale-green laminated silt, from 3 to 5 inches thick, first pointed out by Mr. Binney, and lettered c in the section below.

Fig. 3.

Section of Norbreck Cliff. *

a. Upper Boulder Clay.
b. Sand or Gravel (Middle Drift).
c. Bluish Silt. }
d. Dark-brown Clay. } Lower Boulder Clay.
e. Talus-heap.

The clay is a compact, stiff, dark greyish-brown deposit; sometimes purple. It contains a vast number of erratic stones and boulders, some as much as three yards in diameter, scattered at random through the mass, though here and there, especially near the top, there are some evidences of bedding, the stones lying in definite horizons.

The finest section of the Lower Boulder Clay is that at the base of Red Bank Cliff, north and south of the termination of the lane

---

* Of which Gisborne wrote:—
"For thee, thou worn and billow-beaten cliff,
"Barrier of ocean, Foreland of the Fylde."

leading to Bispham by Cradley Slack, extending about 270 yards northwards, and 160 southwards ; the clay, with its overlying silt disappearing beneath the Middle Sand. The section, Fig. 3, is taken about the centre of the low arch which it forms at the base of the cliff.

Further south another boss of clay occurs, of a more loamy nature, against which the beds of the Middle Sand abruptly terminate, in the same manner as they do on the slopes of the higher and the larger mass of Norbreck. Fig. 4, taken north of Uncle Tom's Cabin in 1872, gives the section of the whole cliff ; the Upper Boulder Clay at the top, and the Middle Sands resting on the smaller boss of Lower Boulder Clay before referred to.

Fig. 4.

Natural Section in Blackpool Cliff, North of Uncle Tom's Cabin.

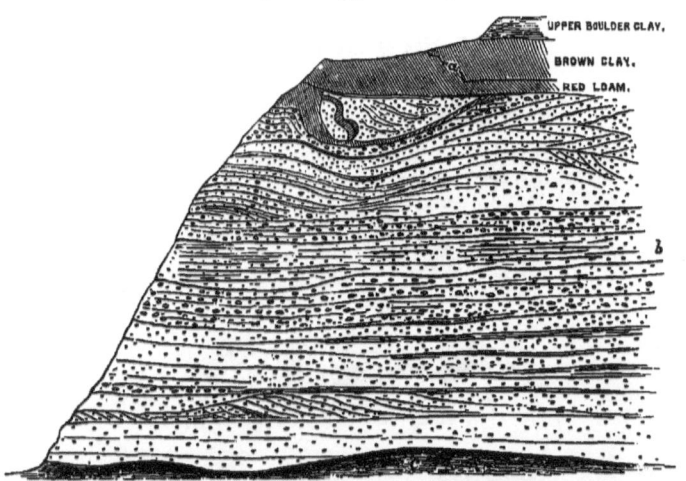

a. Red and brown clays, and red loam (Upper Boulder Clay).
b. Sand and shingle beds, much current-bedded. The shaded portions are beds of loam (Middle Drift).
c. Lower Boulder Clay.

At the top there is an intercalation of Boulder Clay seams in the upper beds of the Middle Sands.

The following notes give an abstract of some of the papers that have appeared on this coast section :—

Rev. W. Thornber[*] described the sands and gravels of that place as containing more than 20 species of marine shells. These sands I have since found to be of the same age as those of Preston.

Mr. Binney, F.R.S.[†]—Notes on the Drift Deposits found near Blackpool. The author describes the following sequence of Drift beds north of the town.

---

[*] History of Blackpool, Lancashire 1837.
[†] Mem. Lit. Phil. Soc., Man. Vol. x., second series, 1852, p. 123.

1. Brown clay, mixed with stones, used for brick-making   - 4 to 5 feet.
2. Brownish-coloured clay, containing stones and much limestone, causing it to be unfit for bricks. It is called
   "good till." The author believes this clay to be often
   replaced by stratified beds of sand and gravel   - 80   feet.
3. Silt of a lightish-brown colour, containing a few pebbles,
   about   -   -   -   -   -   - 2   feet.
4. Brownish-coloured till, mixed with stones, to an extent of
   nearly one-third the whole mass, exposed   -   - 30   feet.

The author gives a section of the cliff from Blackpool to Norbreck, in which he notes the occurrence of a bed of sand and
gravel in the middle of the cliff, south of the Royal Edward (now
Bailey's) Hotel, which cannot now be seen, being covered by the
embankment between Bailey's and the North Pier.

After the severe storm of March 1869 I had an opportunity
of examining this section when the sea-wall was swept away; the
sands appeared to belong to the Middle Drift, noticed in constructing sewers in the road leading towards the Claremont Park
Estate immediately above.

Mr. Binney describes an anticlinal arch of silty clay immediately under the clay, and extending a short distance towards
the Gwyn, which is now concealed by the embankment. His
section represents the larger arch of loamy clay overlying his
clay 4, at Norbreck, which I have described at length as loamy
silt overlying Lower Boulder Clay.

His section also represents a mass of sand and gravel, commencing a little south of the Norbreck arch of loam, and dipping
below the base of the cliff north of the Gwyn, as intercalated in
his clay 3.

An examination of the cliffs at the present time shows that the
sands and gravels have a northward extension over the Norbreck
silt, and a southward extension beyond the Gwyn, joining the mass
described by Mr. Binney as occurring near Bailey's Hotel. The
base of the hollow known as the Gwyn in Mr. Binney's section
is represented as composed of a bed above the sand, which is
believed to have died out, while an examination of the cliff shows
the base of the Upper Boulder Clay resting on the sand to occur a
little above the bottom of the hollow. Having observed these cliffs
at different times of the year, from 1868 to 1875, I find that after the
wash of heavy rains, the sands and gravels become faced over by
clay from above ; which is, no doubt, the explanation of the
junction of the beds not being apparent when Mr. Binney examined
this section.

Garstang District.—A good section is seen beneath the Middle
Sands, and Gravel at Westfield Brook, near Middleton Hall, north
of Broughton, the section being—

	feet.
Upper Boulder Clay - - - -	4
Middle sand - - -	32
Stiff clay - - - - -	4

Further north, in a section of the Garstang and Knott End
Railway, near Taylor's Bridge, 8 to 12 feet of dark reddish-brown
stony clay, extremely irregular, and varied in composition, were

    B

underlying the Middle Sands;—the whole deposit indicating a transitional stage between the Lower Boulder Clay and Till.

MIDDLE DRIFT SAND AND GRAVEL.

In the district lying between Wrightington Park and Haigh Park and Arley Hall, the general level of the country rises eastward from 300 feet above the mean level of the sea to 500 feet at Haigh, where the rock crops to the surface. Between these points the uniformity of level of the country is broken by two deep valleys, separated by a knoll of ground, rising to 385 feet, on the eastern slope of which the village of Standish is built. These valleys are drained by two streams, the river Douglas and Mill Brook, running from north to south.

The Douglas, westward of Shevington and Appley Bridge, flows to the west-north-west, in a deep broad valley, its top water at the bridge being about 45 feet above the mean sea-level, while the level of the ground to the north at Appley Moor reaches 300 feet, and the top of the southern slopes is not much short of 500. On this slope the Middle Sands are well seen at 200 feet west of Cassicar Wood, resting directly on the Shales and Flags.

Lower down on the slope at Fox Holes, Aspinalls, numerous sand-pits occur, the sands being capped by Upper Boulder Clay.

On the side of the valley at Pie Hill Wood, nearly 30 feet of sand is seen, capped by four feet of Upper Boulder Clay, the base of the latter being 75 feet above the mean sea-level.

Northward at Parbold Hill, Appley Row, and at several other places, the rock crops to the surface ; at the edges of the exposure Upper Boulder Clay sets in, the Middle Sand being absent, though present still further to the north-west. On one of these rock-exposures at Noah's Ark occur several large glaciated erratic boulders of Granite, and volcanic altered breccia. There is a curious artificial conical mound, known as the "Boar's Den," resembling the mound near Preesall, on the Upper Boulder Clay near the high road, west of the new portion of Wrightington Park.

The Middle Sand is seen in a pit at Shevington Moor Colliery, overlaid by the Upper Boulder Clay, which spreads over the whole of this country in one uniform sheet. North of this pit, in the road at the Brown Cow Inn, occurs an erratic boulder of quartzite 3 × 2 × 2 feet. Still further north I noticed a boulder of Criffel Granite lying in the lane west of Graham House, about 2 feet long.

These and other Boulders in the district lie on the surface of the Upper Boulder Clay, from which they were no doubt derived ; to the south at Shevington Manor House this clay contained of

Granites	10	
Volcanic rocks from Lake District, &c.	38	in 71 rocks counted.
Coal-measure rocks	20	
Carb. limestones	3	

East of Standish the Middle Sands are well seen on either side of the brook running north of Bradley Lane, the sand containing several seams of shingle.

In a field near the wood west of Coppull Station the following section was observed :—

Fig. 5.

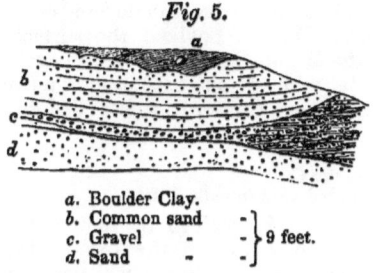

a. Boulder Clay.
b. Common sand -
c. Gravel - - } 9 feet.
d. Sand - -

The pebbles in the gravel, which dips to the E.S.E., consisted of—

	per cent.
Lake District volcanic and Silurian rocks (all scratched) -	4
Coal-measure sandstone and coal - -	85
Ironstone - - - -	6
Yoredale Grits - . - - -	4
Permian Sandstone - - -	1

The Middle Sands occur also in the brook north of Bradley Hall, and there is a small patch of it, north of the Rectory Lane, near the church.

In the London and North-western Railway-cuttings, the Upper Boulder Clay is seen resting on the Middle Sands between Bibbys and the coal-pit to the south, 26 feet of sand being visible; also to the south, at Boar's Head Junction, and east of this station, on the slopes of the valley of the Douglas, on either side of the stream, which runs over rock. So far as I could ascertain, the Lower Boulder Clay was not present.

Soft sand resting on current-bedded shingle, dipping E.S.E., is seen at the end of the railway-siding from Adlington, west of Turbury Lane, Ellerbeck. The gravel I found to consist of :—

	per cent.
Granite - - -	6
Quartz -	2
Volcanic Breccia -	4
Millstone Grit	21
Coal-measure Sandstone -	64
Permian Sandstone -	1
New Red Sandstone -	2
	100

Near the town of Chorley, on the Preston road, there are several deep pits where the sands and gravels of the Middle Drift are worked for building purposes and for gravel for foot-paths, the large pebbles being collected for road-making. The sands are excessively current-bedded, and contain about 14 per cent. of local carboniferous pebbles, the rest being Lake District erratics.

The character of the pebbles of the Middle Drift is mainly determined by the nature of the immediate sub-soil, as may be observed near Chorley, where numerous pebbles of Millstone Grit and coal are spread through the gravel.

In the deep tributary valleys of the rivers Yarrow and Lostock, between Chorley and Leyland, the Middle Sands occur beneath the Upper Boulder Clay. West of Leyland the surface of the sands dips down, so that the Middle Sands are not seen again in any section south of the Ribble, with the one exception of a sand-pit south of St. Mary Eccleston (near Euxton), where the following section occurs :—

			feet.
Upper Boulder Clay	-	-	4
Current-bedded sand (middle drift)	-		12 (+)

Eastward of Leyland, I obtained in 1869 a large number of shells of mollusca from a pit on the top of the hill west of Whittle-le-Woods, and also some bones, which were pronounced by Professor W. Boyd Dawkins, F.R.S., who kindly examined them, to have belonged probably to some herbivorous animal.

From the same pit Mr. Darbishire has since enumerated[*] a large number of species of shells collected by Miss ffarington, of Worden Hall, which I have added to the list of the shells of mollusca from the various Lancashire Drift-deposits, at the end of this Memoir.

The Middle Sands are well seen in the banks of the valley of the river Yarrow, where it flows through Cuerden Park. A particularly good section occurs in a sand-pit at Town's Brow, Clayton-le-Woods, on the south side of the Park, the beds consisting of the following :—

Upper Boulder Clay.

				ft.	in.
Hard brown clay	-	-	-	- 6	0

Middle Drift Sands.

Consolidated sand	-	-	-	- 0	3
Sand	-	-	-	- 0	4
Consolidated sand	-	-	-	0	1
Large-grained ,,	-	-	-	- 1	2
Consolidated ,,	-	-	-	- 0	1
Stiff brown clay	-	-	-	- 0	4
Consolidated sand	-	-	•	- 0	2
Sand	-	-	-	- 10	0
Loam	-	-	-	- 4	0
Sand	-	-	-	- 4	0
Loam	-	-	-	- 3	0
Sand (to road)	-	-	-	- 3	0

The great number of bands of consolidated sand are a marked feature in this section. In some of the sections in the deep valleys or cloughs north of Preston they may be traced running for considerable distance, with a slight dip to the S.S.E., and generally holding up the sheets of water.

The undulations of the surface of the Middle Sand and Shingles, which are observable beneath the Upper Boulder Clay, point to the method of deposition of these banks being similar to that now to be observed in the formation of modern sand-banks in the estuaries of the Lancashire coast.

Thus, between the outcrop of the Middle Sands at Leyland to the India-rubber Works at Golden Hill, the sands have sunk 85 feet in a horizontal space of only 2,000 feet; and the actual fall is pro-

* Quar. Jour. Geol. Soc., vol. xxx., 1874, p. 38.

bably often more abrupt, for in Shaw Brook, south of Leyland, the base of the Upper Boulder Clay is 95 feet above the sea, while in the adjacent Park, sands are found at 156 feet,—the Upper Boulder Clay not being present, and possibly the top of the sands having been more or less denuded.

In a great number of instances, the Middle Sands crop to the surface in the plains, and form a sort of knoll, surrounded by Upper Boulder Clay, at a far higher level than the junction of the two deposits in adjacent valley or brook sections ; proving apparently that the present brooks and modern drainage have a tendency to flow along the lines of natural depression in the surface of the Middle Drift. But this may be partly due to the fact that rain falling on sand would have a tendency to sink, rather than to flow away as a stream ; and that therefore the thicker the clay, the less the depth that rain would percolate, and the more likelihood of a stream forming along the line of thickest clay, or, in other words, along the line of *lowest* Middle Drift.

At Preston, the Middle Sand occupies a very large area in the town, one of these knolls rising to the surface, surrounded by the Upper Boulder Clay to the north-west and east, the western boundary running by Maudlands Bridge Lane, between Friar Gate and Lune Street, across the middle of Fishergate, the north side of Winckley Square, top of Avenham, to Bank Parade ; thence it runs to the north-east to Church Street, whence it turns to the north, running to St. Thomas s Church, to the north of which it joins that portion which runs up by Deepdale.

The following buildings in Preston are upon the Middle Drift :— the Town Hall, Avenham Institution, Dr. Shepherd's library, &c., St. John's, St. Peter's, St. Thomas's churches, and the Roman Catholic cathedral ;—a thin bed of Upper Boulder Clay overlies it under the Preston and Lancaster Banks and the Post Office. In the excavations for the latter, six yards of sand were found resting on loam heavily charged with water. This water-charged bed was also present under the Avenham Institute and the greater part of Ribblesdale Place, giving much trouble in constructing foundations. The surface of the sands is extremely undulating, often causing the Upper Boulder Clay to come in somewhat unexpectedly. Thus, in excavations for the Theatre on the south side of Fishergate, I observed 12 feet of stiff clay, of a reddish-brown colour, the bottom of the bed remaining unexposed. This Upper Boulder Clay probably extends westwards a considerable distance, as 16 or 20 feet of stiff clay rests on sand and bedded silts in the recent excavations (1874) for the rebuilding of the Railway Station. These sands, I am informed by Mr. Rofe, F.G.S., are those from which the late Mr. Gilbertson obtained several species of shells of mollusca ; the discovery of which was alluded to by the late Sir Roderick Murchison in 1836.* The Middle Drift dips suddenly westward on the west side of the tract described above, reappearing near the foot of the bluff which forms the margin of the

---

* Sir R. I. Murchison, " On the Gravels and Alluvia of S. Wales, and Siluria, as distinguished from a Northern Drift covering Lancashire, Cheshire, North Salop, &c." Proc. Geol. Soc., vol. ii., p. 230. In this paper Sir Roderick describes the detritus spread over these counties as being derived from the mountains of Cumberland.

Ribble valley, running from Tulketh Hall, by Stanley Terrace, Avenham Park, to Fishwick, where it has been cut back into a remarkable semicircular cliff by the action of the Ribble. Between this outcrop and the Middle Drift at the top of the plain and the top and edge of the bluff, there is generally an overlap of Upper Boulder Clay; in fact, at Avenham Park it descends nearly to the alluvium below. Near the Wheatsheaf Inn an artificial section of the bluff was exposed, and the sand has been recently cut into in the cliff below Stanley Terrace.

The Middle Sand is well shown in the sand-pit south of the canal near Tulketh Factory, 30 feet of sand being overlaid by 22 feet of Upper Boulder Clay, the former being current-bedded to the S.S.E. and traversed by hard consolidated seams. On the opposite side of the canal the sand crops to the surface, but a little to the south the clay again thickens to 10 feet.

In the Fylde Road, near St. Mary Magdalen's Church, the following section was observed:—

> *a*. Vegetable mould.
> *b*. Upper Boulder Clay.
>
> *Middle Drift.*
>
> *c*. Yellow sand.
> *d*. Shingle (gravel).
> *e*. Sand.

Further east, in a pit N.E. of Deepdale Station, the following sequence of deposits occurred:—

Upper Boulder Clay.

		feet.
a. Red stiff clay, with erratics	- -	6

Middle Drift.

b. Yellow sand, surface undulated	- -	4
c. Shingle (with marine shells)	- -	3
d. Soft yellow sand	-	27
e. Loam	- - -	0½
f. Sand	- -	6¼
g. Loam (used for brass castings) -	-	0¼
h. Sand (base not seen) -	- -	1 (+)

The surface of the Middle Drift is 124 feet above the mean sea-level; the sands are current-bedded, generally dipping S.S.E., but sometimes to the S.S.W. Shells occur plentifully in the sands of Moor Brook, and I noticed one shell of *Ostrea edulis* in the loam occurring beneath 30 feet of sand in Deepdale Brook. Towards Moor Park, and south of Deepdale, the Upper Boulder Clay comes on, and is largely worked for bricks.

In many of the brook valleys running east and west, the steep side of the section falls to the south, which has given rise to a country saying, that "Sand faces 12 o'clock sun." This may possibly be due to the general dip of the current-bedding being to the S.S.E., causing the beds to slide to the south, and be more easily denuded than those on the southern sides of the brook-valleys, which have an inward dip.

West of Preston a good section was seen in 1870 near the Wheatsheaf Inn, consisting of—

Upper Boulder Clay.   feet.

Clay	- - - - -	- 8
Sand	- - - - -	- 8
Clay	- - - - -	- 1

Middle Drift.

Sand	- - - -	- 3
Loam	- - -	2
Sand	- - - - -	- 3
Clay	- - - -	1
Sand	-	13

Lower Boulder Clay.

Stiff red clay	- - - -	- 12 (+)

In the above section it will be noticed that the Shingle Bed present in the Deepdale section is absent; nor does it occur again, westward of the former section, (with the exception of the conglomerate at New Lea Hall,) until the cliffs of Blackpool are reached, when several beds of Shingle occur, some of them of considerable thickness. The pebbles appear to be derived from the pebbles and boulders of the underlying Lower Boulder Clay ; which is also the case in the masses of pebble-gravel met with in the fine section of Glacial deposits occurring east of Preston, at Redscar, and figured in Fig. 35 of the Memoir on the Burnley Coal-field.

The long winding bluff forming the northern margin of the Ribble valley, between Preston and Redscar, exhibits many fine sections of the Middle Sands. Here and there, as at Alston Hall and Fishwick, the seams of shingle are present, in which case shells of the species *Turritella terebra, Cardium edule, Tellina Balthica* invariably occur.

The sands and shingle are well seen at the bottom of the marl pit near the edge of the cliff at Red Scar. Their surface beneath the Upper Boulder Clay appears to have been denuded before its deposition. The base of the Upper Clay is about 70 feet above the sea-level, which is there not less than 130 feet in places.

Northward of Fishwick, at Ribbleton Lane, the following section was obtained during the construction of the new gas-works in 1869 :—

Upper Boulder Clay.   feet.

Reddish clay, with erratic pebbles	-	- 12
Wet loam	- - -	4
Red clay, in part brown, with a few erratic pebbles -		9

Middle Drift.

Sand, wet-running	-	- 5

A similar section to that of Redscar occurs at Spring Wood. North of Lower Hall the thickness of the Middle Drift is about the same, but there is more Sand, and less Shingle. The Clay beneath is stiffer, and of a deep-blue colour. Its level is 50 feet above the mean sea-level, while that of the Lower Boulder Clay at Redscar is only 27 feet. The sand from Spring Wood runs round by Bezza Farm to the brook of that name, where it is seen on both sides of the valley. Eastward towards the Blackburn district the Middle Sand is exposed in many sections, especially along the line of railway from Preston to Blackburn. In one of these the current-bedding, which is so characteristic of the Middle Drift, is so well shown that I give the following section of it, which I made in 1871. It affords evidence of the successive depositions of different beds of sand round a central boss of the same material, but of older date, which affected to a certain extent the latest layer formed, and caused the Upper Boulder Clay to increase in thickness both to the right and left of the section.

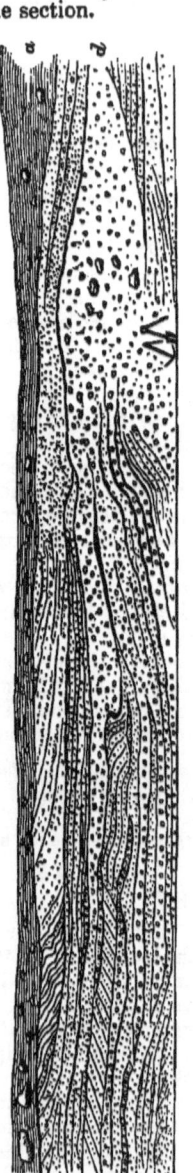

Fig. 6.

Section on the Preston and Blackburn Railway, near Pleasington.

Scale, 16 feet = 1 inch.

a. Upper Boulder Clay.　　d. Sands and gravel (Middle Drift).

In Tun Brook, a little north of the margin of the sheet, a bed of sand occurs precisely similar to the Middle Drift Sand, 10 feet in thickness, capped by 10 feet of Boulder Clay, 28 feet of which occurs between the sand and the Middle Drift beneath. Small seams of sand also sometimes occur near the base of the Upper Boulder Clay, and, when dug under, they are generally found to communicate with the surface of the Middle Drift below, apparently proving the still-water conditions under which this clay was formed. At the same time the occasional occurrence of perfect specimens of *Turritella terebra*, *Cardium edule*, *C. echinatum*, *Tellina Balthica*, and the constant presence of fragments of shells, as well as of oblique lamination caused by currents, show that the sea in which it was deposited was of no very great depth.

The surface of Middle Drift, on which the clay rests, though often minutely eroded, is sometimes a perfectly smooth and level surface as far as regards a small space, though invariably dipping westward as a whole. Whether the Middle Drift was elevated above the sea, and again submerged in the Upper Boulder Clay period, it is difficult to say ; but it appears more probable that the surface of the sand became here and there eroded, when, through great deposition of sand, the crest of the bank at certain points rose above the level of the sea, causing it to experience sub-aërial denudation, which furrowed and minutely eroded its surface; this surface, when again submerged, had sufficiently hardened and consolidated to resist the action of the waves ; and, through alteration of the direction of the currents bearing sand, it was never again covered with this deposit. That some such sequence of events took place is partly proved by the fact that in the midst of the Middle Drift, when two beds are seen resting on each other, it is not uncommon to find the surface of the lower bed eroded, and having the appearance of being sub-aërially denuded ; and also that in modern sand-banks exposed to the action of the tides the surface is often denuded.

In Boilton Wood Brook the upper surface of the Middle Sand is not higher than it is in the escarpment of the valley ; but in the next valley the stream rises at an elevation of 170 feet above the mean sea-level in a col in the watershed. The next valley, Brockholes Wood, is longer, and the Middle Sands disappear under the Boulder Clay at 144 feet, while in the adjacent bluff the junction is at 120 feet.

In a small cutting on either side of the road at the top of the hill, north of Sunny Hill, the Upper Boulder Clay is seen resting on the Middle Sands, but their eastward extension is cut off a few yards further, by a bed of loam, which has every appearance of having been let in by a small fault, and still further east the loam bed is cut off by another fault, and the Upper Boulder Clay again brought in. Whether these are undoubted faults it is difficult to say ; but good examples of faulting in Glacial Drift have been recorded by Mr. Aitkin, F.G.S.,* so that it is possible that these also may be examples of it.

Immediately south of Thatched House Tavern a small tract of Middle Sand is exposed, but it rapidly dips down to the south, so

---

* " On Faults in Drifts at Stockport."—Geol. Mag., vol. viii. p. 117.

that it is overlaid by 15 feet of Boulder Clay in the railway cutting west of the station.

It is worthy of note that many large patches or small sheets of Middle Drift have been chosen for the site of a town by the Northmen when they first colonized the district, as Preston, Kirkham, Chorley, and Leyland, the four largest towns and villages in this district. This may possibly be due to the presence of the springs of water which issue from above the thin beds of loam occurring in the sands, which would be of extreme value to the population settling in an impermeable clay country like that of the Fylde and Amounderness.

Middle Sands occur at the Willows, and have a continuous outcrop by Wrongway Brook to the large exposure at Kirkham, where 24 feet of current-bedded sands are seen, in the pit behind Preston Street ; the various beds being divided by hard seams, the result of the action of waters charged with calcareous matter on the loose sand, which appears specially to take place immediately over impermeable layers of loamy clay.

These hard seams occur in many of the valleys intersecting the continuation of the Boulder Clay plain ; described in the Burnley Memoir, as running from the foot of the Yoredale Grit Fells, at an elevation of 500 feet, by Preston (175 feet), and Kirkham (100 feet), to Blackpool, where it is abruptly terminated by the sea, forming a cliff 70 feet high, which is being worn back into the country, at an average rate of nearly a yard a year, by the combined action of frost, rain, and wind ; vast quantities of sand being swept away, causing large masses of the Upper Boulder Clay to fall to the base of the cliff, from which they are removed by the spring tides.

A portion of the town of Kirkham is built on the Middle Sand, and part on the Upper Boulder Clay, the northward extension of these beds being cut off by a bluff forming the southern limit of a large "swamp hollow," through which the Roman Road and the modern railway have both been carried. Between Church and Mill Streets the bluff is very steep, and has been worn back into a cliff about 50 feet high, entirely composed of sand, the base of which is concealed by peat, so that the Middle Drift here attains a thickness of at least 60 feet.

At Salwick the surface of the sand is 84 feet above the mean sea-level,—capped by only 4 feet of Boulder Clay, which to the west rises to the surface, and forms knolls at Great Plumpton.

North of the latter place the sand is seen in the railway cutting ; but to the south-west in the Lytham railway cutting, north of Moss side, the Upper Boulder Clay has thickened to 31 feet, without the base being exposed, and still further south the level of the surface of the sand has still further diminished.

There are several wells penetrating the Upper Boulder Clay at Blackpool, near the Market. When the drains in Queen Square were made, the Upper Boulder Clay was not penetrated, but only 16 feet of it rested on the Middle Sand higher up on the cliff on the Park Estate.

In 1872 I descended a well in process of sinking at Mr. Ormerod's Brewery, Blackpool, and observed the following sections :—

		feet.
a. Clay and marl (Upper Boulder Clay)	-	18
b. Sand (dry, sharp), with fragments of shells (Middle Drift)	-	47
c. Hard loamy bed, with sharp gritty particles, base not reached (Middle Drift?)	-	12
		77

In the Cemetery several borings were made, in which the Middle Sand was reached after passing through a few feet of Upper Boulder Clay.

The modern town of Blackpool is called after a small stream, now the Spen Dyke, flowing from Marton Mere over the Moss, from the peat of which it derives its black colour ;—" pool " being often used in the the Lancashire dialect instead of "stream," as in Liverpool, and Bromborough Pool in Cheshire, &c.

The Spen Dyke forms the existing boundary between the township of Layton Hawes in the parish of Bispham, and that of Southshore in Marton.

At Blackpool the Middle Sands were described by Mr. Binney as occurring in the cliff under what is now Bailey's Hotel. This is not now visible, through the face being embanked. On the Claremont Park Estate I noticed in the excavation for drains that the sand was met with at a depth of 16 feet beneath the Upper Boulder Clay. In a well at Mr. Ormerod's brewery I found 18 feet of Upper Boulder Clay to overlap the Middle Sands. From the Gwyn to Norbreck very fine sections of the sands and shingle occur, exhibiting every form of current-bedding imaginable ; thick beds of shingle occur, containing many shells of mollusca more or less perfect, and beds of loam intercalated. Fig. 7 will give some idea of the general arrangement of these beds. It is taken near Uncle Tom's Cabin ; not far from the base of the cliff. The current bedding is generally to the S.S.E. ; and both loam and shingle beds come on and thin out with great rapidity.

Fig. 7.

Section South of Uncle Tom's Cabin.

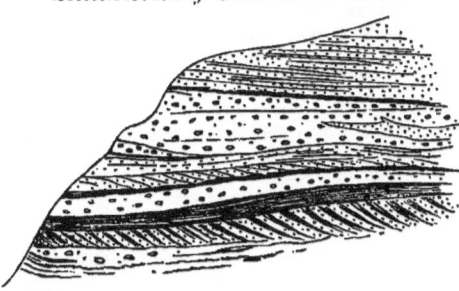

The fine dots represent sand ; the shaded portion, thin bands of loam. The height of the section is about 10 feet.

Very good sections are exposed in the gap, down which the steps from Uncle Tom's Cabin are carried ; alternations of thin beds of sand and shingle, dipping at low angles to the south; current planes intersecting the beds, dipping in the same direction, or to the S.S.E. at higher angles. Amongst the beds of shingle at this place shells are, perhaps, more common than at any point along the cliffs; but everywhere shells, whether perfect or fragmentary, are more common in the pebble beds than in the sand.

Stiff loamy clay, with few pebbles, may be seen on the beach, a little distance to the north of the steps, rising abruptly five feet in a cliff, with a steep escarpment to the north, about 11 yards in width; northward a thin bed of this clay forms the base of the cliff, until it thins out against a bed of the ordinary type of the Lower Boulder Clay. The latter abruptly rises from the base of the cliff to a height of 5 feet, and is overlaid by a bed of loam, which further north becomes a purple Boulder Clay, about 4 feet in thickness. At the gap where the Upper Boulder Clay synclinal occurs, the purple clay has much thinned away, and rests on 4½ feet of brown clay.

A few yards north of the gap the brown clay thins to two feet; and the general thickness is maintained by a thickening of the purple clay to 7 feet, its surface being slightly undulating, and covered with gravel on white rich patches of loam.

Further north the Lower Boulder Clay rises in a mound-like boss, and is overlaid by a thin bed of loam, the following being a characteristic section:—

		feet.				feet.
a. Sand	- - -	16		f. Gravel	-	4
b. Gravel	-	2		g. Sand -	- -	1
c. Sand	-	2		h. Loam	- -	0½
d. Gravel	-	2		i. Lower Boulder Clay		9
e. Sand -	-	3				

At Bank Gap, beds c to g have thinned out, and are replaced by others; h is absent; and a thin ferruginous gravel rests on 7 feet of Lower Boulder Clay.

Twenty yards south of Bank Gap I noticed the following section at the base of the cliff:—

	feet.
a. Compact bed of shingle, dipping S. - -	15
b. Small shingle and sand, where thickest - - -	9
c. Small mass of Boulder Clay, with rounded edges in b, and resting on d - - - -	4
d. Reddish loam, without stones, dipping north, and thickening south, about seven feet north of the mass of Boulder Clay. The loam throws out a narrow curved mass, which describes nearly two-thirds of a circle, nearly touching the mass c, and enclosing between it and the mass much coarser shingle than b	2
e. Dark purple clay, with erratic stone - -	6½
f. Dark reddish brown clay, exceedingly compact and stony, to the base of the cliff - - - -	3
(Exposed on the beach is about 3 feet more.)	

The ferruginous gravel thins out about 40 yards to the north, and is overlaid by narrow bands of sand and shingle, arranged in an anticlinal manner, in a hollow of the Lower Boulder Clay. At 16 feet above the base of the cliff a compact bed of shingle

4 feet in thickness may be seen. A hundred yards still further north the following section occurs:—

	feet.
Shingle	6
Sand	6
Laminated Loam	3
(thinning to the south, where it is replaced by sand)	2
Lower Boulder Clay	5½

Some 80 yards further north the following section occurs at the top of the cliff:—

	feet.
a. Upper Boulder Clay	11
b. Sand	46
c. Lower Boulder Clay	3

. A few yards further north the Lower Boulder Clay disappears beneath the sand on the beach. Northward from this point, up to the hedges, on the Blackpool side of Fanny Hall, the cliffs are much obscured by landslips. Thin loam and gravel beds, dipping S.S.E., rise a few feet in low mounds above the level of the base of the cliff. The Middle Drift mainly consists of sand, and the Upper Boulder Clay is very compact, often overhanging the tumbling masses of sand beneath; it varies in thickness from 8 to 16 feet, the sand being from 30 to 40 feet.

Under the third hedge visible from the beach, after leaving the gap, the second hedge north of Fanny Hall, several masses of the conglomerate formed by consolidation of the sand and shingle by the action of water holding carbonate of lime and oxide of iron in solution are to be seen. The Upper Boulder Clay is about 16 feet in thickness, and the sands are traversed by several bands of curved laminated loam.

Further north the Upper Boulder Clay averages 10 feet in thickness. Several seams of loam and sand alternate with each other, and thin out against the Lower Boulder Clay, which here sets in, forming the longest exposure of any on the several bosses rising above the beach in these cliffs. Its surface rises northwards at a very low angle; it consists of a red loamy clay, with a very few pebbles.

Section a little north, of lane end from Banks.

	feet.
a. Sand	6
b. Loam	7
c. Sand, thickening north	1
d. Loam	4
e. Sand, thickening north	5
f. Stiff loam	2
g. Sandy loam	3
h. Blue silt, rises to the S., and thickens north, breaking into several detached masses	0½
i. Loam	0¾
k. Lower Boulder Clay	8

Thickens southwards to 14 feet under the lower end.

South of the lane end, *i* thins out, and *h* rests directly on *k*, which thickens to 20 feet, and contains many pebbles and boulders, from half an inch to 5 feet in diameter, mostly rounded and scratched. Still further south the bed *h* thins out, and a thin bed of sand intervenes between the Middle Sands and the Lower Boulder Clay, which latter rises to its greatest height a few yards further north, as represented in Fig. 3. The projecting mass of Lower Boulder Clay, though wasting less rapidly than the overlying sands, which are daily crumbling away through the action of the wind, splits off in great masses, along planes of division, by the action of frosts and rain.

It is worthy of note that the ground slopes gradually down the lower plains both at the south and north ends of the Blackpool cliffs; and that where the cliffs are highest, near Uncle Tom's Cabin, they are backed by still higher ground; so that as the cliffs have gradually been wasted back, they have increased in height; it is probable that the peat plain of Lytham and Southshore swept round this tongue of high ground, and joined that of Rossal and Fleetwood.

Portions of the base of the old destroyed cliffs remain in the scattered masses of consolidated Middle Drift sand and shingle, between tide marks off the Norbreck coast, some of which are more than 20 feet in length, the best known being called "the Pennystone,"* "Higher Gingle," "Lower Gingle," "Carlin and his Colts," "Silkstone," and "Bear and Staff." In Fig. 8 the bedded lines of pebbles and traces of current-bedding are observable.

Fig. 8.

Waterworn Consolidated Sand and Shingle (Middle Drift) off the Coast of Norbreck.

* According to a local tradition, this stone was called the "Pennystone," from the fact of there having been a public-house there where a gallon of beer was sold for a penny; a ring attached being that to which travellers tied their horses. From the form of the ground it is tolerably certain, that when this spot was land, before the coast was denuded as much as at present, any house that might have been there would have been at the top of the cliff, while the consolidated gravel evidently formed a portion of its base.

North of the point where the Lower Boulder Clay disappears beneath high-water mark, the cliff lowers in height, and its base is concealed by blown sand, the Upper Boulder Clay being about 12 feet in thickness. A little further north there is a gap in the cliff, which has been formed by the washing of springs issuing from some post-glacial beds filling in a hollow in the Upper Boulder Clay, consisting of—

	feet.
Sandy Loam - - - -	1 to 4
Peat - - - - - -	1½
Grey silty clay, resting on Middle Drift gravel - -	2

On the north side of the gap the section is as follows :—

Loam - -	2
Peat - - - -	1
Blue silt - - - - -	3
Upper Boulder Clay - - -	4
Gravel - - - - - -	3
Sand (base not seen, concealed by blown sand)	3

Northward from this point the sections are of great interest in regard to the disappearance of the Middle Sands and Gravels, which Mr. Binney believes 'to wedge out in the Boulder Clay, and to be intercalated with it. From the gap at the Gwyn to the gap now described, thick masses, exhibiting in section very low domes of Lower Boulder Clay, have been seen to rise above the level of the beach, the highest to a height of 21 feet. Most of these have been overlaid more or less entirely by a thin silty bed conformable to its surface, against which various sands and gravels have been deposited entirely unconformably, and heaped up against the domes. These sands and gravels have been overlaid by an Upper Boulder Clay, the base line of which is sharply cut and well defined, but undulating, cutting off the various beds of the sands and shingle. It is a somewhat remarkable phenomenon that the average thickness of the Upper Boulder Clay is maintained independently of the height of the cliff ; in such a manner that the base line of the Upper Boulder Clay, following the lines of the surface of the cliffs, causes the Middle Sands to be gradually cut off; so that the sands and gravels of the whole section may be regarded as a very flat dome, covering the various small bosses of Lower Boulder Clay, and dipping under the Upper Boulder Clay at both ends, which thickens out in the plains, and appears on the beach, both at Rossal and at South Shore.

The small proportion of carboniferous limestone is very marked when it is compared with that obtaining in the gravels at Carnforth, where some of the boulders of white limestone occurring in the laminated current-bedded gravels (to E.S.E.) measure 9½ × 9 × 5 feet. All are more or less scratched, and two-thirds of them rounded. In 100 specimens were the following :—

White carboniferous limestone - -	63
Volcanic ash and breccia - - - -	2
Silurian grits - - - - - -	30
Yoredale grits - - - - - -	5

To return to the gap north of Red Bank, the following are sections at the top of the cliffs :—

	feet.
Blown sand - - - - - - -	1
Peat - - - - - - - -	0½
Blue clay - - - - - -	3
Upper Boulder Clay - - - - - -	4
⎧ Sand - - - - - -	4
⎨ Gravel, with shells - - - - . -	2
⎩ Sand, to blown sand - - - - -	5

Still further north, near the hedge :—

Peaty clay - - - -	3
Upper Boulder Clay - - -	8
Sand - - - - - - -	9

A few yards further north, the base of the Upper Boulder Clay descends, and cuts off the upper bed of the sand and the loam bed, and fills up several hollows in the sand, which conform to sharply curved bands of loam, the bases of which are concealed by sand dunes.

Northward the base of the cliff is concealed by blown sand, which daily accumulates, and the Upper Boulder Clay descends nearer to the beach, as shown in Fig. 9.

Fig. 9.

Section of Norbreck Cliff, South of Bispham.

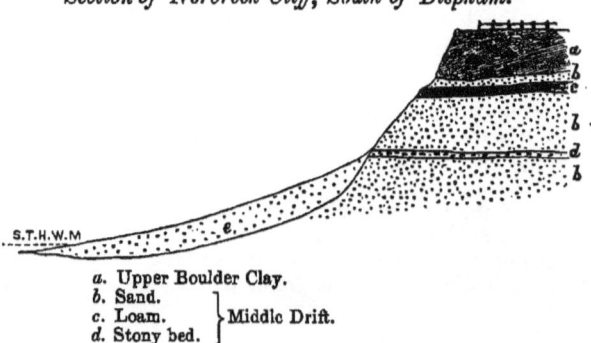

a. Upper Boulder Clay.
b. Sand.
c. Loam. ⎫ Middle Drift.
d. Stony bed. ⎬
e. Recent sand, concealing the base of the cliff.

Still further north, near the hedge north of the gap :—

	feet.
Upper Boulder Clay, with a shingle bed, at a depth of 9 feet, which rises northward, and eventually crops to the surface, while the base of the clay, which here coincides with it, dips northward, so that the clay becomes 12 feet in thickness - - - - - -	9
Sand - - - - - - -	3
Boulder Clay band, thinning out northward - -	2
Sand - - - - - -	4
Loam, laminated and current-bedded, thinning out abruptly against yellow sand to the south - - -	4
Fine sand, including base not seen - - - -	10

A few yards beyond this section the sand, blown up from the beach, has concealed the face of the cliff; so that the Middle Sand is totally obscured, as is the base of the Upper Boulder Clay, which gradually thickens northwards, a good section being visible at Norbreck.

North of Wyre District.—Immediately north of Rawcliffe Hall the Middle Sands crop to the surface, appearing from beneath the Boulder Clay, and forming a knoll beween Riggs Wood and Hoskinshire ; and another small patch is seen at Light Ash House, Rotten Row. The occurrence of these small patches is of importance, as proving the clay area which forms the long narrow belt of pasture land dotted with houses, with fields separated by hedges, intervening between the great peat mosses to the north, and the river Wyre to the south, to belong to the upper division of the Glacial Deposits.

The height of the top of these knolls is about 32 feet above the Ordnance datum-line ; that of the alluvium to the south, about 19 or 20 feet; that of the peat, at the line of junction with the Boulder Clay, averages 16 feet. From this line the moss rises inland until it reaches more than 50 feet at Rawcliffe Moss. The whole of the southern portion of this moss appears to lie directly on the Boulder Clay, which appears at the surface at several points in the midst of the moss. The clay in one of these patches at Frances Lane, near Wilson House, is used for the manufacture of tiles. On the eastern margin of the moss, at Hool Lane, brick and tile works are also carried on. Considerable numbers of erratic pebbles and boulders occur in the Boulder Clay, which are carefully picked out, collected in heaps, and used for mending the roads. Of these I found 70 per cent. to be Upper Yordale Grit.

Eastward of the large knoll of Upper Boulder Clay extending from Hudson's Farm to Moss Side, between the moss and the river, a strip of alluvium runs from the river at New Skitham to the moss at Tithe Barn Lane; but eastward of this another Boulder Clay tract forms the eastern margin of the moss as far as Raby House, west of Churchtown. Northwards of this point to Humblescow Lane the peat comes directly in contact with the alluvium of the Wyre, which overlies it.

Small exposures of Preesall Shingle occur, overlying the Middle Glacial Sand, at Way Hill in the peat-area, and at Sharples and Humblescow Lanes, at the north end of Kirkland Wood, in the alluvial area.

A line of Upper Boulder Clay inliers divides Rawcliffe from Pilling Moss at Trashy Hill, Old Eskham House, and New Eskham ; and to the east, at Gibson's Farm, Primrose Hill, and Gilbertson's, several patches of clay of various sizes rise above the moss. The northern termination of the latter area was cut through by the Garstang and Knot End Railway at Helen's Farm, 8 feet of Boulder Clay being exposed. A few yards to the east of this, the following section of peat is seen.

Fig. 10.

*Section in Railway Bank, Winmarleigh.   Base 5 feet above
the rails.*

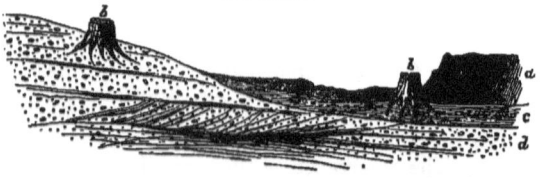

a. Peat.	*c.* Upper Boulder Clay.
b. Stumps of trees older than the peat.	*d.* Middle sand and gravel.

The Boulder Clay would not appear to be very thick, for immediately to the west, on the same line of railway, 12 feet of Middle Sand and Gravel is seen rising in a mound flanked and overlaid by the clay. These Sands and Gravels were used in the construction of the line for ballast, and a still larger quantity was obtained at another hillock, a mile further west, at Cogie Hill. The sand is also seen underlying four feet of peat in Pilling Brook, between Cogie Hill and Bone Hill; but the latter knoll consists of the Upper Boulder Clay, which is worked for the manufacture of tiles. The Middle Sands, however, cross to the surface at Birks, a mile and a half to the S.W. of Bone Hill, and about half way between that place and the Boulder Clay exposures near Rawcliffe Hall; so that it is clear the Upper Boulder Clay had suffered extensive denudation before the growth of the peat, which probably never covered the knolls of Boulder Clay and Middle Sand which rise above the moss in different localities.

The section in the sand pit at Birks gives Middle Drift of the ordinary type, the Upper Boulder Clay thinning out abruptly against the sand on all sides; the clay is covered with five feet of peat, which also thins out against the Middle Sand slope.

West of Birks a deep sluice, Ridgy Pool, carries off the drainage of Pilling Mosses to Morecambe Bay. I was not able to observe what formed the subsoil of the peat in its sides, but half a mile to the west, at Lousanna, the sand crops to the surface. At a short distance from the latter place occurs the following section:—

	feet.
Peat	3
Upper Boulder Clay	1
Middle Sand	2

The occurrence of these Middle Sands and Gravels under the peat is interesting as bearing on the origin of the Preesall Shingles, which also crop to the surface from beneath the peat, but which overlie the Boulder Clay instead of appearing from beneath it.

It is probable that a certain amount of the denudation which the Upper Boulder Clay has experienced in this area took place at the time of the deposition of the Shirdley Hill Sand and Preesall Shingle, and these sands and shingles are redeposited Middle Sands, &c. From the fact that I observed fragments of hæmatite in the post-glacial shingle of Preesall, I infer that the set of the currents was across Morecambe Bay, at the time of the deposition of this shingle, as it was in Middle Glacial times.

At Lousanna, Rawcliffe Moss, the peat, though wrapping round the islet of the Middle Sands, does not directly rest upon them; the following section occurs in a sluice 300 feet from the house:—

	feet.
Peat - - - - -	3
Upper Boulder Clay, with erratic pebbles - -	1
Middle sand - - - -	2 (+)

The same method of occurrence is also noticeable at Birks ; a boss of Middle Sand rising above the peat which slightly overlaps the Boulder Clay cropping around the boss of sand.

During the construction of the Garstang and Knot End Railway, I observed good sections of the Upper Boulder Clay overlying the Middle Gravel, which here consisted of rounded blocks and large stones of Yoredale Grit and Lake District erratics. The whole would appear to have been deposited in very shallow water around the knoll of Permian Red Sandstone, exposed in the railway cutting between Taylor's Bridge and the town. The junction of the Clay and Gravel with the Red Sandstone is seen in the following figure.

Fig. 11.

Section in Garstang and Knot End Railway.

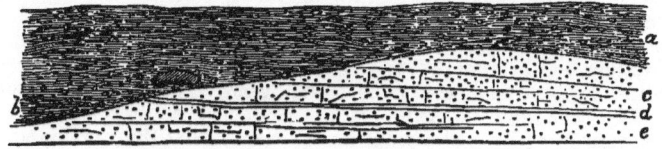

a. Upper Boulder Clay.
b. Middle Drift with large Yoredale Grit Boulders, 8 × 3 × 2.
c. and e. Red Sandstone. } Permian Sandstone.
d. Yellow   „

Good sections of the Middle Sands, though somewhat obscured by grass, may be seen in the railway cuttings from Scorton to Bay Horse. The sand contains many bands of shingle, and is overlaid by the Upper Boulder Clay. In these sections the sands for the first time proceeding northwards begin to contain a great number of Carboniferous Limestone Boulders, some of them very large ; so much so, that one which was met with in constructing the railway was of sufficient size to be sawn into blocks for the mantlepiece of the waiting room of Galgate Station.

At Cleveley Bridge, near Shireshead, the following section occurs:—

	feet.
Gravel - - - -	5
Sand, current-bedded to the S.S.E. -	2
Gravel - - -	3
Sand, current-bedded -	16

The Boulder Clay comes on to the south, and the surface of the Middle Drift slopes down.

Between Goosnargh and Grimsargh the Middle Sand forms the banks of Blundel Brook between the copse a little west of New Chingle Hall and Sudell House, near Dale Brow. It was found under the Upper Boulder Clay, near the new Whittingham Lunatic Asylum,—the surface of the clay being extremely uneven, and running down into the sand 20 feet or more, filling up the hollows in the original curved surface of deposition of the sand.

One or two of these hollows have their sides so extremely steep and sudden as to lead to the idea, that, where valleys bounded by this sand occur at lower levels, springs, or rather underground watercourses, may run along determinate lines in the sand, gradually abstracting and carrying away matter to the valley beneath, and that the clay above sinks by gravity into the space thus left vacant. That this is really the case is supported by the fact that in numerous instances I have observed a hollow in the ground surface of the Upper Boulder Clay correspond to a hollow or depression in the surface of the Middle Sand beneath it; in other words, the surface of the sand beneath rises with the surface of the ground on either side. This is often noticeable on a large scale in the cliff sections forming the sides of valleys, the sand there being much thinner than in neighbouring well-sections in the plain above, and its upper surface much lower, being perhaps only half way up the valley cliff, while in the adjoining plain it rises to the surface and forms a knoll.

One of these occurs between Goose and Gander Halls, and is about 800 yards in length, containing a few pebbles, all rounded.*

The Middle Sand and Gravel underlies, with a very few local exceptions, the whole of the great sheet of Upper Boulder Clay forming the surface of the Fylde. It is generally seen in the sides of valleys, but in several places considerable tracts of it are exposed at the surface, and every here and there forms knolls, rising a little above the level of the plain of Boulder Clay.

Several of these knolls occur on the west side of the London and North-western Railway, between Broughton and Brock stations; the sand is also seen in the railway cutting at several points, and in the side of the valleys of Barton and Dean Brook,—that at Barton, north of Tunstedd, containing a shingle bed.

Though the surface of the Middle Drift generally rises inland, the contour of equal level does not range north and south, but rather runs from N.E. to S.W., following the western slopes of the Pendle range; thus, at Brindle it is seen in a deep pit, at an elevation of 450 feet, while at Bezza Brook to the due north it is only 118 feet: proving that this deposit invariably conforms to the level of the rocky floor beneath, as might be expected from the shallow-water conditions observable in it,—successive lines of Middle Drift sand and shingle being formed as the country gradually subsided, offering higher and still higher coast-lines to the denuding action of its breakers. Thus, in the lowlands the included stones are invariably such as might be found in the Lower Boulder Clay, while higher up pebbles of Coal, Millstone Grit, and Yoredale Grit first make their appearance, the whole character of the gravel becoming more and more local as greater heights are reached.

* I am informed by Mr. J. Tullis, of Preston, the contractor for the building of the new Lunatic Asylum at Whittingham, that a drain-pipe, with a very steep incline, with one of these sand-pockets, became entirely choked with the running sand, and necessitated the fixing of a wire inside, to periodically shift the sand filling the pipe.

CHAPTER II.

UPPER BOULDER CLAY.

The Boulder Clay of Western Lancashire, lying between the Mersey and the Douglas, generally rests directly on the rock surface beneath; and though beds of sand occasionally occur in it, they are not of sufficient thickness and importance to be considered the representatives of the Middle Sands occurring in the country to the north and east, and it is therefore doubtful to which division the clay of this area belongs ; but, on the whole, there is reason to believe that the greater portion of it is the Upper Boulder Clay.

Litherland, Orrell, and Ford District.— At Hatton Hill the Keuper Sandstone almost crops to the surface, and appears to have been worn into a bluff or escarpment facing west, before the deposition of the Boulder Clay, which not only caps the hill but conceals and diminishes the steepness of the bluff, which is further effected by the Boulder Clay being overlaid by 15 feet of Shirdley Hill Sand (Field Lane, north of Litherland Mount). At the top of the hill the sand is thinner, but it thickens again to the east to about 6 feet north of Moss Lane, where it is here and there overlaid by a thin deposit of peat, and rests on Boulder Clay. The latter has thinned out at Sefton Quarry, and the sand rests almost directly on the Keuper Sandstone.

In the line of ponds on the slope between the quarry mentioned above and Park Gate House, the clay is seen to be perfectly impermeable, the water standing at a different height in each case ; the highest top-water being determined by the level of the overlying sand on the lowest side of the pond or down slope.

In the Orrell Railway-cutting, Shirdley Hill Sand, with rolled pebbles, fragments of land and sea shells, and bones, rests on the Boulder Clay overlying the Keuper Sandstones, and reaches from Orrell Lane to Captain's Lane. Here the sand thins, and 20 feet of Boulder Clay forms the railway bank ; but about 50 yards to the east, near Park Gate House, the sand again sets in, reaching 15 feet in thickness.

A well was sunk a few yards S.E. of the railway in the Orrel road into the Lower Keuper Sandstone, a plentiful supply of water being met with at a depth of 40 feet.

Melling.—In the brickfield at Pye's Bridge, over the Leeds and Liverpool Canal, the following section occurs :—

	ft.	in.
Alluvium and Shirdley Hill Sand - -	2	0
Red clay, with very few pebbles, used for bricks and tiles (Upper Boulder clay) - -	8	0 (+)

In an adjacent well the clay was found to be 14 feet thick, when water was reached ; but whether it occurred in the Middle Sand, or the Pebble Beds of the Bunter, I could not ascertain.

At *Kirkby*, in the Earl of Sefton's brickfield, a well was sunk 14 feet in depth, at the corner of the brickfield next the lane, which reached the Pebble Beds, with a supply of water.

In a boring on the north-east side of the field the following beds occurred :—

	feet.
Boulder Clay	- 15
Sand - - - -	- 3
Boulder Clay - - - -	3

In a great many sections similar thin bands of sand occur. They are probably not representative of the Middle Drift, but mere sandy beds, intercalated in the Upper Boulder Clay.

Very fine-grained sand, of doubtful age, occurs between Clock House and Alder's Bridge. It is of a pale-yellowish colour, and may be referable either to bands of sand in the Upper Boulder Clay, or to the Shirdley Hill Sand.

I observed the following section near Preston Road railway station, near Liverpool :—

	feet.
a. Boulder Clay -	- 16
b. Fine sand - - -	- 3 (+)

In the adjacent cemetery I found the beds to consist of—

	feet.
a. Boulder Clay - - -	- 12
b. Sand - - - -	- 6
c. Boulder Clay similar to a, but without pebbles	- 14

From the section I saw, and from the information I obtained from the superintendent, it appears that the sand *b* is a bank 80 yards in width, abruptly terminating at the sides, and running for an unknown distance in either direction beyond the cemetery.

In an adjacent brickfield 24 feet of Upper Boulder Clay is to be seen above the brook, where 4 feet of Alluvium caps the Boulder Clay, and is mixed with it in the manufacture of the bricks.

The upper portion of the following section was seen in a brick-field near Litherland Bridge and Gas-works :—

	feet.
Sand (Shirdley Hill Sand) - -	- 6
Boulder Clay (upper 9 feet worked as a brick-earth)	31

The lower portion was seen in a sinking for the gas-works ; in sinking for the bed of a gasometer, the following section was observed :—

	feet.
Blown sand, and Shirdley Hill sand -	- 6
Boulder Clay, with erratic pebbles -	12
Boulder Clay, red marl, no pebbles	- 7
Sand, fine running, light coloured -	- 3
Boulder Clay, with a few pebbles (base not seen) -	2

In a boring made immediately south of the brickfield by Mr. Humphrey, he failed to find the base of the Boulder Clay, after sinking through it to a depth of 40 feet.

In Mr. Humphrey's brickfield near End Butts Lane, Great Crosby, the following was seen in the north-east corner :—

	feet.
Soil 1 foot, Shirdley Hill sand 4 feet	- 5
Boulder Clay, reddish, with erratic pebbles -	- 10
Sand - . - -	- 3
Boulder Clay, without pebbles - -	- 2½
Lower Keuper sandstone (visible)	- 5

In this pit water was found to stand uniformly at a depth of about 12 feet, at an elevation of about 16 feet above Ordnance datum-line.

In a quarry at Great Crosby, on the south side of the National School play-ground wall, the surface of the Lower Keuper Sandstone is about 36 feet above the Ordnance datum-line, and is capped by about 5 feet of Boulder Clay, of a reddish colour, with many water-worn pebbles disseminated through the mass. Some of them have been more or less striated before being water-worn, especially those derived from the Lake District, which compose about 70 per cent. of the whole. Resting on the surface of the clay is about 4 feet of Shirdley Hill Sand, composed of extremely fine grains of a very light-yellow and orange-red colour in about equal proportions.

In Barr Moss Lane Marl Pitt occurred the following section :—

		ft. in.	
a.	Peat - -	0 10	
b.	Ashey-grey sand - -	- 0 9	⎱ Shirdley Hill
c.	Yellow sand, with seam of pebbles at base -	1 6	⎰ Sand.
d.	Peat - - - -	- 0 3	
e.	Light red-coloured clay, with boulders of granite, and altered volcanic ash and breccia	11 0 (+)	⎱ Upper ⎰ Boulder Clay.

Between Ormskirk and Scarisbrick the character of the Upper Boulder Clay is identical with its appearance in the Liverpool district. Numerous sections are seen in the marl pits, which occur in almost every field around Aughton Hall, Spout House, and White Rails. At the latter place the clay is worked for brick-making. Immediately to the south it has been bored through at the corner of Brookhouse Lane, west of the bridge; in the wells of the Southport Waterworks, the sands of the Middle Drift were found with numerous shells of mollusca.

Mr. Binney records the fact that Mr. Harkness obtained marine shells from the Boulder Clay of Ormskirk, which he found to be 150 feet in thickness.

Nearer Southport, at Brown Edge, the Middle Drift has thinned out, and the Upper Boulder Clay rests directly on the older rocks, as seen in section, Fig. 12.

Fig. 12.

Section in Trench near Brown Edge, Southport.

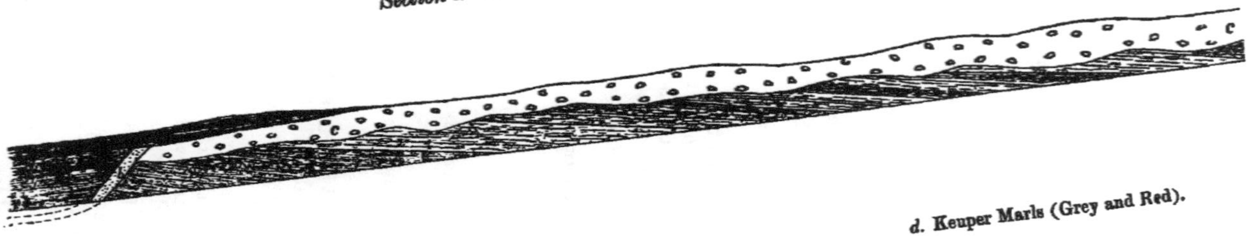

a. Peat.

b. Shirdley Hill Sand.

c. Upper Boulder Clay.

d. Keuper Marls (Grey and Red).

When the pipes of the Southport Waterworks were laid across this district, I noticed the occurrence of several thin beds of sand intercalated in the Upper Boulder Clay.

South of the Ribble and west of the river Lostock, from Farrington to Croston, no section of the Middle Drift is seen, and, as far as I am aware, it has never been bored into. But there appears strong reason to believe that the Boulder Clay of the Hoole district belongs to the upper division, because it has every appearance of being continuous with the undoubted Upper Boulder Clay of Charnock Moss to the north, and Eccleston to the south; but, at the same time, it is certain that the Hoole Clay rests directly upon rock (Keuper Marls) at several points in the river Douglas, and the Middle Drift and Lower Clay must therefore be absent. This is however often locally the case, both in the Euxton and other districts, for in a quarry near Euxton undoubted Upper Clay is seen resting on the Lower Coal-measure Sandstone, which is glacially striated in a S.S.E. direction (first observed by my colleague Mr. Tiddeman).

The Boulder Clay at Farrers near the bottom of Hutton is very deep-coloured, and contains a large number of subangular and angular pebbles from one to six inches in length, some with very sharp edges. The trees in this neighbourhood are remarkably turned in the direction of the prevalent wind, W. 10° N., many resembling trees struck by lightning.

East of the Douglas the Boulder Clay is well seen in the cliff called Red Bank, about 30 feet in height, and the beach beneath, the cliff being a notch cut in the clay by the tides of the Ribble. A little to the west a well-marked combe has been excavated by springs in the cliff.

West of the river Douglas there is a tract of Boulder Clay extending from Hesketh Bank to Sollom, being about three and a half miles in length, and a mile and a half in breadth, at the former place and at Tarleton. There can be little doubt that this clay is a portion of the same bed as that occurring on the eastern bank of the river; and if the latter is true Upper Boulder Clay, this bed must be so also. This view is the more strengthened by the fact that the true Upper Boulder Clay, seen at Freckleton Point, on the north side of the river Ribble, opposite Hesketh Bank, rests on the red marl without the intervention of the Middle and Lower Drifts. But in these low tracts of country, including that between Southport and Liverpool, it is difficult to know whether a clay belongs to the lower or upper division; because even when both happen to be present, divided by the Middle Drift, they are found to be precisely similar in character, the Lower Clay only becoming distinct when higher elevations are reached.

Preston District.—Between Preston and Longridge the character of the upper beds of the Upper Boulder Clay is well seen; from the bleaching effects of the atmosphere they are generally of bright-yellow colour or pure white, instead of the dark-purple, red or chocolate tint obtaining in the lower beds. In the upper part, in the fields near Grimsargh, faint traces of stratification* may be seen, small stones running in definite lines. Such traces are extremely rare. Rude lamination is, however, to be seen in pits in Penwortham, west of Preston; that between the letters " t " and " h " of Penwortham, and the other west of the word " New Gate," on the one-inch map. The basement bed, which is of the darkest colour and stiffest consistence, is well seen in the section at Red Scar, where it is 20 feet in thickness : the bed above is of a lighter tint, and contains a great number of erratic stones, mostly derived from the Lake District of Westmorland and North Lancashire.

The junction of the Upper Boulder Clay with the Middle Sands in the Canal-section, south of Brookhouse Mill, is marked by the intercalation of red shaley loam, a few inches in thickness, resembling, except in colour, the silty bed holding the same position at Norbreck.

Good sections of the Upper Boulder Clay, resting on the Middle Sand, occur in the deep valley of Tun Brook. At one point on the east side, near the top of the cliff, a bed of sand 12 feet in thickness, precisely similar to that of the Middle Drift, is intercalated in the Upper Boulder Clay before referred to.

Returning to the brooks between Tun Brook and Boilton, with short courses running immediately into the Ribble, the first to the west is small; rising at an elevation of 150 feet, it only flows eastwards 450 feet before reaching the Ribble plain at a level of 60 feet, falling therefore 90 feet in 450, or one foot in five, the gorge thus excavated being V-shaped in plan and section. In plan the V being longer and longer in these valleys, in proportion as there is a greater and a greater distance between the source and the outfall, as the springs gradually work backward, so this lengthens, and the angle of the fall of the stream becomes less and less steep. On examination of the brook-valleys with long courses flowing west from Grimsargh and Fulwood to the Ribble plain east of Clifton, I found the gradients of their beds to be one uniform slope from the source to the plain; in other words, these brooks have cut their channels as low as it is possible, so long as the level of the sea (and therefore of the plain on which they debouch) and that of their sources remain at their existing level.

In these streams denudation appears to be threefold,—*vertical*, cutting the channels downwards, always acting from below upwards, or from the outfall towards the source ; *longitudinal*, cutting away the banks on both sides when the streams flow straight, and the outer side only when it flows in a curve ; and *horizontal* where the stream or river, through excessive curving, in addition to wearing the edge of its channel, wears it completely backwards, causing the water to be thrown diagonally at the hill or bluff forming the limit of the valley, which thus receives the whole horizontal width of the stream.

In streams supplied by springs flowing out of the hill sides, it follows that if the strata dip inwards into the hill, that the further back the stream is cut the lower will be the level of the springs.

---

* I have recently found traces of stratification, in the Lower and Upper Boulder Clay, to be very common in the Wigan district ; and my colleague, Mr. Strahan, has noticed it around St. Helens.

(which must necessarily issue at the junction of permeable with impermeable beds). In these instances the cutting back of the stream by denudation will have the effect of lowering the level of the source. If, on the contrary, the strata have an outward dip, the source will be raised until it reaches the line along which the water-bearing stratum crops to the surface on the top of the hill, the slope corresponding to the dip of the bed, and not to the gradient of the stream below.

In the Glacial Drift beds the water-bearing seams occur at the surface of the Lower Boulder Clay, and on thin beds of clayey loam which occur in the Middle Drift as well as above the seams of consolidated sand and gravel found in that formation. The boss or mound-shaped arrangement so often found in these beds,—an envelope of Upper Boulder Clay covering a central mass of Middle Drift, or a thick bed of the latter covering an internal core of Lower Boulder Clay,—resembles to a certain extent the outward dip of strata; and the sources of nearly all the small brooks intersecting the Boulder Clay plain running to the Ribble occur in beds with this arrangement, and have no tendency to cut down their channels at their source, but rather in cutting back to ascend the hill. The ground above a spring is generally steep, and from 10 to 30 feet in height, up to the top of the plain, or to the undulating hollow which forms the upper portion of most of the brook-valleys running into the Ribble. It is particularly well seen in the valley behind Fishwick Hall, of which Fig. 13 is a diagram.

Fig. 13.

Sketch Map of Brooks near Fishwick Hall.

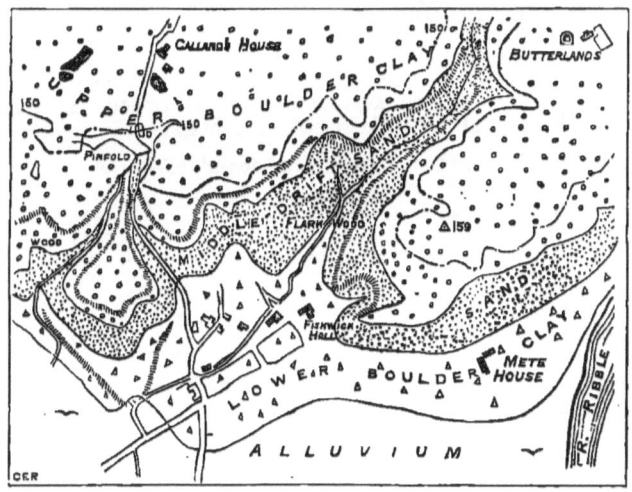

(Scale, 6 inches = 1 mile.)

At Moor Lane, in a pit at Moor Park Inn, I noticed a bed of Boulder Clay, of ordinary character, from 2 to 4 feet thick, containing erratic pebbles, intercalated in the Middle Sand, near the top of the section, and probably not far below the horizon of the top of the Middle Sand. In this and several other sections it would appear that the Upper Boulder Clay conditions set in, in advance of the period of deposition of the main mass ;—which, taken with the fact of the occasional occurrence of sand beds in the Upper Boulder Clay, as at Tun Brook, and in a brickfield north of Marsh End Preston, where five feet of sand is intercalated in the brick-clay, points to the interwedging and intercalation of these deposits, from the recurrence of similar conditions. This recurrence would account for the phenomena observable in the Bury district, where an interbedded clay occurs in the Middle Sand, and occupies a considerable area, and in the Manchester district, where several Boulder Clays and sand-beds alternate with each other ; though, at the same time, there is little doubt that the Boulder Clay found at the surface in different areas overlying sands and shingle-beds is of the same general age.

West Fylde District.—Between Preston and Kirkham, and Kirkham and Blackpool, the Upper Boulder Clay varies but little in its consistence, colour, or in the nature of the included fragments.

At Robbins I noticed a boulder of volcanic breccia derived from the Lake District, $6 \times 3\frac{1}{2} \times 3$ feet in size; and at the Fold, one of Trap, $4 \times 3 \times 3$ feet.

At Little Marton Windmill I found the pebbles in the brickfield to consist of—

Granite - - - -	1
Lake District volcanic series - - -	32
Quartz rock - - - -	4
Silurian grits - -	52
Permian breccia - - - -	4
Coal-measure sandstones - - -	7
	100

This locality, as well as the two last-mentioned, is in Lancashire Sheet 59 of the Ordnance Survey Map.

At Old Bank, in (Lan.) Sheet 51, I found, of—

Pebbles of Old Red Sandstone - - -	1
Carboniferous Limestone - -	12
Silurian grits - - -	36
Lake District volcanic series - - -	28
Trap - - - - -	3
Granite - - - -	20
	100

In the same 6-inch map, a good section of the Boulder Clay is seen in the cliff section of the River Wyre. The clay contained, of—

Carboniferous Limestone - - -	20
Silurian grits - - - - -	60
Granite - - - - -	8
Volcanic series - - - - -	12
	100

At Little Singleton, in the same 6-inch map I noticed an angular boulder containing about 48 cubic feet, and probably not weighing less than four tons.

The base of the Upper Boulder Clay resting on the Middle Sand is well shown on the north side of the Gwyn. Advancing towards Norbreck, very coarse current-bedded gravels are seen at the base of the cliff, resting on a boss of stiff loamy Lower Boulder Clay, without pebbles; which latter has only recently (1874) been exposed through the wearing back of the gravels, which rested against the mound of Boulder Clay on the seaward as well as on the north and south sides.

There are some traces of stratification in the Upper Boulder Clay at the top of the cliff, near the lane end, by Bank Farm—

				ft.	in.	
Loam	-	-	-	-	2	0
Red Clay, with two horizontal layers of pebbles				3	2
Upper Boulder Clay:						
Layer of stones in clay	-	-	-	0	4	
Band of large stones in clay	-	-		1	0	
Layer of small stones in clay	-	-		0	3	
Boulder Clay, without stone	-	-		1	6	
Stratified loam	-	-	-	0	9 —9	0
Bed of sand, with very large pebbles	-	-		—2		0
Sand	-	-	-	-	—1	0

A sort of synclinal arrangement of both deposits, the post-glacial and glacial, is seen in the gap near to Fanny Hall; the section being as follows:—

	feet.
a. Blown Sand at top of the cliff - - -⎤	4
b. Peat - - -⎬	1
c. Layer of stones - - - -⎮	0¼
d. Grey post-glacial clay - - - -⎦	4
e. Red Boulder Clay, to bottom of gap, 6 ft. -⎫	
„ „ „ below the bottom of the gap, 4 ft.⎬	10
f. Synclinal of loamy stratified clay - - -	5
g. Red Boulder Clay in the line of the gap - -	—
but thickening to the south, and still more to the north, at the expense of e, and resting on a nearly level floor of - - - - -	
h. Sand, dipping slightly south	-

The north end of the stratified bed dipping more strongly than the south, causes it to be more quickly cut off by the over-lying post-glacial beds. But this section is of great interest, through the stratified deposit entirely separating the one bed of Boulder Clay from the other, and from occurring so low in the Upper Boulder Clay section as nearly to be deposited at its lowest point on the Middle Sands,—pointing to sudden and unequal deposition of clays after the deposition of the sands, and immediate tranquil deposit of finer and more sandy material. From the loamy nature of the latter, springs are thrown out, which in 1873 produced an extensive land-slip of the bed e, causing the section, when I last visited it, to be not so clear as when I took the above note in 1870.

In 100 specimens of stones from the brick-clay, No. 1, near the Royal Edward (Bailey's Hotel), Mr. Binney[*] found that the stones there thrown out of the clay were of the following descriptions; viz. :—

A. Granites, greenstones, porphyries, &c.		- 42
B. Slates and silurians	-	- 44
C. Mountain Limestones	- - -	- 4
D. Coal-measures, sandstones	- -	- 8
E. New Red Sandstones and other newer rocks		- 2
		100

In another brickyard near the railway-station at Blackpool, Mr. Binney observed :—

Of	Total.	Angular.	Partly Rounded.	Rounded.
A.	49	17	20	12
B.	32	5	16	11
C.	6	3	2	1
D.	9	4	3	1
E.	4	1	2	1
	100	30	43	26

Six of the Slates and Silurian specimens (B.) were striated.

From the sand beds the author gives a list of 11 univalve and 8 bivalve shells.

In the bed No. 4. the author found one-half of the stones to be angular, nearly all striated, and some to weigh a ton. Out of 100 small specimens examined—

1 was New Red Sandstone. (Permian ?—C. E. R.)
10 were carboniferous limestones.
4 were   „   gritstones.
49 were silurian and slates.
36 were granites, greenstones, porphyries, &c.

The author also found fragments of shells, *Nucula, Buccinum, Dentalium, Tellina, Cardium, Psammobia,* and *Turritella,* two specimens of Liassic rock, containing *Gryphœa incurva* ; and pieces of chalk flint; which latter the author believed to have been derived from Ireland.

Since writing the above, I have had opportunities of examining the chalk flints of the north-east of Ireland *in sitû,* and think there is no doubt of the correctness of Mr. Binney's opinion. Several worked flints I obtained at the top of the Giant's Causeway exhibited the same peculiarities. Liassic fossils have also been picked up on the Blackpool beach by my colleague, Mr. Tiddeman, by Mr. Mackintosh, F.G.S., and by myself.

At the end of this Memoir I have noted the shells found in the clays and sands by Mr. Binney, as well as those collected by other observers who have published their results, supplementing the list by that of the species collected by myself.

---

[*] Mem. Lit. Phil. Soc. Manchester, Second Series, vol. x. p. 121.   Binney, E.W., F.R.S.:—"Notes on the Drift Deposits found near Blackpool."

The thickness of Upper Boulder Clay is small, but eastwards it thickens very rapidly, the surface of the sand beneath sinking and undulating. The top of the Upper Boulder Clay, though inclining inland, maintains a constant level, being apparently a surface of deposition.

The uniformity of the slope of the country towards the sea, though subject to undulations below the plane, is constant in the district, stray hills never rising above. These undulations, though unimportant in the greater part of the Preston sheet, increase in number and depth in the country to the north and west, where they form "swamp-hollows," generally filled in at the bottom with peat, occasionally underlain by lacustrine clay. The hollows are entirely excavated in the glacial deposits, and the rock-surface is invariably at a considerable depth below the bottom of the hollow, trending, like the surface of the Drift, in an inclined plane from the Grit Fells at Chipping, at 500 feet, towards the sea; but, unlike the Drift, its surface is at least 20 feet below the Ordnance datum-line instead of nearly 100 feet above it. It is clear, therefore, that though the rock and the Drift surface start from the same point, the fall of the latter is less than that of the former by nearly 120 feet, and that the whole of the space intervening between the two planes must be filled in with drift of that thickness. And thus it is that in the Preston quarter-sheet, 89 N.W., the rock in the western portions is found only at the bottom of the Ribble valley and near the mouths of its immediate tributaries, and that in all the deep brook-valleys north of the Ribble, including even that of Tun Brook, near Redscar, which is 80 feet in depth, the base of the drift is not seen; and it is only on approaching the Fell country that the rock crops to the surface at the bottom of the deep brook-valleys.

If it be admitted that the surface of the Glacial Drift plain owed its inclination to deposition, and not to denudation, then it is easy to understand that the surface would be subject to a certain amount of undulation, and hollows would be left, the level of the entrances to which would be often above that of the central part of the depression, resembling in this respect the "Rock-basin" of Prof. Ramsay, though due to so entirely different a cause. And it would also explain the fact that these swamp-hollows, when numerous, are separated from each other by "cols," and are entirely unconnected with the drainage of the country;—as may be well seen east of Blackpool, where the bottom of every swamp-hollow is found to be filled with peat, and to receive and not discharge the drainage of the more immediate area. Even in the largest of these, Marton Mere, the present drainage is entirely artificial;—the Lake being due to the collection of water in a Boulder Clay basin, and not like Martin Mere on the south side of the Ribble, merely the result of obstruction of drainage of a flat country, much of which is below spring-tide high-water mark.

East Fylde* District (Broughton).— Stiff reddish-brown coloured Upper Boulder Clay is seen at the brick-field near Savick Brook,

---

* The district called the "Fylde" or field of Lancashire is noted for its grain-growing capabilities, and has been called "the Cornfield of Amounderness." The latter name, that of the Hundred, or Old Wapentake, is said to be derived from the promontory or projection of Almund or Edmond, while the district to the north was called the Further-ness, contracted into Furness.

south of Haighton Hall. The joint-partings, and portions here and there, are of a deep bluish-grey colour. Of the included pebbles and boulders, 25 per cent. are sub-angular; the rest quite rounded. They consist of Scratched Limestone, 3 per cent; Yoredale Grits, 20 per cent. ; Lake-district Traps and Volcanic Ashes, 70 per cent.; Granite, 5 per cent. A little to the south, towards Gander Hall, the clay thins out, and the Middle Sand forms the surface.

In the excavations for the new Lunatic Asylum at Whittingham, and in the brick-fields there, I observed the following per-centage of included fragments :—White Quartz, 6 per cent. ; Criffel Granite, 4 per cent; other Granites and Trap, 70 per cent.; Black Chert, 2 per cent.; White scratched Mountain Limestone, 2 per cent. ;* Yoredale Grits, 10 per cent. A large boulder, of Lake-district origin, was discovered in the clay during the excavation, and will be preserved in the garden of the Institution.

Smaller boulders occur by the road side near Haighton Hall, and south of Brabiner, near the brick-field, the former being Trap, and the latter Greenstone.

A per-centage of the included pebbles in the fields south of Withy Trees gave—Trap, 8 per cent., all scratched ; 90 Silurian Grits, of which 5 were scratched ; and 2 Yoredale or Millstone Grits. This tendency for one sort of rock to prevail in the erratics of one field, or tract, is rather marked, and points to local (erratic) freights of floating ice. The heights on which these boulders occur are respectively 225 and 205 feet above the sea-level.

North Fylde.—At Lane, Hardhead, west of Garstang, 3 feet of Boulder Clay is seen overlying the Permian Red Sandstone. The surface of the latter is more or less rounded, but no distinct traces of ice-action are visible.

At High Crookey a well has been sunk through the Upper Boulder Clay into the Permian. The Middle Sands were very thin, and the Lower Clay absent ; the drift was 30 feet thick; the level of the surface of the ground, more than 50 feet above the mean sea-level ; so that the surface of the rock must be about 25 feet above the mean sea-level.

Fig. 14.

Section near Berries Hill, Bay Horse.

| a. Soil. | b. Peat. |
| c. Boulder of Yoredale Grit. | d. Gravel, with sand bed e. |

f. Yoredale Grits.

In the above section, Fig. 14, the Upper Boulder Clay rests on a slightly smoothed surface of the Yoredale Rocks, which above have

---

* Northwards, at Carnforth and Morecambe, limestone pebbles and boulders in the Upper Boulder Clay are very numerous and of great size.

been worn and eroded, as well as the Boulder Clay overlying them; the latter has been denuded away on the slope-side, beds of gravel, probably of the age of the Preesall Shingle, having been deposited in the space thus left vacant.

In the railway-section at Garstang, the character of the Upper Boulder Clay is seen to be changing, for though containing many erratic blocks, the included fragments are far more local than in the country to the west. The following, Fig. 15, shows the manner of its occurrence in regard to the Middle Sands and the underlying rocks.

Fig. 15.

a. Upper Boulder Clay, graduating downwards into
b. Loamy gravel with many pebbles, and large stones.
d. Red Sandstone,   } Permian.
e. Red shaly marl-seams, }

The following villages and hamlets in this district are situated on the Upper Boulder Clay:— Blackpool, Poulton-le-Fylde, Layton, Staining, Newton, Little Marton, Mythorpe, Dagger's Hole, Great Plumpton, Weeton, Swarbrick Hall, Hardthorn, Warbreck, Great and Little Carleton, Bispham, Norbreck, Thornton, Great and Little Singleton, Hambleton, Stainall, Stalmine, Preesall, Wrea Green, Warton, Freckleton, Treales, Newton, Scales, Lund, Clifton, Ashton, Fullwood, Ribbleton, Samelsbury, Penwortham, Howick, Hutton, Longton, Farrington, Bamber Bridge, Moon's Mill, Houghton, Hesketh Bank, Hesketh with Becconsall, Much Hoole, Tarleton, Bretherton, Eccleston, Euxton, Brindle, Whittle-le-Woods, Heapey, Duxbury, Coppull, Maudesley, Rufford.

ESKER DRIFT.

North-east of Chorley there are several remarkable mound-like hills which rise abruptly from the surface of the Upper Boulder Clay, and apparently rest upon it. One of these, known as Pickering Castle, is 75 feet in height.

Immediately north of the district described in this Memoir, at Carnforth, occur a great number of mounds of Shingle and Sand, the former containing a large quantity of Mountain Limestone Boulders. These were long ago described by Dr. Buckland, who, however, attributed them to glacier action.

Whether they are Eskers of the Esker period is doubtful ; but whether they rest on the Upper Boulder Clay, or on an older deposit, it is clear they owe their present form to deposition, and not denudation. Whether they belong to the Middle Sand series is a point which my colleague, Mr. Tiddeman, who is surveying that district, will doubtless be enabled to make out.

Glaciated Rock Surfaces of Western Lancashire, and their Geological Date.

Since the year 1816, when Playfair declared, after his visit to the Alps, that no power could have transported the great angular erratics of Switzerland but glaciers which formerly extended far down the valleys, several theories have been promulgated as to the origin of the thick beds of clay containing erratic boulders, associated with smoothed and scratched rock surfaces, occurring over the greater part of Scotland, and Northern and Central England.

One of the first, of which Sir James Hall was the chief exponent, was based on the assumption that these phenomena were due to violent floods or debacles, which, sweeping over the country from the north-west to the south-east, deposited the clay, smoothed the hills, and scored the rocks.

Another, that of Mr. Maclaren, first published in 1828, assumed the effects to have been produced by great oceanic currents, sometimes carrying icebergs laden with earth, stones, and boulders, moving from the north-west to the south-east ; this may be considered as the germ of the iceberg theory of the origin of Boulder Clay, still held in part by many geologists.

Agassiz, after visiting Scotland in 1840, suggested that the whole of that country had been the home of glaciers, which descended every valley from the hills above, as is now the case in Switzerland, scoring, smoothing, and scratching the rocks beneath, and carrying on their surface erratic blocks derived from the rocks above, far up the valley ; and indeed went further than this, stating that the whole of Britain was covered by an ice-sheet, which passed over hill and dale, as is now the case in Greenland, and that it was only towards the close of the Glacial Epoch that this ice-sheet so far dwindled away as to consist of isolated valley-glaciers, such as now exist in Norway and Sweden.

For a great many years after the publication of this "ice-sheet theory" geologists shrank from accepting it; and, though admitting the period of glacial cold, and the possible presence of small glaciers in the deeper valleys of mountainous tracts, attributed the formation

of Boulder Clay, as well as the scratched and smoothed rock surfaces beneath it, to the action of icebergs borne by currents from
the North; but in 1851 Professor Ramsay found evidence that
though marine deposits existed amongst the mountains of North
Wales, which proved that country to have been submerged to a
depth of nearly 2,000 feet, yet beneath these marine beds the
rocks were smoothed and striated in a manner which could only
have arisen from the action of Glaciers before the submergence.
These glaciers again filled the valleys, though on a smaller scale, on
the re-elevation of the land, often scooping out the marine drift,
and often depositing a moraine in the space thus left vacant;
the sequence of events being—Glaciers, submergence with marine
drift, and Glaciers with later moraines.

In 1852, Mr. Robert Chambers described the whole of Northern
Britain as having been covered by an ice-sheet derived from the
circum-polar ice, moving from N.W. to S.E., grinding down the
country in that direction, the resulting débris forming the Boulder
Clay. A nearly similar opinion was held in a paper read 10 years
later by Mr. Jamieson, F.G.S., who stated that no icebergs running aground, nor pack-ice driven by the winds, nor coast-ice lashed
by the breakers, could explain the worn and polished surfaces
always found on the land side of rocks, which he believed to have
been produced by a continental ice-sheet like that of Greenland.*

But the same author, writing of Scotland, now states that the
great development of snow and ice around a mass of mountains
caused a localization of weight, which resulted in a *radiated* ice-
flow in all directions ; which ice, on its outward progress, would
never have reached the limits of its drainage-basin had it not
received fresh snow-falls on its journey seawards. He comments
on the great rain-fall of the western side of Britain, which would
be represented by a greater snow-fall in glacial times, and the
greater amount of peat growth in later times, which was the result
of the rain.†

A similar radiate direction of the flow of the glaciers was
observed by myself in the Lake District of Cumberland and Westmoreland in 1869, and has since been made out in detail by
Mr. Clifton Ward. From an examination of the map accompanying
Mr. Tiddeman's paper on the glaciation of Western Yorkshire, it
would appear that no glacial striæ have been observed in the district described by him at elevations above 1,500 feet; that striæ
only occur on watersheds, where the ice was passing from one
valley into another by the lowest col; that the striæ point to
the ice going round, being deflected by all high hills, such as
Ingleboro', and that there is a tendency for all the scratches to
run parallel to the valleys.

The ice would appear not to have covered the whole of the
Penine ridge up to the snow-shed, but to have gathered in the
valleys, and thence poured seaward over the plains. During its
progress, it is probable the stiff dark-coloured clay with sub-angular
local boulders, the waste of the underlying rocks, occurring on the

---

* Quar. Jour. Geol. Soc., vol. xviii., 1862, p. 164.—" On the Ice-worn Rocks of
Scotland."

† Quar. Jour. Geol. Soc., vol. xxx., 1874, p 317. T. F. Jamieson :—" On the Last
Stage of the Glacial Period in North Britain."

western slopes of the spurs of the Penine chain, came into existence. The Till was probably formed at the same time as the Lower Moraine Drifts of the mountains of North Wales and Cumberland. To this era may be attributed the formation of those polished and scratched rock-surfaces occurring at various points on the lowlands skirting the coasts of Lancashire and Cheshire. The vast glaciers emerging from the valleys of the Duddon, the Leven, and the Kent coalesced into one sheet, probably swept southwards over Western Lancashire and Cheshire, and what is now sea, until their progress was stopped by the Welsh mountains, or by the barrier formed by the glaciers extending northwards from them, the level of the land being probably much as at present. Summed up, the sequence of events in north-western England and Wales appears to have been as follows, in descending order :—

Moraines. *Glaciers* in N. Wales and Lake District, and deeper valleys of Penine Hills.

ELEVATION.
Upper Boulder Clay. *Coast-ice.* Drift from the north-west.
Middle Drift Sand. *Tidal-currents.* Local Drift.
Lower Boulder Clay. *Sea and ice-foot.* Drift from the north-west.

SUBMERGENCE.
Till. Lower Moraine Drift. Large *Glaciers* and *Ice-sheet.*

The subsidence probably commenced at the beginning of the Glacial Epoch, and possibly before it ; but it was not until the Lower Boulder Clay period that the lowlands became submerged, when some denudation of Till took place, and the deposition of loam brought down by rivers into the sea from the Permian and Triassic districts to the east and south commenced, and was spread out by the flood tide, which then probably flowed to the S.S.E., as it still does on the Cumberland coast.

The clay and till beneath the Middle Sands may have been formed simultaneously ; for when the lowlands of Lancashire were submerged beneath the sea, an ice-sheet covered the land, and an ice-foot surrounded the sea-margin, which received vast quantities of rocks from the Cumberland and North Lancashire mountains. On the ice-foot breaking and melting whilst being carried by currents from the N.W. to the S.E., these Lake District fragments would be deposited amongst the sediment, and form the erratic pebbles and boulders of the low-level Lower Boulder Clay.

Everywhere in the Lake District of Cumberland, Westmoreland, and North Lancashire, we meet with traces of land-ice. Not only do the Lakes Windermere, Rydal Water, Grasmere, Thirlmere, Wastwater, &c. &c., lie in rock-basins scooped out by ice to a depth of hundreds of feet below the present sea-level, and the valleys and gorges in which they lie exhibit scratchings, scorings, and rounded rocks, but the comparatively flat and high ground intervening between the various valleys and gorges exhibit the marks of glaciation. The snow gathered round the pikes of Sca Fell and other peaks, from which the ice radiated in every direction—pouring from the plains, over the edges of the cliffs, whenever an indentation or hollow occurred, into the valleys below.

The immense masses of ice poured down from above, uniting in the main gorges, scooped out the various lake-basins referred to ; the resulting deposit of this grinding by land-ice being true Moraine

Drift, often of enormous thickness. Much of this, however, has since been denuded away, partly by the sea, but chiefly through later glaciation. Possibly many of the older Moraines of the Lake District may have been formed by glaciers under the sea when the valleys were submerged beneath it; but, in any case, it is probable that, in the periods occupied by the deposition of both the Lower and the Upper Boulder Clay, glaciers reached the sea, and, breaking off in fragments, floated off in stone-laden bergs southwards, and that during the export the land-ice had retreated from its former position over the Irish sea bed, back to the entrances of the valleys of the Lake District and the Penine chain.

Glacial Striæ near the S.W. Coast of Lancashire and Cheshire.

Locality and Elevation.	Direction.	Discoverer.	Trans. and Date.
Ordsall, Old Clough, near Manchester.	N. 40 W.	J. Plant, F.G.S. -	Trans. Man. Geol. Soc., vol. vi.,1868.
Mellor, near Blackburn	E. 10 N. -	J. Eccles, F.G.S	
Euxton, near Preston	N.N.W. -	R. H. Tiddeman,	Quar. Jour. Geol. Soc., 1872, vol. xxviii, p. 489.
Grey Heights, east of Chorley.	N.N.W.	F.G.S.	
Near Burnt Edge Colliery, Horwich Moor, 1160 ft.	W. 12 N. -	E. Hull, F.R.S.	Geological Survey.
Middeshurst's Delf, near St. Helens.	W. 33 N. -	A. Strahan, F.G.S.	,,
St. Helens and Wigan Railway, near Garswood.	W. 30 N. -	,,	,,
St. Helens and Huyton Quarry Railway, near Thatto Heath.	W. 35 N. -	Dr. Ricketts, F.G.S.	Brit. Assoc. Liverpool, Meeting 1872.
Ditto.	N.W. -	C.E. De Rance, F.G.S.	Geological Survey.
Runcorn Gap Viaduct, bed of the river Mersey.	W. 8 N. -	A. Strahan, F.G.S.	,,
Near Appleton Quarry.	W. 8 N. -	,,	,,
Farncombe Churchyard.	W. 8 N. -	,,	,,
Liverpool District: Toxteth Park, Liverpool, 120.	N. 42 W. -	G.H. Morton, F.G.S.	Quar. Jour. Geol. Soc., vol.18, p.377.
Boundary Street, Kirkdale.	N. 15 W. -	,,	,,
New Road, Kirkdale, 80 feet.	,, -	,,	,,
Stanley Road, Liverpool.	N.E. by E. and 22 W. of N.	Mellard Reade, C.E., F.G.S.	Proc. Liverpool Geol. Soc., 1872.
Ditto. -	E.N.E.; N.N.W		
Flayhrick Hill, ½ S.E. of Telegraph on Bidston Hill, 120 feet.	N. 30 W. -	G. H. Morton, F.G.S.	"Geology of Liverpool."
Bidston Hill, Cheshire.	N.N.W.; N.10 W.	E. Hull, F.R.S. -	Trans. Man. Geol. Soc., vol. iv. p. 288. 1864.
St. Patrick's Chapel, Heysham.	S. - -	R. H. Tiddeman	Quar. Jour. Geol. Soc.,vol.xxviii, 1872.
Ingleboro Hill at 1375 ft.	S. 35 W. - -		

Transport of Erratic Boulders occurring in the Lancashire Boulder Clays and Sands.

Not only are the Middle Sands and Shingle of Lancashire of marine origin, but a vast number of the pebbles and boulders of the great Upper Boulder Clay of Lancashire and Cheshire are more or less waterworn, many of them having been previously scratched, and occasionally they even lie in continuous lines in the midst of the fine reddish sediment derived from the waste of Permian and Triassic strata making up the Upper Boulder Clay of the district. There can be little doubt that the reason why stratification is so seldom seen, is that the fineness of the material makes the lamination extremely minute.* The Lower Boulder Clay of Norbreck Cliffs and the Ribble Valley at Preston occurring at low-levels, also contains rounded pebbles; and in both clays shells occur of the same species as those found in the Middle Sand.

After the submergence commenced the climate ameliorated, and the Middle Sands were deposited around the coasts of an open but gradually deepening sea. Everywhere the current-bedding of the sands is in a south-easterly or east-south-easterly direction, proving the existence of great north-westerly tidal currents. This is the present direction of the flow tide in the northern part of the Irish Sea, and would, I presume, be that of nearly the whole of that sea, were a large portion of Ireland submerged.†

It is in the highest degree probable, looking to the numerous alternations of clay with sand seen in many colliery and well sections, that all the large exposures of sand and shingle seen at various points of the country do not all represent the same precise period, though conditions prevailed at one particular time, which led to a very large deposition of sand over a very extensive area during the Middle Drift era; but, at the same time, it is unlikely that all sand and gravel exposures are referable to that precise epoch. Alternations of climate of minor extent may often have caused changes of the matter deposited at the sea bottom; and this may still more often have been effected by pauses in subsidence, during which denudation went on along the sea-coast, producing sand and shingle beds.

In Cumberland, North Wales, and Derbyshire, beds of the age of the Middle Sands and Shingle rise to heights of 1,200 and 1,500 feet. Everywhere they are composed of the waste of the rocks of the immediate neighbourhood, produced by the action of the breakers upon successive lines of coasts; which breaker action probably exerted an important detaching influence on the exposed granite of Wastdale Crag in the Shap Fells (an elevation of 1,600 feet), more especially in breaking up the great masses brought down by the ice of the first glaciation.

---

* Near Wigan and also near Garston, exceedingly laminated bands of clay occur both in the Boulder Clay and associated with the sands. When the eye is trained to observe this minute stratification, banded structure is found to be generally observable in most sections of Boulder Clay.

† Since writing the above, I have had the opportunity of examining several sections of the Middle Sands in the North-East of Ireland, and have noticed several in the counties Down and Antrim, which distinctly showed traces of current-bedding to the S.S.W.

The masses and boulders would remain lying on the beach lines of the Middle Drift period, until on the refrigeration of the country, coast-ice surrounded them, and floated off fragments of the Granite southward into Lancashire, and south-eastward into Yorkshire, where they are described by Messrs. S. V. Wood, junr., and Rome, as occurring so frequently in their "Purple Clay without chalk," which is possibly merely the deep-water condition of that "with chalk," and the shallower water "chalky Boulder Clay."*

In the purple clays of the north-east of England, as in the red (purple?) Upper Boulder Clay of the north-west, the included fragments appear to have been brought by flow tides, and the fine sediment constituting the matrix of the clay by the ebb;—a similar process to that now going on on the South Lancashire coast, where sand is carried south, and pebbles north. The direction of the largest amount of Lake District erratics in Lancashire and Cheshire appears to run from the mouth of the Leven.

At Blackpool a considerable number of flints occur in the Middle Sands, which have every appearance of having been derived from the Irish chalk. At Crewe, Mr. J. E. Taylor, F.G.S., found a great number of flints in the sand underlying the Upper Boulder Clay, but whether they were derived from the Irish or English Chalk is not stated.

---

* The result of the gradual deepening of the sea-bottom, exposing first the chalk, then chalk and red rocks, to the action of the waves and coast-ice.

ABSTRACT NOTES OF SOME PAPERS ON THE GLACIAL DRIFTS OF THE VALLEYS OF THE MERSEY AND IRWELL.

When revising for publication the proofs of the Drift Edition of the one-inch maps around Manchester, viz., 89 S.E., 88 S.W., and 81 N.W., which were surveyed by Prof. Hull, it appeared to me that the great detail in which the various drift deposits are represented required some further explanation than that afforded by the already published "Memoirs" on those sheets, which were designed to illustrate merely the solid geology of this county, and I have been led to add the following abstracts of some of the important papers that have been written on the District.

Dr. Bostock* in 1823 described the occurrence of rounded pebbles and boulders, which have undergone a great degree of attrition, found in clays overlying the New Red Sandstone of S.W. Lancashire, and nearly the whole of Cheshire. The fragments include portions of basalt, greenstone, and other igneous rocks. The upper portion of the clay, for about 10 inches in depth, is more sandy than the great mass of it, and is called "ravin."

Mr. Joshua Trimmer,† in a paper "On the discovery of Marine Shells of existing species on the left bank of the river Mersey and above the level of high-water mark," describes sand with clay below, which contains erratic fragments of granite, syenite, and greenstone, some weighing a quarter of a ton. In the lower part occurred shells of *Cardium.* At Runcorn he found shells of *Turritella* and *Buccinum.*

Sir R. I. Murchison,‡ "On the Gravel and Alluvia of South Wales, and Siluria, as distinguished from a Northern Drift covering Lancashire, Cheshire, North Salop, &c.," describes the detritus over these (Northern) Counties to have been derived from the Cumberland Mountains, and mentions the occurrence of marine shells in gravels at and near Preston.

The Rev. Prof. Buckland,§ "On the evidence of Glaciers in Scotland and the North of England," describes the signs of glaciation in the valleys of the English Lake District; attributes the presence of Criffel Granite at Carlisle and Cockermouth to floating ice, and considers the gravel mounds at Carnforth to be glacier moraines. He mentions the occurrence of Shap Granite on the Scottish shores of the Solway Firth.

Mr. Binney, ‖ in a paper entitled "Sketch of the Drift Deposits of Manchester and its neighbourhood," divides the foreign drift into, (1) Lower Sand and Gravel ; (2) Till ; (3) Upper Sand and Gravel ; (4) Valley Gravel.

---

* Geol. Soc. Trans., 2nd ser., vol. ii. p. 138, March 1823.
† Geol. Soc. Proc., vol. i., p. 419, Jan. 1833.
‡ Proc. Geol. Soc., vol. ii. p. 230, Feb. 16, 1836.
§ Proc. Geol. Soc., vol. iii. pp. 332, 345, Nov. and Dec. 1840.
‖ Statistical Society of Manchester, 1841.

The same author, in " Notes on the Lancashire and Cheshire
Drift," 1842.*, describes foreign drift as high as 1,200 feet above
the sea at Pikelow, near Macclesfield, which passed over the
Penine chain through the valley of Todmorden to Hebden
Bridge, by the summit-valley above Littleborough, 610 feet above
the level of the sea.   Near the coast, a brown Till is covered by
thin "forest sand," while at Manchester there is both an upper
(No. 3) and a lower sand and gravel (No. 1).   The latter contains
pebbles of granites, syenites, greenstones, slate, mountain limestone, and coal-measure rocks.   No. 2, known in the country as
" marl," and near towns as "brick-clay," is a stiff brown clay, with
pebbles and blocks varying from the size of a pea to blocks 6 tons
in weight; some of which are angular, and scored with striæ,
derived from the Lake District and Scotland.   The clay, when
allowed to dry in the open air, cleaves vertically, the faces
exhibiting a dull blue colour, probably owing to the presence of
carbonate of iron.

In the gravel, No. 3, at Kersal Moor, rounded blocks of granite
occur, and no striated or perfectly angular blocks were found in it
by the author, or in beds 1 and 4.

The country between Manchester, Bury, and Stockport is one
great sand-bank extending into Cheshire.

Mr. Binney mentions the occurrence of marine shells at Preston,
Ormskirk, Blackrod, Haigh, Bowdon, and Swettenham, and mentions
that the sands have sometimes a decided dip to the S.W.

He describes beds (No. 4) of fine and coarse gravel and sand in
the bottoms and sides of valleys and low lands now traversed by
the rivers Irwell, Roche, and Mersey, the pebbles of which are
derived from deposits Nos. 1, 2, and 3.

The same author† divides the deposits in and about Manchester into the following sequence:—

No. 1.—Coarse gravel, with layers of fine sand,—most frequently
stratified, sometimes unstratified,—with erratic pebbles, 0 to 12 yards,
on the sides of the three great valleys near Manchester.

No. 2.—Sharp Forest sand, parted with layers of gravel, containing the same rocks as No. 1., but generally more regularly
stratified, and occasionally containing thin seams of Till, 0 to 25
yards.

No. 3.—"Till" (the brick-clay of Manchester, &c.), a mass of
strong brown clay, with rocks similar to those in Nos. 1 and 2,
0 to 30 yards.

No. 4.—A bed of sand, or coarse gravel, with pebbles of the
same kind of rocks as Nos. 1, 2, and 3 above, well-rounded sometimes, 0 to 11 yards, in the valley of the Irwell.

Mr. Binney gives sections showing the undulation of the surface of the sand and gravel beneath the Till in Manchester.

He attributes the formation of the sand and gravel to marine
currents and coast action ; that of the Till being due to still sea
waters, occasionally agitated by violent currents.

---

* Trans. Man. Geol. Soc. vol. viii. p. 30, containing paper read before the Society
in 1842–43.

† Proc. Lit. Phil. Soc. Man., second series, vol. viii., 1848, p. 204:—"Sketch of
the Drift Deposits of Manchester and its Neighbourhood."

He gives the following table of the rocks from the Till near Manchester.

	Salford.	Cheetham.	Openshaw.	Mean.
Granites, Greenstones, &c. -	21	15	27	21
Angular	3	5	7	5
Partly rounded	12	7	11	10
Rounded	6	3	9	6
Slates and Silurian Rocks -	19	27	17	21
Angular	3	4	4	3·66
Partly rounded -	11	8	8	9·0
Rounded	5	15	5	8·33
Mountain Limestones	5	6	7	6
Angular	1	2	0	1
Partly rounded	3	2	4	3
Rounded	1	2	3	3
Coal Measures	49	50	49	49·33
Angular	22	31	23	25·33
Partly rounded	21	16	20	19
Rounded -	6	3	6	5
New Red Sandstone	6	2	0	2·66
Angular	4	2	0	2
Partly rounded	2	0	0	0·66
Rounded -	0	0	0	0
	100	100	100	100
Striated Rocks	2	2	1	1·66

Mr. Binney attributes the presence of erratics in the Manchester Till to the falling of blocks from floating icebergs drifting from the Lake District, which he believes to have been probably covered with icebergs.

On the elevation of the land and consequent shoaling of the sea, the ice ceased to enter the latter, but strong currents brought down sand and gravel No. 2. The land still rising, the deposits 2, 3, and 4 were cut through by currents, and the gravels No. 1 were formed.

Dr. J. B. Edwards* described "The Titaniferous Iron of the Mersey Shore," from the Boulder Clay.

Mr. G. H. Morton,† F.G.S., ("Traces of Icebergs near Liverpool,") describes the occurrence of stones and boulders striated by the action of ice.

The same Author,‡ in a Report "On the Pleistocene Deposits of the District around Liverpool," divides the Drift into three subdivisions.

A year later§ he also describes glacial surface-markings near Liverpool.

---

* Report Brit. Assoc., Glasgow, 1855.
† Proc. Lit. Phil. Soc., Liverpool, 1859; and Proc. Liverpool Geol. Soc., 1859.
‡ Report Brit. Assoc., Manchester, 1861, p. 120.
§ Quar. Jour. Geol. Soc., vol. xviii,, 1862, p. 377.

Prof. Hull,* in his " Memoirs on the Country around Bolton," describes the occurrence of Glacial Drifts on Winter Hill, at an elevation of 1,380 feet, containing scratched, polished, and grooved pebbles and boulders of granite, slates, and trappean rocks, derived from the Lake District of England. He adopts Mr. Binney's classification of the Drift, and describes the " Upper Sand " (Middle Drift) as reaching a thickness at times of 150 feet.

Prof. Hull, in his " Memoir on the Geology of the Country around Wigan," 1862, gives a similar description of the drift deposits which wrap round the whole of the lower region, and rise to the summit of Ashurst Beacon, 560 feet.

Mr. E. W. Binney,† in his "Geology of Manchester and its Neighbourhood," gives the following sequence of drift deposits :—

		yards.
1.	Valley ground, two well marked terraces above present rivers	0—12
2.	Forest sand and gravel - - -	0—25
3.	Silt, with occasional bands of silt and sand -	0—30
4.	Lower gravel, stratified and unstratified, pebbles well rounded, 0—11 yards, average 2,	

The Lower Gravel yields a bright lime (hard ?) water, known at Haelds as "brandy-and-water water," in the wells between Spring Gardens and Piccadilly.

The author repeats the table of erratic rocks given in his paper read in 1842, abstracted above, and attributes the valley gravels to marine origin.

Mr. J. Whitaker,‡ of Burnley, in 1863, described the occurrence of chalk flints at Barrowford, at the foot of Pendle Hill.

Mr. Binney, F.R.S.,§ " Recent Marine Shells near Mottram-in-Longdendale," had visited the locality with Messrs. Bateman, C.E., and Prestwich, F.R.S., and found in the excavations of the Hollingworth reservoir shells of the species *Turritella terebra, Fusus Bamfius, Purpura lapillus, Tellina sp.,* and *Cardium edule.* Marine shells were also discovered by Mr. Prestwich in the gravels near Macclesfield, from which large numbers were afterwards procured by Messrs. Sainter, Darbishire, and Green.

Prof. E. Hull, F.R.S.‖ "Additional Observations on the Drift Deposits and more recent gravels around Manchester." The author establishes the following sequence for the Glacial Drift of Lancashire, Cheshire, and Derbyshire :—

1. Upper Boulder Clay.
2. Middle sand and gravel.
3. Lower Boulder Clay.

Beds 2 and 3 had been previously described by Mr. Binney (Mem. Lit. Phil. Soc., vol. viii., 2nd series), whose lower sand-bed the author shows to be local. He believes the River Terrace of

---

* Mem. Geol. Survey, 1862, p. 29.
† Trans. Man. Geol. Soc., vol. iii., 1862:—Geology of Manchester and its Neighbourhood.
‡ Trans. Man. Geol. Soc., vol. iv. p. 176, 1863.
§ Proc. Lit. Phil. Soc. Man., vol. iii. p.15, 1864. Binney, E. W. :—Recent Marine Shells near Mottram-in-Longdendale. Read Dec. 1862.
‖ Op. cit., p. 212 ; and Third Series, vol. ii. p. 499. Read Dec. 1863.

the valley of the Mersey and Irwell, from Didsbury and Manchester westward to near Warrington, and from Altringham to Eccles, to have been formed when the land stood lower than at present, and the rains during floods covered a far wider area than they do now.

The apparent wedging of sand into Till, alluded to by Mr. Binney, Prof. Hull attributes to the thinning out of the sand causing the upper clay to rest on the lower, and calls attention to the great denudation the Middle Sand has often experienced before the deposition of the Upper Boulder Clay. He suggests that the gravels of Bispham, described by Mr. Binney (1852), belong to the Middle Sand and Gravel, which has yielded so many shells at Macclesfield. Prof. Hull attributes the valley gravels (1) to a period when the tides extended as far up the Mersey as Manchester and Didsbury ; the two rivers having thus a very slight fall, covered the plain with gravel.

Prof. Hull,* in his " Geology of the Country around Oldham," gives the same classification, and a detailed description of the various drift deposits.

Mr. Binney,† " Lancashire and Cheshire Drift," states that out of 11 Manchester well-sections, 10 show a lower sand and gravel, and that he has observed it in other parts of Lancashire. He gives a section at Hyde, exhibiting six beds of Boulder Clay, and another at Outwood, showing only three.

Mr. Morton, F.G.S.,‡ in his " Geology of Liverpool," described the glacial deposits of the valley of the Mersey, and the direction of the glacial striæ at Liverpool.

Mr. R. D. Darbishire, F.G.S.§ " Notes on Marine Shells' found in Stratified Drift at Macclesfield." Specimens were found at the cemetery 500 feet above the sea, in sand and shingle, exhibiting current-bedding. He records 50 species of mollusca, including the rather southern species *Cytherea chione, Cardium rusticum, C. aculeatum,* and *Arca lactea.* The author mentions the occurrence of nine species of shells, at an elevation of 1,200 feet above the sea, on the east side of Macclesfield.

Prof. Hull, F.R.S.,‖ " On the Occurrence of Glacial Striations on the Surface of Bidston Hill," describes groovings in the New Red Sandstone at, (1) Kirkdale Jail, running N. 10° W., with a small number of cross groovings pointing east; at (2) Gore Street, on the north side of Liverpool, running north ; at (3) Park Hill House, on the south side of the town, running N.N.W., with a few cross striæ from W. to E. ; and (4) at Bidston Hill, Cheshire, at an elevation of 150 feet above the sea; first observed by Mr. J. Cunningham, F.G.S., who pointed out similar scratches to Dr. Buckland when he was examining the glacial phenomena of the British Isles.

Mr. J. Taylor, F.G.S.,‖ " On the Drift Deposits of Crewe, Cheshire."—At Barthomley, near Crewe, occur gravels containing

* Mem. Geol. Survey, 1864.
† Proc. Lit. Phil. Soc. Man. vol. iii. Binney, E. W.: —Lancashire and Cheshire Drift : Read Jan. 1864. p. 214. And Third Series, vol. ii., 1865, p. 462.
‡ " Geology of the Country around Liverpool." Liverpool, 1863.
§ Proc. Lit. Phil. Soc. Man., 1864–65.
‖ Trans. Man. Geol. Soc., vol. iv., 1864, p. 288.

pebbles of granite, trap, &c., and nearly 30 per cent. of flints. These rest on sand, with marine shells, overlaid at Crewe by a layer of stiff clay, which, half a mile north of the town, was distinctly laminated, and contained pyritized organic remains. Below the sand-beds, 7 feet in thickness, occurs loamy clay (Lower Boulder Clay?).

Mr. R. D. Darbishire, F.G.S.,[*] describes the gravels near Macclesfield, with marine shells, giving the height of Mr. Prestwich's patch as 1,150 feet above the sea. In 1865 he published a list of the species, which is incorporated in Appendix I.

Mr. John Plant, F.G.S.,[†] informed the Society of his discovery of deep glacial striæ beneath 20 feet of Boulder Clay at Ordsall Old Clough, Salford, in Pebble Beds.

Mr. James Eccles, F.G.S.,[‡] " On some instances of the Superficial Curvature of Inclined Strata near Blackburn." Gives sections of Millstone Grits and Lower Coal Measures dipping to the S.S.E.; the surface ends of which are turned completely back, so as to dip N.N.W. at a high angle ; the whole being capped by Boulder Clay, which in one instance is forced into the space left between two curves of the Grit. In two instances the curvatures were uphill.

Mr. Morton,[§] " On the presence of Glacial Ice in the valley of the Mersey during Post-pliocene times."

Mr. Plant,[‖] " On the Glacial Groovings on the Bunter Sandstone at Ordsall Clough, Salford." The grooves were 5 inches across and 3 inches deep, with polished surfaces. They ran N. 40° W., were capped by 12 feet of Boulder Clay, and occurred at an elevation of about 96 feet above the mean level. Seven out of 10 boulders in the Boulder Clay were limestones.

Mr. J. A. Aitkin, F.G.S.,[¶] describes a bed of drift gravel on the southern end of Holcombe Hill, at an elevation of 1,150 feet, containing 21 per cent. of trappean rocks, and 3 per cent. of granite.

Mr. J. Eccles[¶] drew attention to Glacial Striæ running E. 12° N. at Mellor, between Preston and Blackburn.

Mr. Plant,[**] " On a Stone Axe found in the valley of the Mersey at Flixton, near Manchester, in 1846." It occurred in the flat terrace of gravel which occurs on both sides of the Mersey, lying, according to Prof. Hull, on the Lower Boulder Clay, and rising 40 feet above the ordinary alluvium of the river.

Mr. Binney,[††] " Notes on some high-level Drifts in the Counties of Chester, Derby, and Lancaster." Describes erratic blocks at a height of 1,000 to 1,400 feet, on the crescent of hills between Chilow Cross, through Cheshire and Derbyshire, to Rivington Pike in Lancashire, and other localities ; including a section exposed in making the Hollingworth Reservoir, west of Glossop, where

---

* Proc. Lit. Phil. Soc. Man., Third Series, vol. iii.; and Geol. Mag., 1865.
† Trans. Man. Geol. Soc., vol. vi.; May 28, 1867, p. 128.
‡ Op. cit., vol. vii. p. 20.
§ Proc. Liverpool Geol. Soc., 1866-7.
‖ Trans. Man. Geol. Soc., Jan. 28, 1868, vol. vii. p. 40.
¶ Op. cit., Feb. 25, 1868, vol. vii. p. 62.
** Op. cit., March 31, 1868, vol. vii. p. 65.
†† Proc. Lit. Phil. Soc. Man., vol. x. Read Dec. 1870.

gravel resting on Boulder Clay contained several marine shells at a height of 568 feet above the sea. He also refers to the rare occurrence of chalk flints on the gravels of the high levels, and their presence in those of the Isle of Man.

Mr. Aitkin, F.G.S.,* in November 1870, describes the occurrence of glacial striæ, under 15 feet of Boulder Clay at Thatto Heath, near Prescot, running N. 45° W.

Mr. Kerr, "On Traces of Glacial Phenomena in the Valley of the River Irwell and its tributaries in Rossendale." Describes a large number of mounds of re-assorted drift, which he believes to have formed during a second glaciation, after a submergence of from 1,200 to 1,400 feet. They occur at elevations of from 900 to 1,000 feet.

Mr. Binney, "Notes on the Lancashire Drift Deposits."‡ describes the sequence of glacial beds between Liverpool and Manchester, and on the Lancashire and Yorkshire Railway as far north as Todmorden. Near the latter line he gives a section of a boring at Boarshaw; giving 243 feet of drift, the last 161 being hard sand, at an elevation of 450 feet; and another, at about the same height, at Three Gates, which exhibited no less than 227 feet of drift, consisting of 10 seams of marl, six of sand, and two of loam. The boring is near Tandle Hill, which rises to 750 feet, with sand and loam to the top, so that the drift may be 510 feet in thickness.

Mr. Binney,§ "Additional Notes on the Drift Deposits near Manchester," also gives several sections in and near Manchester, showing a lower sand and gravel beneath the Lower Boulder Clay, and still considers the Upper Boulder Clay of Prof. Hull to be intercalated in the Upper Sands and Gravels (*i.e.* Middle Sand and Gravel of Prof. Hull, F.R.S.)

---

* Trans. Man. Geol. Soc., vol. x. p. 26.
† Op. cit., p. 116.
‡ Proc. Lit. Phil. Soc. Man., vol. xi. p. 139. "Additional Notes on the Lancashire Drift Deposits;" by E. W. Binney, F.R.S., President, March 19, 1872.
§ Proc. Lit. Phil. Soc. Manchester, Nov. 12, 1872. "Additional Notes on the Drift Deposits near Manchester;" by E. W. Binney, F.R.S.

CHAPTER III.

POST-GLACIAL DEPOSITS.

High-Level Alluvium.

The valleys of West Lancashire are cut down deep through the Glacial Deposits, and terraces of alluvium hang on the bluff of Glacial Drift overlooking the valley ; but no fluviatile deposit ever occurs in sheets on the plains above the valleys. In the south of England terraces of high-level alluvial gravel occur not only on the slopes forming the limits of the valley, but high up on the plains above, sheets of gravel running from one valley-margin to another.   Of these latter deposits there are no representatives in Lancashire.

In the Drift Edition of the maps around Manchester* extensive alluvial terraces are seen ranged in tier after tier from the level of the ordinary alluvium of the Irwell and the Mersey to a considerable height up the slope of the hills of Glacial Deposits forming the limits of those valleys.

In the district now under review, traces of the old terraces are more rare, denudation having been more complete. The rivers have worn their beds to their lowest possible gradient, and have, in travelling from side to side of their valleys, nearly obliterated all their old depositions at higher levels.

At a few points in the valley of the Ribble, such traces still remain, as shown in the following interesting section ; from which it will be seen how much newer the older terrace is in geological time than the Glacial Deposits, and how much later again is the modern alluvial flat than the old terrace.

Fig. 16.

Diagram of Banks of the Ribble, in Mete House Wood.

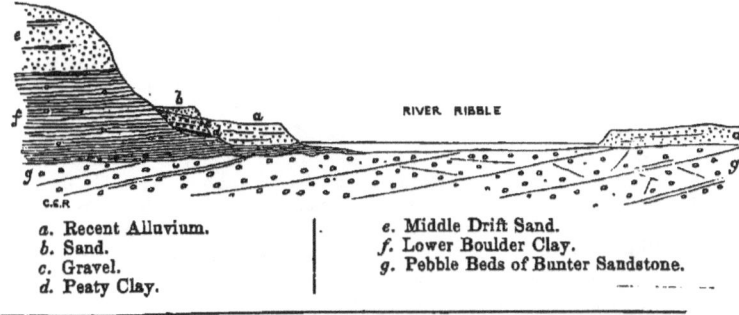

a. Recent Alluvium.	*e.* Middle Drift Sand.
b. Sand.	*f.* Lower Boulder Clay.
c. Gravel.	*g.* Pebble Beds of Bunter Sandstone.
d. Peaty Clay.	

* One-inch maps, 89 S.E., 88 S.W., and 81 N.W.

A little to the south of the above section, where a small brook crosses the wood, the following occur :—

	I.			II.	
		feet.			feet.
a. Sand	-	- 8			
b. Gravel	- -	- 13	b. Gravel	- -	- 0
c. (Absent)	-	- 0	c. Clay	-	6
d. Peat and clay	-	- 2	d. Peat	-	- 2
e. (Absent)	-	- 0	e. Gravel	-	- 1
f. Boulder Clay	-	- 6	f. Boulder Clay	-	- 2
					10 (+)

It is noteworthy that the conditions of deposition of these old terraces, as exemplified in the above section, appear to be closely analogous to those obtaining during the formation of the modern alluvium, consisting broadly of—

    I. Fine sediment (sand, fine gravel and clay). (*Deposition.*)
    II. Peat. (*Obstruction of drainage.*)
    III. Coarse gravels. (*Great denudation of valley above.*)

And this sequence appears to be repeated in every terrace. Accumulation of fine sediment goes quietly on, until a barrier breaks; denudation of the old terrace then goes rapidly on, and deposition of coarse material at a lower level takes place further down the stream, until at length the outlet becomes completely choked, and more or less peaty conditions prevail.

Similar terraces of high-level alluvium forming long slopes occur above the alluvial flat of the river Darwen below Roach Bridge, and a terrace of sandy ground, probably derived from the waste of Boulder Clay, occurs from Woodcock Hall to Pinfold House on the Lostock river.

A deposit of yellow loamy sand occurs at Golden Hill, near Leyland. Its age is doubtful ; it has probably resulted from the waste of sandy beds of Boulder Clay.

Shirdley Hill Sand and Preesall Shingle.

The deposit I called Shirdley Hill Sand in 1869,* from its marked development at a knoll of that name, rising above the peat-plain, and flanking the Boulder Clay plain to the east, is current-bedded at the base, and contains perfect shells of mollusca of the species *Turritella terebra* and *Cardium edule*, together with pebbles of white quartz, and has every appearance here of having been deposited by the sea. I have been led to believe that the Shirdley Hill range represents an ancient line of sand dunes from the character of the upper portion, and from the fact that sands are found at higher levels irregularly distributed over the surface of the Boulder Clay, on the one side of a valley and not the other, and occasionally containing land shells as well as fragments of sea shells. The extremely irregular deposits of sand found spread over the country from Bootle to Ormskirk, and running up the valley of the Douglas, have been blown from the Shirdley range westward. Sand, deposited

---

* "Explanation of the Country between Liverpool and Southport, and description of one-inch map 90 S.E."

probably under the sea, is often found underlying the peat and grey estuarine clays, from the margin of which the sands on the higher land to the east were blown.

The peculiarly isolated appearance of Shirdley Hill has probably led to the local legend, that a certain person, having made a compact with an evil spirit to build him a house at Lydiate, and seeing the spirit flying over the country with an immense load of sand from the coast, exclaimed " God be praised," which caused the said spirit to break his agreement, and to throw down the sand, which formed the hillock now known as Shirdley Hill.

The whole of these sands being of one general age, and it being impossible in all cases to separate the sub-aërial portion from the marine, I have classed them together; but, speaking broadly, it may be stated that nearly all the Shirdley Hill Sand represented on the maps is of sub-aërial origin, the marine portions being concealed by later deposits in the lowest plain.

At the period when this belt of ancient sand dunes surrounded the lowest plain, then covered by the sea, considerable quantities of sand must have been blown over the adjacent country to the east; which is, no doubt, the origin of the sand so generally found capping the slopes and plains of Boulder Clay between Liverpool and Ormskirk. The peculiarly capricious manner of its occurrence, —sometimes on one side of valley, and not on the other,—sometimes capping a rising hill or knoll, at other times only occurring in the hollow beneath,—and its uncertain thickness,—is well explained on the assumption of its sub-aërial origin, and also explains its occurrence beneath Rainford and mosses situated in hollows of the Boulder Clay above the level of the lowest plain.

In most instances the sand rests on the Boulder Clay; but in a few sections, a thin bed of peat intervenes, as at the base of Shirdley Hill; and when the rock comes through to the surface, and forms projecting knolls, a thin capping of the old blown sand often occurs. At Sefton Quarry the capping consists of—

	feet.
Ashy-grey (Shirdley Hill) sand - - -	1
Dark yellowish-brown (Shirdley Hill) sand -	3
Lower Keuper Sandstone (base not seen)	- 12

In the railway cutting near Orrel, in the link between Seaforth and Aintree, 5 feet of the sand caps the laminated grey sandstone.

The sand exposed on the south side of Orrel Hill Lane at Orrel Hill Wood is of a deep-red colour, tinged with oxide of iron. The following is the section:—

	ft.	in.
1. Vegetable mould mixed with sand	1	3
2. Ashy-grey sand - -	1	0
3. Dark-red indurated sand - -	3	0 (+)

In most of the sections, when a peaty layer overlies the sand, the sand appears to have been bleached, as it is either an ashy grey or white. At Blundell Arms Inn, west of Moss, a quarter of a mile from the last section, there is an exposure of—

	feet.
1. Vegetable mould - -	1
2. Dark-red indurated sand - -	- 6
3. Yellow sand, soft - - -	4

The compact nature of some of these sands makes it somewhat difficult to be certain that all these sections are Shirdley Hill Sand, and suggests a possibility that, in some cases, they may be of Middle Drift age, or, still more probably, that they are sands derived from the Middle Drifts and afterwards re-deposited.

At Aintree Race-course, in a sand-pit on the east side, the following sequence occurs :—

				feet.
a.	Dark-brown rusty sand	-	-	- 3
b.	Orange-coloured ,,		-	0½
c.	Bright-yellow ,,	-	-	- 1
d.	Dark-brown ,,	-	-	- 0¼
e.	Light-yellow ,,		-	3
f.	Hard, black, indurated sand		-	- 0¾
g.	Yellow ,, ,,		-	- 3 (+)

A patch of this sand extends from Holmes in Tarleton to Mere Side and Mere Windmill at Rufford. The centre of this tract rises so much as to form a ridge or sandy cliff running S.E.,—probably marking an older cliff of Boulder Clay which crops to the surface at Holmes.

North of Holmes Wood, the sand dips under the peat occupying the site of the old lake Martin Mere, to which the cliff or ridge at Holmes Woods must formerly have formed the southern limit.

North of the Boulder Clay of Holmes occurs a knoll of the same deposit, surrounded by peat, running from the farm south of Moss Side to that called Wignalls, round the slope of the clay as well as round the knolls of clay. At Clay Brow and Tarlscough occur thick deposits of Shirdley Hill Sand, especially on the western sides.

Good sections occur at Black Moor between Mawdesley and Rufford, various coarse-grained yellow and ash-grey sands alternating with finer beds, traversed by thin seams of peroxide of iron, and containing peat-holes, in which peat has grown afterwards, covered by more sand ; which conditions appear to have been frequently repeated, sand and peat alternating several times.

Between the Boulder Clay of New Lane, St. John's, and Burscough, and the peat, a tract of Shirdley Hill Sand intervenes, running from Tarlscough to St. John's, occupying an area of two square miles ; and to the east, several patches of sand rise to the surface through the peat.

Southward of the patch of sand at Black Moss none is seen, it having been apparently all swept away by the denudation of the river Douglas as far as Parbold Hill,—which here and there, as at Wilbrahams and Low Meadows, has formed a true fluviatile alluvium,—most of that overlying the peat, through which the river runs to the west, being estuarine, the tides still flowing up as far as Wanes Blade Bridge in map 89 S.W.

Dr. Harison, chaplain to Lord Cobham, describing the course of the Lancashire rivers nearly 300 years ago, mentions that "the Duglesse meeteth also on the same side with Merton Meere water, in which Meere is an island called Netherholme, besides others," which was probably Holme Wood Hill, in which case the channel from the Lake to the Douglas must have been between the Boulder Clay knolls of Rufford Park and that of Sollom.

Preesall Shingle.—This deposit is well seen in several shallow pits, where it is worked for gravel, at the foot of the steep bluff called Preesall Hill.

The shingle is well rounded, and contains pebbles of Red Hæmatite and Permian Red Sandstone, probably derived from the opposite side of Morecambe Bay. I also noticed shells of the species—

Cardium edule.	*Cardium rusticum.*
Purpura lapillus.	*Natica monilifera.*
Turritella terebra.	*Tellina Balthica.*

These shingles must occupy a considerable area in the plain, as they crop to the surface at several points on the eastern edge of the peat; but they form a comparatively small exposure at the surface, being immediately overlaid by grey scrobicularia clay underlying peat.

Lower Scrobicularia and Cyclas Clays.

In 1868, when I examined the coast of Wirral, in order, if possible, to correlate the post-glacial deposits described there by Messrs. Morton,[*] E. Smith, and others, with those of Lancashire, I noticed that though there were several horizons of peat and grey clay, that the thickest clay underlying the thickest peat was tolerably persistent, and contained large numbers of *Scrobiculariæ*; finding the same shell in a clay occupying the same position with regard to the main or thick peat at Eccles Place, Crossens, Lancashire, I called the deposit the Lower *Scrobicularia* Clay, from the fact that another Scrobicularia Clay occurs above the peat at Crossens, and is even now in process of deposition.

Mr. Morton gives the following section of the Old Dock, Liverpool, under the Custom House, recorded in 1829 :—

	feet.
Water	- 19
Dock silt	- 3
White sand	- 0
Blue silt	- 6
Peat or forest bed	- 1
Blue silt (with remains of stag)	- 10
Peat or forest bed	- 1
	40

the lower peat resting on sandstone. He gives a figure of another section at North Docks, Bootle, where the lower silt and lower peat were alone present, the sandstone occurring at 35 feet below the high-water mark.

In the grey clays beneath the peat at Birkdale, and at several other points, I observed many detached shells of *Cyclas cornea*, associated with stems of rushes. This deposit I described as the Lower Cyclas Clay, from the fact that ordinary alluvial clay of the Ribble and the Alt lying above the peat often contains that shell in great abundance.

The Lower Cyclas and Scrobicularia Clays represent, each to a great extent in time, frequent alternations of estuarine and lacus-

[*] Geology of Liverpool, 1863.

trine conditions; but, on the whole, it would appear that the Cyclas Clay is slightly newer than the Scrobicularia, the deposition of grey mud with Scrobicularia going on in salt or brackish water, which gradually became shallower and more fresh, so that *Cyclas cornea* was able to exist until the water became so shallow, and the drainage so obstructed, that the growth of peat ensued.

The grey clays seldom crop to the surface, being concealed below the peat, and are thickest on the western or seaward side of the peat plains, both in those of Lytham, and in those extending from the Alt to Crossens; the peat in the eastern portion of the mosses resting directly on the Shirdley Hill Sand which caps the Boulder Clay.

The eastern boundary runs from the end of the lane N.W. of Bridge Hall to the point where Long Ditch joins the Great Martin Mere Sluice; thence turning N.W. it disappears under the estuary of the Ribble at Crossens, re-appearing on the north side of the river, where it also underlies much of Lytham Moss, Marton and other mosses.

It was well seen, in March 1869, on the beach at South Shore, cropping out from beneath the peat. Its upper portion was traversed by numerous seams of rushes, and other freshwater plants.

Northward its extension is cut off by the high cliffs of Glacial Deposits, which terminate the peat plain; but it re-appears north of Blackpool, cropping out on the beach from under the peat at the edge of the Rossall and Fleetwood alluvial plain.

The Lower Scrobicularia Clay is seen on the east side of the Wyre, resting on the Preesall Shingle, and underlying the peat. Eastward in Rawcliffe Moss it appears to have thinned out, the peat resting directly on the Glacial Deposits, or on the Preesall beds.

The unequal deposition and denudation of Glacial Drift over portions of Western Lancashire produced an inequality of surface, instrumental in causing the " Swamp-hollows " and the peat-covered flats extending over so large an area in the north-west of England. Barriers of clay to the west appear to have obstructed the flow of the streams running off the Boulder Clay slopes bounding the lowland plain. Traces of these streams may be seen in the channels excavated in the Shirdley Hill Sands near Halsall, as shown in the accompanying section.

Fig. 17.

Section of Carr Moss, Halsall, exposed in a Sluice.

Scale 16 feet.

a. Peat, with trunks and roots of oaks, pollard ashes, &c.
b. Dark-brown sand. } Shirdley Hill Sand.
b. White and yellow sand.

After the deposition of the Shirdley Hill Sand in the area south of the Ribble, and of the Preesall Shingles to the north, it is evident that the land rose slightly, so that fluvio-marine or rather estuarine conditions prevailed, during which the Scrobicularia and Cyclas Clays were thrown down; and occasionally, during this deposition of clay, portions of the surface were elevated above the water, and formed a soil for plants, and in some cases for trees. The surface of the marine 'sands and fluvio-marine clay became covered with large forests; while in other portions, the drainage being entirely obstructed, and the influx of mud produced by the denudation of Glacial· Clays cut off, the growth of peat at once ensued, causing endless intercalations and wedging out of Scrobicularia ·Clay with peat, and peat with freshwater Cyclas Clay. Elevation still continuing, deposition of clay ceased ; and the ground having sufficient slope to the sea, the obstruction to the drainage was removed, and the growth of peat stopped.

A considerable alluvial tract occurs at Linacre, extending from the finger-post at the corner of the Litherland Road to Seaforth View, where it divides into two spurs,—the shorter running up to Orrell church by Kemp, the other lying at and occupying the depression between the sand-covered Boulder Clay area at Waterloo or Seafield House on the one side, and the bluff of Hatton Hill on the other. Seaforth Station and a portion of the Liverpool and Southport Railway is situated on this alluvium,—which, in sections in Rimrose Brook and its tributary, both above and below the station, is seen to rest on peat.

Near 'Seaforth parsonage I observed the following section in 1868:—

				feet.
a.	Blown sand	- - -		1
b.	Alluvial-sand	- - -		3
c.	Peat	- - - -		1
d.	White Boulder Clay		- -	1
e.	Reddish ,, ,,		-	- 11 (visible.)

On the adjacent coast, immediately below high-water mark, I found an exposure of peat which was considerably thicker than in the above section, and rested on a bed of grey silty clay in which occurred roots and snags of trees. Portions of the trunks lay embedded in the peat. I was not able to observe any shells of mollusca in the clay, but Mr. M. Reade has since recorded the presence of—

Scrobicularia piperata.	Natica monilifera.
Tellina Balthica.	Cardium edule.*
Turritella terebra.	

From the fact that the Shirdley Hill Sand is here absent, it would appear probable that these estuario-marine clays of Seaforth are partly the representative in time of the marine sands of Shirdley, which were evidently not thrown down in this area.

* Geol. Mag , vol; x, 1873, p. 239

Mr. Reade gives the following section, met with in constructing the outlet sewer for Crosby Hall :—

	ft.	in.
1. Soil and brown sand - - - - -	3	4
2. Hard peat - - -	0	4

(3–7. *Shirdley Hill Sand?—C. E. R.*)

3. Yellow sand - - -	3	0
4. Sand, with occasional trees, about as thick as a man's thigh, rooted in - -	0	6
5. Yellow sand -	3	6
6. Gravel and sand -	1	0
7. Sand -	3	0 (+)
	15	0

which shows that the occurrence of the grey clays is extremely variable, and that they are often replaced in a very short distance by sandy beds, probably partly of the age of the Shirdley Hill Sands, and partly of the period immediately following their deposition.

Mr. Reade gives another section in the Seaforth alluvial flat, referred to above, of the excavation for the North Docks and Aintree railway-bridge over the Southport line, communicated to him by Mr. A. Holme, C.E. 22 feet of peat was found to rest directly on Boulder Clay; so that east of the Rimrose depression, both the sands and grey clays have thinned out. But at Seaforth Station, in an interesting well-section communicated by Mr. J. Sawyer to Mr. Reade, the following sequence occurred :—

	feet.
Peat -	30
White sand with shells - - -	1
Peat - - -	9
Blue clay (Slutch?) - -	10 (+)
(Water fetid.)	50

The finest exposure of grey clays in the district is that to be seen between tide-marks at Hightown, at the coast opposite the Old Light-house (*b*), of which the Frontispiece, Figure 18, is a diagrammatic sketch. From beneath the sand dunes (*c*) fringing the coast, appears a broad extent of peat (*d*), interspersed with trunks of trees with their roots embedded in the grey clay (*e*), beneath, which has been cut into a steep bank, 8 feet in height, by the scour of the river Alt (*a*) at low-water.

Though a few of the trees have evidently grown *in situ*, by far the largest proportion of the trunks appear to have been drifted for a certain distance, and deposited upon the stumps of other trees, often of different species. The roots and lowest end of most of the trunks point southwards, the general direction of the trunks being from N. 10° E. to N. 30° E.; but a few range about N.N.W., and in various other directions.

In the surface of the grey clay immediately beneath the peat are several horizons of rushes and other aquatic plants, indicating a succession of marsh-growths immediately preceding the growth of the peat.

In the lower portion of the peat the conditions appear to have been estuarine. Shells of the species *Cardium edule* and *Tellina solidula* have been discovered by Mr. M. Reade in sinking a trench 5½ feet deep.

The following are the details of Mr. Reade's section:—

	ft.	in.
1. Peat, soft at top, lower part made of twigs, &c. -	2	4
2. Laminated clay, and silt with balls of peat	3	2
3. Shell bed, mixed with blue silt -	1	6
4. Sandy silt, not bottomed - -	1	6
	8	6

The beds I have numbered 2, 3, 4 would appear to belong to the Grey Estuarine Clay, the peat being particularly thin at tho point chosen by Mr. Reade. From the same paper[*] I quote the following journals of borings.

Section disclosed in excavating Alt floodgates in 1830, by the late Christopher Houghton, surveyor to Alt Commissioners:—

| Marsh clay, with thin peat bed | - | - | - |
| Peat and forest | - | ~ | - |

Estuarine Clays?

	feet.
Blue clay - - -	- 3 to 4
Blue silt (total depth of this group) -	18
Clay -	3

Shirdley Hill Sand?

Red quicksand. (Foundation of piers built on timber cradles.)

Section exposed in foundations of the Earl of Sefton's windmill for working the second set of pumping engines for draining Altcar:—

	feet.
Soil and marsh clay, about -	- 5
Silt - - - - -	- 11
Peat - - - - -	- 4
Silt, not bottomed - - from surface	- 25

The Engine Sluice cut in 1842, 12 feet in depth, at the south end, was entirely excavated in the upper silt, and contained horns of stag, shells, &c.

Trial-bore for sewerage works, Blundellsands Road East, communicated by Messrs. Dixon and Co. Level of surface, 36 feet above mean sea-level.

---

[*] Post-Glacial Deposits of Lanc. and Cheshire. Proc. Liverpool Geol. Soc., Nov. 1871, p.49, section 6.

(1–3. *Blown Sand and Old Beach?*—C. E. R.)

		ft.	in.
1. Soil and sand	- - - - -	2	3
2. Wet sand	- - -	9	8
3. Running sand, and pebbles	- - -	3	4
4. Wet bog	- - - -	5	6
5. Blue clay -	- - -	2	0
		22	9

Higher up the Alt, at the floodgates, eight or nine feet of grey clay, capped by sand dunes, form the left bank of the stream; while on the opposite side there is a small alluvial flat, extending up to the sand dunes, the alluvium being about 10 inches in thickness, resting on two feet of peat lying on the grey clay, which also forms the bed of the river.

Still further up the stream, at the foot-bridge between Old Crosby Lighthouse and Grange Farm, the following section is seen in the bank of the stream :—

		feet.
a. Alluvium of sandy clay -	- -	1
b. Blown Sand, with fresh-water shells	- -	5
c. Peat	- - - -	1
d. Grey clay (base not seen)	- -	8

The grey clay is the impermeable layer that supports the water held by the peat throughout the western portion of the great mosses south of Crossens. In a pit at Gorsey Lane, half-way between Moss Farm and New Houses, the following is seen :—

		feet.
a. Blown Sand, resting on an extremely irregular surface of	- - - -	3
b. Peat (above water 2 feet)	- - -	6
c. Grey clay (base not seen)	- -	1

When at Southport in Nov. 1872, I observed the following section in the excavations for the new gas-works :—

		feet.
Blown Sand	- - - - -	3
Peat -	- - -	4
Grey clay	- - -	3 (+)

In another section, the base of the sand was of a greyish colour, and appeared to have been blown into fresh water. In one of the grey silty beds, locally called " scotch," a skull, horns, and several bones of deer were found, which are now preserved in the Town Hall, Southport.

Describing this tract, Mr. M. Reade, in his paper " On the Post-Glacial Deposits of Lancashire and Cheshire," from which I have abstracted several well-sections and other artificial sections, (to which I had not access at the time of my survey, or that have been made since,) states that 39 borings were taken in five acres of ground, previous to the construction of the new gas-works, "all of which sections differed in the depth, number, position, and thickness of the peat beds."

The following gives the details of two of these borings :—

	ft.	in.			ft.	in.
a. Blown Sand -	- 2	1				
b. Peat (Pasture) -	- 0	4				
c. Blown Sand -	- 1	0	a–c. Blown Sand	-	8	0
d. Peat -	- 2	6	d. Peat -	-	2	0
e. Light Scotch -	- 2	9	e–f. Scotch -	-	1	6
f. Dark ,, -	- 3	9				
g. Peat -	1	6	g. Peat -	-	2	0
h. Light Scotch -	- 5	0	h. Scotch - -		1	6
			i. Loam and sand -	-	28	0
	18	11			42	0

Eastward of these sections, the various beds of grey clay appear to unite, and underlie the peat, until the clay eventually thins out, and peat rests on a thin bed of Shirdley Hill Sand.

The section given in Fig. 12, seen in a deep ditch at right angles to the Scarisbrick and Southport. road at Brown Edge, shows that channels have been excavated in the surface of the Shirdley Hill Sand before the growth of the peat.

In the adjacent road I observed—

	feet.
Peat, dark black mass of, with the roots of large trees - - - - -	2½
Sand, light ashy-grey coloured, loose and large-grained - - - - -	2½
Boulder Clay, brown and reddish-coloured, with seams of bluish-grey marl (base not seen) -	6

In the brick-field at Brown Edge the same superposition is seen, but the ash-grey sand is 4 feet in thickness, and contains shells of the species *Cardium aculeatum.*

Near Crossens, the grey clays beneath the peat are again seen. At the west side of Smith Lane the following occurs:—

	feet.
a. Alluvial clay (Upper Scrobicularia) - -	4½
b. Peat (base not seen) - - -	2

Pilling Moss.—In the district north of the Wyre, beds of grey clay occur under the peat in places, or intercalated with it in some sections. One of these, near Cogie Hill, exhibits the following:—

	feet.
a. Laminated peat, the curves of the various beds rolling over the broken trunks of trees, the roots of which are in the beds beneath - -	3
b. Grey stony clay - - - -	2
c. Peat, with prostrate trunks of trees - - -	1
d. Compact peat - - - -	1
e. Boulder Clay - - - -	1

Ancient Low-level Fluviatile Alluvium.

At the base of the ordinary alluvium of the river Ribble, and overlying the coarse gravel which forms the actual base of the alluvium of the lowest plain, there generally occurs a peaty seam, often exhibiting trunks of trees, more or less rolled, resting on a grey fresh-water clay (which resembles that underlying the peat of the plains).

A careful examination of the banks of the Ribble from Preston seaward discloses the fact that this thin seam of peat is continuous with the thick peat of the plains, which relegates the probable age of the underlying gravel to that of the Shirdley Hill Sand, and proves that the valley of the Ribble had already been denuded, and received its present lines before the growth of peat in West Lancashire.

A good section of these beds is seen at Mete House on the Ribble, of which the following is a section.

Fig. 19.

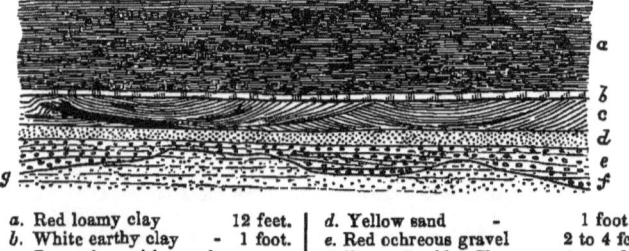

a. Red loamy clay	12 feet.	d. Yellow sand	-	1 foot.
b. White earthy clay	- 1 foot.	e. Red ochreous gravel		2 to 4 feet.
c. Grey clay, with much vegetable matter, and young trees	4 feet.	f. Lower Boulder Clay		0 to 3 feet.
		g. Sandstone (Pebble Beds)		- 1 foot.

(Both *f.* and *g.* are generally below the water-level.)

A peaty-bed resting on gravel forms the base of the alluvial plain of the River Darwen, near Walton-le-Dale. The gravel is more or less cemented together by oxide of iron, and rests on the Pebble Beds of the Bunter series.

The gravel supports a sheet of impure water, which was reached by several shallow wells, and used by the inhabitants of the village prior to the outbreak of fever in 1868. In one of the largest of these the water-level was found to be 2 feet 4 inches above the ordinary top-water of the river Darwen, the well being 16 feet 4 inches in depth.

CHAPTER IV.

PEAT.

In 1686, Dr. Plot, after referring to the various opinions held by different persons regarding the origin of trees found embedded in peat mosses, concludes that as the trees have no branches, they could not be true trees at all, but disports of Nature, and states, " I must distinguish between those found near the sea-coasts and " those in the inland countries; the former, no doubt, being over- " thrown and covered, either by the violent encroachments of the " sea, if near the shore, as those on the coast of Pembrokeshire." And he adds " that these morasses were the products of the woods " that grew upon them, which, by the putrefaction of the leaves " rains, and dews, may . . . . be converted into bogs or morasses ; " and that the firs found there were not brought thither by any " deluge, but were the product of the soil, and in all probability " ruined by the Britains,* in revenge to the Danes, the pines being " their darling tree."

Dr. Leight† in 1700 described peat mosses as occupying large areas in western Lancashire, and states " the postures the Firr-stocks ' are found in, evince they were brought thither by a Deluge."

The submerged forest and peat beds fringing the coast of Wirral have been described by many observers. In 1846 the Rev. A. Hume, F.S.A.,‡ described a section at Poulton Bridge, showing 6 feet of alluvium resting on 6 feet of peat, with trunks of trees, bark, decayed leaves, and a large number of nuts.

In 1849 Mr. J. A. Picton, F.S.A.,§ read a paper before the Lit. Phil. Soc. of Liverpool, quoted by Mr. Morton,‖ in which he described a submarine forest at Leasowe, with several hundred stumps of trees, some of which appear to have been cut by an axe, especially the oak trunks ; and also a submarine forest north of Prince's Dock, known as Wycherley Wood, which existed 70 years ago.

In the same year, Mr. J. P. G. Smith,¶ described the section exposed by cutting a sluice, 14 feet deep, between Poulton and Bidston Road towards Leasowe lighthouse, consisting of—

> Alluvium.
> Peat, wet rushes, equisetum.
> Forest trees (oaks, elms, alders, &c.) in soil.
> White sand.
> Boulder Clay.

---

* Natural History of Staffordshire, p. 215.
† Natural History of Lancashire and Cheshire, 1700.
‡ Proc. Lit. Phil. Soc. Liverpool, May 1846.
§ Op. cit., 1848-9.
‖ Proc. Liverpool Geol. Soc., 1871.
¶ Proc. Lit. Phil. Soc. Liverpool, 1848-9.

Mr. Nisbit[*] described how runners of grass had completely penetrated the soft trunks of the trees in the peat; and Dr. Inman[†] states that he believed the trees to have been snapped off by violent winds after being made rotten by saturation of their bases.

Mr. J. Cunningham, F.G.S.,[‡] "On the Submarine Forest at Leasowe," gives two sections of bores.

Mr. J. Boult,[§] "On some recorded Changes in Liverpool Bay, previous to the year 1800."

Mr. T. J. Moore,[‖] "Notice of Mammalian Remains discovered in the Excavations at Wallasey for the Birkenhead New Docks."

Rev. Dr. Hume,[¶] "Ancient Meols, Antiquities of Dove Point and Sea Coast of Cheshire."

General the Hon. Sir Edward Cust, D.C.L., "The Pre-Historic Man of Cheshire, or some Account of a Human Skeleton found under the Leasowe Shore, in Wirral."[**]

Mr. Morton,[††] in his "Geology of the Country around Liverpool," describes the following peat beds:—

Lancashire	Custom House, peat and forest bed	-	39	feet below
	Nelson Dock	„	„	35	high-water
	Wallasey Pool	„	„	29	mark at
Cheshire	Lower Leasowe, submarine land surface		9	spring-tide.
	Upper Leasowe	„	forest bed	3	

The same author also describes the recent shell beds at Wallasey.[‡‡]

Mr. J. Boult, F.R.I.B.A.,[§§] "On the Alleged Submarine Forests on the Shores of Liverpool Bay and the River Mersey." He endeavours to prove that the trees found in the peat were drifted to their present position.

Rev. Dr. Hume,[‖‖] replied in "Fallacies and Incorrect Statements on the Subject of the Local Submarine Forest," and in his "Changes in the Seacoast of Lancashire and Cheshire."[¶¶]

In 1865–6 Mr. Boult[¶¶] published "Further Observations on the Alleged Submarine Forests on the Shores of Liverpool Bay and the River Mersey;" and a year later, "Speculation on the former Topography of Liverpool and Neighbourhood."[***]

Mr. H. Ecroyd Smith,[†††] in his "Record of Archæological Products of the Seashore of Cheshire in 1864," describes two sub-

---

[*] Proc. Lit. Phil. Soc. Liverpool, 1848–9.
[†] Op. cit.
[‡] Report Brit. Assoc. Liverpool, 1854.
[§] Trans. Hist. Soc. of Lancashire and Cheshire, 1855–6.
[‖] Op. cit., 1857–8.
[¶] "Ancient Meols." Liverpool, 1863.
[**] Proc. Liverpool Geol. Soc., 1863–4.
[††] "Geology of Liverpool," Liverpool, 1863.
[‡‡] Proc. Liverpool Geol. Soc., 1864–5.
[§§] Polytechnic Soc. of Liverpool, 1865.
[‖‖] Op. cit. 1866.
[¶¶] Trans. Hist. Soc., Lancashire and Cheshire, 1865.
[***] Polytechnic Soc. of Liverpool (Parts 1 and 2), 1866–7.
[†††] "Reliquary," 1865.

marine forest-beds as occurring where the human skeleton was found in that year. These two forest-beds have since been found to be absent near Leasowe Castle, Mr. Isaac Roberts having bored to the Boulder Clay in several places without finding them. Mr. Smith* also published " Notabilia of the Archæology of the Mersey District, 1865."*

Mr. C. Potter,† in "Observations on the Cheshire Coast," describes the various peat beds, and adopts Mr. Boult's theory that the trees found embedded were drifted by currents.

Mosses north of the River Mersey :—Seaforth.—In 1796 Mr. George Holt,‡ of Walton, described the submerged forest at Crosby "as " extending upwards of a mile towards Formby . . . . vestiges of it " are visible, dipping westerly into the sea, which doubtless covers " a great part of the land on which a considerable portion of it " grew. There are numberless trunks." At the time of my survey in 1868, peat, with the roots of trees *in situ*, were visible on the shore at the mouth of Rimrose Brook, beneath the sand, and connected with the peat underlying the alluvium of the brook inland. In 1815 it is recorded that hundreds of trees and stumps were exposed.

Halsall Moss.—One of the earliest references to the peat tract of Western Lancashire, is one by Dr. Leigh, in which he describes the occurrence of a bituminous turf, which will burn on water, with a smell resembling that of amber. He also mentions the large number of fir trees found in this moss, which were split and dried and by the poorer people made use of instead of candles.

Messrs. Binney and Talbot § describe deposits of peat that occupy the low lands west of Downholland and Halsall, extending through Formby to the sea. In the upper part of the Moss the peat is black, and much decomposed from two feet to a yard in thickness, and resting on a bed of white sand from an inch to two feet thick, based on blue or brown clay resembling Till. In the peat occur boles of oak, pine, and willow lying prostrate by their roots, which are still embedded in the clay and sand where they grew. In the tract of peat land between Barton and Fleam Brooks occurs a fluid bituminous matter, which burns with a bright white flame, known to the farmers as "light turf," being used for lighting fires, and many years since pronounced by Baron Thenard to be petroleum. The authors found a hard pitchy mass beneath the decomposed peat-soil in an oat stubble field, which, on exposure to the atmosphere, lost its inflammable principle, and was converted into black mould. This substance was also found under green sward, where it had an empyreumatic smell like that observable in the oily iridescent petroleum found floating on the

---

* Trans. Hist. Soc. Lancashire and Cheshire, 1866-7.
† Proc. Liverpool Geol. Soc., 1868-9.
‡ Gentleman's Magazine, July 1796.
§ Trans. Man. Geol. Soc. vol. viii. p. 186, (containing papers read in 1842-43),—
" On the Petroleum found in the Downholland Moss near Ormskirk ;" by E. W. Binney and J. H. Talbot, 1843.

water of the adjacent ditches. With a 6-inch boring instrument they obtained the following section :—

	ft.	in.
1. Surface, black decomposed peat, lower part of a pitchy nature - - -	0	3
2. Black peat, moist, and full of petroleum, lower part called " pipy moss," from compressed reeds in it - -	3	10
3. Soft blue silty clay -	3	6
4. Dry mouldy peat, with apparently mustard seeds, of a brown colour when freshly exposed, base reedy like No. 2 - -	4	0
5. Blue silty clay - -	0	6
6. Blue sandy clay (+) - -	3	6
	16	0

By other borings the upper peat was found to thicken to the west and north-west. The parting of the silty clay gradually diminished, and finally disappeared to north and east.

At the mouth of the river Alt, near Hightown, the peat covers much of the beach running out seawards from beneath the sand dunes, until cut off with the grey clay beneath it by the channel of the river, as shown in the diagram, Fig. 18. The snags and roots of trees, many of them of large size, are scattered over the whole area, the roots going down into the underlying clay. One of these I measured was over 40 feet in length, the trend of the trunk being about north-north-east.

Mr. Baines* states that portions of the many large masses of oak dug up at Halsall from under the moss have been used for window frames; and that the library of Leasowe Castle, and the handles of the doors of Hoylake parsonage, were made from bog oak.

The thin bed of whitish sand resting on the Boulder Clay in the eastern parts of Halsall and Downholland forms the substratum of the peat, but to the west the latter rests on the silty clay that lies above it.

On the bank of the Alt the lower bed of the peat is seen resting between two beds of silty clay thinning out to the south, so that the two beds of silty clay run into one.

The pitchy peat from bed 1, analysed by Mr. J. E. Bowman, of King's College, gave of organic constituents—

Carbon	60·31	while common	60·89
Hydrogen	8·86	peat analysed by	6·21
Oxygen	30·83	Regnault gives	32·90

The authors believe the petroleum to be formed by the decomposition of the peat under the underlying sand, which, they are informed by Mr. R. Harkness, is occasionally subject to infiltration of sea-water.

North of Great Altcar, where Doctors Lane joins Wood Lane, I noticed the following section :—

	feet.
Peat - - -	2
Grey clay - - - - -	1
Peat - - - - -	2

* History of Lancashire, vol. iv.

In the sections at the back of Town Lane the intercalated clay has thinned out, and from 3 to 5 feet of peat rests directly on the thick grey clay; which latter, at Middle Within Lane, (at a height of only 9·8 feet above the mean sea-level,) crops to the surface. Westward at Tongues Watercourse it is overlaid by the more recent alluvial clay.

In the tract now covered by blown sand there was an extensive moss in the 17th century, which is shown on Smith's map, 1588, in Speed's, 1610, and in Morden's, 1660. In making excavations through the sand, cultivated land and the old Formby streets are met with at a depth of 15 feet, forming the surface of the peat, then the moss.

Before the sand was so thick as at present between Crosby and Hightown, eels were speared at the Old and New Sniggery, in swamps in the peat,—" snig " being in the Lancashire dialect an eel.

To the east the underlying grey clays entirely disappear, and the peat rests on Boulder Clay ; while still further east, near the slope lying above the peat moss, the Shirdley Sand intervenes between the peat and the Boulder Clay.

Sefton Moss.—The alluvium of the Alt rests on peat, which crops to the surface.

At the base of the peat is a submerged forest, which is continually being met with in agricultural operations, no less than 50 cart-loads having been removed from one acre. Most of the trees appear to have been blown over from the west.

The direct juxtaposition of peat and Boulder Clay is well seen at Colonel Holt's, where 6 feet of the former rests on the latter ; at Ollery Hall, where the peat is only 4 feet in thickness; and at the adjacent lane, where the peat has thinned to 1 foot.

At Carr Moss Lane, east of the Holt, 6 to 8 feet of Shirdley Hill Sand rests on the Boulder Clay, which has been dug for marl ; and round this knoll the peat rests on the sands, on a layer of trunks of trees, which appear to have grown round the knoll, before the deposition of the peat, with their roots in the sand.

At North End, Birkdale, a pit was dug, in the autumn of 1868, through the peat, in order to experiment with the underlying grey clay as a brick-making material, which proved a failure. At the time of the excavation I noticed the following section :—

		feet.
1. Dark blown sand, with much vegetable matter, roots of recent plants - - -		3 to 4
2. Fine blown sand, very light coloured		2 to 3
3. Dark greyish-blue sand, with peaty matter		3
4. *a.* Peat, brown colour - - }		
b. Seam of hazel and red wood - - }		9
c. Black dense peat, with snags and roots at base in 5 - - - }		
5. Grey estuarine clay, with a few shells of *Cyclas cornea* in upper part - - -		20
6. Reddish coarse sand (Shirdley Hill Sands), depth not ascertained - - -		1 (+)

Mr. Reade gives some interesting sections which he observed in carrying out the Birkdale Outlet Sewer from Fine Jane's Brook to the west of the railway, which shows the peat below the blown sand to be rather thicker in the tanks than I observed it in the section at Fine Janes' Brook. But the grey clays do not appear to have been fathomed. According to Mr. Reade they contained shells of *Scrobicularia piperata, Turritella communis, Cardium edule, Tellina solidula, Buccinum undatum,* and *Natica monilifera.* The peat was found to contain thin stems of birch and alder, and large quantities of *Iris pseud-acorus.*

An interesting section occurs in Smith Lane, east of Crossens, about 4 feet of grey scrobicularia clay resting on peat, of which about 2 feet is visible at the western end. The peat gradually thins eastwardly, is seen to rest upon grey clay, and eventually disappear, the upper clay resting directly on the lower one.

The western extension of the peat under the alluvium will be seen by the following sections, which I observed in 1868 :

1. Water Lane.		2.		3. Sluice Bridge.	
Alluvial Clay	3 feet.	Alluvial Clay	- 2 feet,	Alluvial Clay	3 feet.
Peat - -	1 „	Boulder Clay	- 2 „	Peat -	1 „
Grey Clay	- 1 „			Boulder Clay	2 „

4. Brickkiln Lane.		5.		6.	
Alluvial Clay	- 3 feet.	Alluvial Clay	- 3 feet.	Alluvial Clay	- 3 feet.
Boulder Clay	- 4 „	Peat -	2 „	Boulder Clay	2 „
		Boulder Clay	1 (†)		

7. Bank Lane.		8.		9.	
Alluvial Clay	- 5 feet.	Alluvial Clay	2 feet.	Peat - -	6 feet.
Boulder Clay	- 2 „	Peat -	1 „	Grey Clay	1 (+)
		Boulder Clay	- 0½ „		

In sections 4 to 9 the peat is either absent or very thin, the Boulder Clay being near the surface, cropping at Guinea Hall, immediately to the south, where it is worked for bricks. Eastward of No. 9, towards Brandy Hill, the grey clay thins out, and the peat rests on the Boulder Clay.

The following are representative sections :—

10. West of Smithy.		11. West of 10.		12. West of 11 at corner of lane.	
Peat -	- 2 feet.	Peat	- 7 feet.	Peat	- 0 feet.
Grey Clay	- 8 „	Grey Clay	- 1 (+)	Grey Clay -	- 5 „
Boulder Clay -	- 2 „			Boulder Clay -	- 3 „

West of section 12, at corner of Bank Place, 5 feet of grey clay is seen, the level of the surface being 14 feet above Ordnance datum, sections 10 to 12 being about 12 feet above the same.

13. *Crossens Marsh, near Bank.*	14. *N.E. of* 13.	15. *N.E. of* 14.
ա. Reddish Yellow Clay with marine shells 5 feet.	Peat - - 3 (+)	Blown Sand - - 3 feet. Peat - - - 3 „ Grey Sand, marine shells - - 0½ „ Peat - - 4 (+)

16.	17.	18.
Blown Sand - - 3 feet. Peat - - 4 „ Grey Sand - - 0½ „ Peat - 6 (+)	Peat - - - 4 feet. Grey Clay with marine shells - 4 „	Sand - - Peat Grey Clay - -

Westward, in Ralph's Wife's Lane, from 2 to 5 feet of grey clay intervenes between the peat and the Boulder Clay, and at Hoole the peat itself is overlaid by blown sand.

Several small lakes or meres were formerly scattered over the Moss, which, by the process of draining, have gradually become extinct. One of them, Church Mere, near the site of the old church at Formby, was filled up by the blowing of sand. There was a larger lake near the village, known as Barton Mere. In Halsall there were three tarns,—White Otter, Black Otter, and Gethern Mere.

From the adjacent moss Mr. Binney[*] has described a remarkable bed of "non-blazing peat" found 300 yards east of Mr. Linaker's house. On the moss east of Churchtown are the drains, where the author by digging found the following section :—

	ft.	ins.
1. Black decomposed peat -	3	6
2. Reddish-brown peat, full of the impression of reeds, containing near the bottom " jelly peat," from half an inch to two inches in thickness - - - -	1	0
3. Blue silty clay, locally called "Scotch"	(+)	

The base of No. 2 has a black jelly-like appearance, something similar to coagulated blood, when first dug up, but becomes brittle, shining, and possesses a conchoidal fracture like bright pitch, burning like charcoal without flame. The reddish-brown peat rapidly becomes black, when exposed to the atmosphere, by absorption of oxygen. The jelly peat rests on 2 inches of peat, containing many impressio. of leaves resembling *Typha latifolia* and *Acorus calamus*, which impressions do not occur in the upper decomposed peat. Mr. Linaker informed Mr. Binney that the

---

[*] Trans. Man. Geol. Soc. vol. iii., 1862, p. 19. In the same volume it is stated that Mr. E. W. Binney, F.R.S., read a paper entitled "Observations on Down-holland Moss," a copy of that read by him in 1842. The author adds that the peat must have been partially putrified before it was covered with sand, which excluded the air, when a part of its carbon would combine with the oxygen in it and in the water, while its hydrogen and that of the decomposed water were liberated. These gases being unable to escape, and the oxygen not being in sufficient quantities to consume all the hydrogen, new hydrocarbons would be formed, such as petroleum.

"jelly peat" occupies an area of 50 acres, that the ignis fatuus is still seen on the moss near Martin Mere; a number of antlers, probably of red deer, have been found in the blue silt under the moss; under which a second bed of peat had been occasionally found at Downholland. Near the house the peat is overlaid by 2 feet of blown sand, and traces of oily fluid occur on the surface of the adjoining ditches.

At New Cover, east of Churchtown, I noticed the following section :—

	feet.
Alluvial clay - - - -	- 6
Peat -	- 4
Grey clay - - - -	- 4 (+)

The Grey Clay is also seen in the Crossens Sluice, under the peat on the west side of the Churchtown Moss. The peat here does not appear to be more than 6 or 7 feet thick.

Martin Mere.—The bank of Shirdley Hill Sand at Holmes Wood has been described as formerly constituting the northern limit of Martin Mere, which old lake was described by Leland as "the biggest meare in Lancashire, iiii. miles in length and ii. in breadth ;" and in 1692 it had an area, before it was drained, of 3,000 acres. In that year Mr. T. Fleetwood, of Bank Hall, began the great work of reclaiming it by cutting a sluice 24 feet in width from the sea through the salt marsh bordering the coast near Crossens (which at that early period was already embanked), through a thick deposit of peat for a mile and a half, up to the margin of the lake, employing at times 2,000 workmen. The water gradually flowed away into the sea, which before only escaped during floods into the river Douglas.

Dr. Leigh describes large quantities of roach, pike, perch, and bream being left by the retiring waters, and mentions the discovery of eight canoes, each scooped out of a single tree, one having attached to it plates of iron. He also mentions the finding of great numbers of trunks of ash, birch, oak, and pine, in separate and distinct plots, as if they had been planted.*

This flood-channel appears to have run between the Boulder Clay patches already described at Tarlscough and Rufford, following the line of "Boundary Lane" joining the Douglas at the point where a sort of arm of alluvium juts out in the direction of Lathom Windmill. In a small portion of the area occupied by the peat in the south-west corner of the sheet it is found to rest on the grey Estuarine Clay, as in map 90 S.E.; but all around this tract (between the "M" of Martin Mere and the "L" of Longditch) the peat rests directly on the Shirdley Hill Sand lying directly on the Boulder Clay plain.

Further operations were undertaken in 1714, and Mr. Fleetwood died in 1717. To prevent the sea entering the sluice at spring-tides he had built flood-gates, which in 1755, five years after

---

* Natural History of Lancashire and Cheshire. Oxford, 1700.

his lease expired, were thrown down by a high tide. The sea rushing in, these were again rebuilt, but the sluice was neglected, and in the winter of that year the site of the lake was again covered with water; but in 1781 Mr. T. Eccleston, of Scarisbrick, procured the assistance of Mr. Gilbert, of Worsley, who had worked for the Duke of Bridgewater. Mr. Gilbert commenced operations in 1783 by making sea-gates at the coast, "stop gates" half a mile from it, and "flushing gates" at the junction of the sluice with the lake. In the following year these were so far successful that several acres were sown with corn; and Mr. Eccleston was voted a gold medal by the Society for the Encouragement of Arts, Manufactures, and Commerce; and when he died in 1809 an elaborate Latin inscription recorded how he, with immense pains, had drained the great Martinesian lake. But, unfortunately, in 1813 the sea destroyed the two outer gates, since replaced by cast-iron cylinders with valves instead of flood-gates, which, though often choked, have answered well. Immense damage has since been done on several occasions through the sea breaking down the banks and flooding the country, most of which is 10 feet below spring-tide high-water mark. A small stream, called Merebrooks, flows from Bickertaffe by the south side of Ormskirk into the Mere.

Leigh mentions the discovery of an elk's head "4 yards within Marle," under the Moss between Martin Mere and Meales (now North Meales), the antlers of which were thicker than a man's arm, the beams being two yards long. The head of a stag found at Larbrick, "eight yards within Marle," which he describes as larger than that of any stag now in England or Canada, was probably the Irish elk, *Megaceros Hibernicus;* and another elk, found in Ellel Moss, "five yards within Marl," was preserved in Ellel Grange, near Lancaster.

From Midge Hall up to the Great Sluice there is a great thickness of peat; and though the mere is drained, during rainy seasons the moss is extremely wet, and the long narrow sluices are not sufficient to carry off the water, which flows over their tops.

The level of the peat at the top of the bank of the Great Sluice in the centre of the old mere is 8 feet above the mean sea-level. Here the peat appears to rest on a thin bed of Shirdley Hill Sand lying on Boulder Clay.

Many legends still linger in regard to Martin Mere amongst the inhabitants of the district, who believe that it was inhabited by a mermaid, seen only a short time before the lake was drained.

By the side of its waters, according to tradition, Sir Lancelot du Lac had his habitation. The round table of King Arthur still exists at Lowther Bridge, near Penrith.

Rufford and Croston Mosses.—A committee was appointed to drain the lowlands of Rufford, Croston, Tarleton, and Mawdesley, with power to levy a rate on the property in the district. In carrying out their operations large quantities of decayed vegetable matter, chiefly composed of oak and yew, were found, some of the trunks of which appeared to have been burnt.*

Hesketh and Tarleton Mosses.—West of Hesketh Moss the peat is seen on the beach cropping out from beneath the Salt Marsh Clay near Cottam's Houses. South of Pipe House the peat rests on the Boulder Clay, but rapidly thickens southwards. North of Boundary Meanygate are two pits, called "Bottomless Holes," locally believed to be unfathomable. Trunks of oak, elder, yew, and ash occur in and under the peat near this tract. The peat to the east is a slope peat, rising from 11·44 feet above the mean sea-level at Sugar Stubs to 46 feet at Boundary Meanygate. Further to the N.E. towards Becconsall Windmill the level of the surface of the peat diminishes to 35 feet, where it thins out on the Boulder Clay.

The peat in this tract, and in fact in all the "slope peats" of the district, though reaching a thickness of 12 and even 16 feet, appears to have been nearly entirely formed of heath and small brushwood laid down in successive thin layers, which can be separated from each other like leaves of paper. The peat is much drier than that formed on the flat surface, and when perfectly free from moisture is a bright yellowish-brown, while the "swamp-peat" is invariably a very dark-brown colour, and possesses from three to seven times the specific gravity of the heath or slope peat when both are dried at the same temperature.

Mr. Baines mentions that the traces of a submerged forest were formerly visible on the coast at Hesketh, and traces of peat may still be seen at several points between Hesketh and Croston.

Another considerable tract of "slope peat" occurs around Midge Hall Station. It includes the tracts known as Farrington Moss, Longton Moss, Little Hoole Moss, Leyland Moss, and Great Moss, in all about 5 square miles, the boundary of which was traced by my former colleague, Mr. Shelswell, who states that the average thickness is 12 feet, and also that oaks and other trees lie at the bottom of the moss. At one point north of White Houses (the second house from the east in the lane running north of the word "Londonderry" on the 1-inch map) I observed the base of a large oak tree *in situ*, with its roots in the Boulder Clay beneath, the colour of which had been bleached by the humic acid from a bright red colour to white.

Farrington Moss.—This moss is continuous with the last described, rising from 65 feet to more than 100 feet above the sea-level; but the level is constantly being reduced by the cutting of the peat for fuel, and the burning of the newly exposed surface preparatory to bringing it under cultivation, which is rapidly being carried out. The peat here is at least 18 feet in thickness, and extremely dense

---

* The trunks of *Pinus Sylvestris* dug out of the moss have generally a tendency to split up into longitudinal ropes or strips, which are occasionally used, as in some parts of Scotland and Ireland, instead of candles, and in some parts of Aberdeenshire for halters for cattle.

in its lower part, though light and heathy above, nor is the lowest portion perhaps as compact as the peat of Rufford.

Northward in Penwortham several patches of peat occur, but they are of no great thickness, probably having been long under cultivation and much cut, as several names testify to the former presence of moss, as Charnock *Moss*, Hutton *Moor*, Howick *Tarn* Moor.

Mosses north of the Ribble.—Lytham and Marton Moss.—The boundary runs eastward by Moss-side by Marton to Southshore. Its boundary was described in the charter of Lytham Priory, time of Richard I. Large quantities of trunks of oaks and alders have been obtained from it, many of which have been used for roofs, gate-posts, fences, and agricultural implements. In some parts of the moss, from one to three feet of sand is intercalated in the peat, and in a few cases a yellowish-white clay containing plant-growths.

Great numbers of oaks and yews have been found in the Marton moss, some at a depth of 16 feet, and generally in a slanting position.

After the severe storm of March 1869, when the embankment at Southshore was washed away, I observed the following section :—

		feet.
Blown sand	- -	4
Peaty earth	-	1
Blown sand	- -	1½
Peat	- -	13
Grey clay	-	3 (+)

In the moss in the country lying immediately behind, the peat reaches a thickness of from three to five yards; a bed of sand with comminuted shells often occurs at about five feet ; and trunks of oak, alder, yew, ash, and Scotch fir are constantly being met with. At the base is blue and white silt.*

A sheet of peat occupies the bottom of the long swamp valley which connects the Wyre at Skippool with the estuary of the Ribble at Lytham, the soil between the two depressions being low, and covered with at least 10 feet of peat.

Camden describes more than a third of the Fylde as a swampy morass, while Holingshead writes that " the whole county of Lancashire has been forests heretofore."

The bottoms of the numerous swamp-hollows between Blackpool and Poulton-le-Fylde are all occupied by peat. The great depression, at the bottom of which lies Marton Mere, may be regarded as one of these hollows, being due probably to unequal deposition of Boulder Clay. The slightly cliffed and terraced aspect of the slopes above the alluvial plain marking the

---

* Many of the oaks dug up are exceedingly black, the colour being probably due to combination of the tannin matter and gallic acid of the oak with iron, the wood being dyed with a natural ink.

former area of the lake before drainage operations, and the occurrence of gravel at levels above, would appear to indicate subsequent modification by water.

In cutting the main dyke three coracles were found. In the time of Edward III., when a dispute in regard to fishery rights in it arose, it would appear to have been of considerable size. Much turf appears to have been dug, and the pits have become filled up with rotten peat, called "dewon." There were, probably, many woods in Poulton parish in the peat flats, as in a grant to St. Mary's Church, Lancaster, of Poulton Church, pawnage of the woods is given. (Harleian MS. 506.)

Coast of Rossal.—Cropping out from beneath the shingle near Rossal School, a bed of peat is seen resting on grey clay, in which there are many roots of trees, amongst which, Prof. W. Boyd Dawkins, F.R.S., informs me, a large number of Scotch fir cones might formerly be noticed. In 1793 it is recorded that a large number of trunks were observed there, all of which laid in a S.W. and N.E. direction.

Pilling Moss.—This extensive tract of peat* is bounded on the north by the belt of fluvio-marine alluvium which fringes the coast of Morecambe Bay between the rivers Wyre and Cocker, and conceals the peat moss, which formerly extended northward into the bay, where small patches of the peat may still be seen resting on Boulder Clay at several points between tide-marks when uncovered by the sands.

Westward a series of knolls of Boulder Clay between Knott End, Hambleton, and the Wyre at Shard Bridge, rise up through the peat, the slopes of which, having been worn back by the Wyre, constitute cliffs forming the eastern boundary of that river.

This area is very thinly inhabited, and those who live in it are, I am informed, often subject to idiotcy† and rheumatism. The soil is excessively damp, and the water obtainable from the peat extremely impure and turbid. In several farms Abyssinian pumps are used, and a tolerably plentiful supply of water is obtained of a rather brackish character.

Under the peat of Pilling Moss are the trunks of oaks, yews, and alders, the presence of which is recorded in many of the names of the hillocks rising above the moss,—Black Hill, Hurst, Wood Hill, Dunock, Alder field. These mounds appear to have been connected by a path under the moss, made and supported by alder poles. Many of the trees appear to have been destroyed by burning. Before Rawcliffe Moss was drained by the late Mr. ffrance, heavy floods of the Wyre washed right across that and Pilling Mosses, and escaped into Morecambe Bay. The gravel bed

---

* The inhabitants say, " Pilling Moss, like God's grace, is boundless." Pilling, Rawcliffe, and Stalmine Mosses cover an area of about 20,000 acres.

† This is believed to be produced by the dislike of the people to marry strangers.

at Cogie Hill, which rises above the level of the moss, has given rise to a popular legend:—

       " Once a wood, then a sea;
       Now a moss, and e'er will be."

The Rev. L. Richmond* states that on the 28th January 1744-5 a part of Pilling Moss which had been gradually swelling rose to a surprising height, and after a short time sank, when it commenced slowly moving towards the south, and covered 10 acres of good and improved land with moss and water to a depth, in some places, of 5 yards.

Streams of water appear to have flowed over this area during all the earlier formation of the peat, for rolled pebbles constantly occur in the moss near Stalmine, and thence to Pilling, apparently derived from the Preesall shingle bed, often spread out in layers between the planes of deposition of the peat.

Many instances of mosses overflowing in other districts are recorded; as the moss of Solway, in Dumfriesshire, on 16 Nov. 1771, where 800 acres of land were covered with peat to a depth of 3 to 15 feet; Poulenard, in the county Louth, in Ireland, on 20 Dec. 1793, when the peat covered the ground to a depth of 20 feet; at Kilmaleady, in the King's county, which commenced 26 June 1821, and covered 150 acres of corn-fields, &c. As draining operations extend, these irruptions will probably become rarer and rarer. A portion of Chat Moss, it is related by Leland, grew to a great height, burst, and was carried away into Glazebrook, and thence into the Mersey, the waters of which were so spoilt by the peat, that, according to Camden, great numbers of fish were killed.

Of the vast number of prostrate trunks of trees I have observed at the base of the peat mosses of Western Lancashire, many of them still attached to the parent roots, by far the largest proportion rest on a thin seam of peat intervening between the trunk and the underlying clay or sand; and though this may have been formed after the fall of the tree, as the peat surrounding its sides and entirely concealing it from view undoubtedly has, yet, as the points of contact with the ground are underlaid by peat, it appears more probable that the obstruction of drainage and growth of peat had set in previous to the destruction of the forests. That this was so, is borne out by the fact that the portion of the trunks of the trees still left standing are broken off short and jagged at about the same height,—a result evidently produced by violent winds blowing down the trees, and snapping the trunks at a line of weakness, caused by the trees becoming surrounded by standing water, which rotted their trunks at the line of junction of the air with the water. The fall of the trees must necessarily have produced still further obstruction of drainage, but this was evidently not the cause of the original obstruction and the consequent growth of the peat ; a view which is borne out by the occurrence of higher horizons of prostrate trees of

---

    * Phil. Trans., vol. xliii. p. 282.

smaller size, and of hazel (redwood of the peat cutters) and spurge at almost all levels.*

Much of the peat near its surface is " heath peat," formed of the growth of such plants as *Erica vulgaris, E. cinerea, Myrica gale, Vaccinium myrtillus,* resting on a " swamp-peat " below, which thins out eastwards;—the whole of the peat on the sands and shingle, near the Boulder Clay slope, being dry heath-peat of very low specific gravity

In many of the vast peat mosses of the plains of Northern Germany there is a similar superposition of immersed formed peat, consisting of aquatic plants, reeds, and carices, overlaid by an emerged formed peat, consisting mainly of sphagnum. Basins several feet deep being gradually filled up with water-plants, the growth ot the emerged peat commenced. These emerged peat-mosses M. Lesquereux† found to occur on very highly-inclined slopes, as the Vosges and Hartz mountains, and even rising to the culminating point of the Brocken, where the rocks were but slightly permeable to humidity. The slope-peats of Bleasdale Fells are, no doubt, due to the impermeable clay-wash capping the Yoredale Grit.

In the Isle of Lewis, one of the Hebrides, there is a plain 30 miles long, covered with peat moss, but slightly above the sea level.

Many lagunes of the Baltic and German Ocean are now filled with peat, formed under freshwater conditions, the same plants occurring as are found inland. This affords an existing example of the phenomena obtaining when the peat beds of West Lancashire were formed, especially the alternating and wedging out of peat, marine clays, and peat, exhibited in the neighbourhood of the river Alt at Altcar, which are still observable in the banks of that river and the neighbouring sluices.

In the Lake District of England, in Ireland, Germany,‡ and Labrador, peat moors occur on highlands, in which the atmosphere and ground are kept sufficiently moist to allow the growth of moss. These mosses rise by growth from the centre, and slope from it towards the sides, some 10 and even 30 feet. The extensive moss near Pilling is a good example of this,—the centre or crown gradually diminishing in height, from the drainage now being carried out, but suddenly rising and swelling up like a huge sponge after heavy rains.

Mr. W. Roscoe, who was the first to drain Chat Moss, between Manchester and Warrington, which is about 6 miles long and 3 miles broad, considered it to be due to a sheet of water held up by the underlying bed of clay. and derived from the high ground about Worsley. This being unable to escape except by

---

* In Queen's County, Ireland, I noticed in some of the peat sections no less than four horizons of large forest trees on a table land more than 1,000 feet in height.
† M. Léo Lesquereux, in Bulletin de la Société des Sciences Naturelles de Neuchatel, 1847, vol. i. p. 471.
‡ The Blogsberg, a high mountain in Lower Saxony, is also covered with peat. Prof. Robert Jameson, Mineralogical Travels through the Hebrides, &c.

overflowing the moss, makes its way up through holes, (locally called "ring pits)" believed to be unfathomable, but in reality only reaching to the clay, down to which he afterwards carried deep drains. Mr. Roscoe commenced his drainage and improving operations in 1805, and in 1813 had 160 acres under cultivation, and afterwards marled 100 acres per year without further expenditure of capital.

The mosses on the site of Martin Mere also sensibly rise when the quantity of the water flowing off the clay country is larger than the existing steam-pumping arrangements can carry off. Before the drainage of the lake was carried out, large portions floated or rested on a cushion of water, and prevented access to the edge of the mere, resembling the floating moors called *hangesak* in Zealand and which in the Ural are sufficiently thick to support forests of large fir trees.

Both on the coast of Wirral and West Lancashire thin seams of peat occur at the base of the sand dunes overlying the main mass of the peat. In one section near Leasowe Castle I noticed 15 thin peat-seams within a space of 5 feet. The base of the vertical blown sand is invariably stratified, and generally contains shells of *Bithynia tentaculata* and other fresh-water mollusca, associated with rolled marine shells that have been blown into the fresh water with the sand.

At a depth of from 3 to 4 feet from the top of the peat there is, both in Lancashire and Cheshire, though more persistently in the latter county, a bed of fine-grained grey or greenish sand, plentifully charged with shells of *Tellina Balthica* and *Cardium edule*. This is particularly well seen at Eccles Place, near Crossens, north of Southport, where the peat beneath it rests on Grey *Scrobicularia* Clay.

The various varieties of peat depend partly on the nature of the plants of which it is composed, which are mainly governed by the character of the subsoil, and partly on the stage of decomposition at which it has arrived. The "pitch peat" described by Mr. Binney as occurring near Churchtown is probably the ripest, *i.e.* the most perfectly decomposed ; in Germany it is called *pitchy-peat* or *fat peat (pechtorf, specktorf)*,—a firm sticky mass, plastic while moist, and hard and lustrous when dry.*

Peat which has been more recently formed is more fibrous, the structure being more and more apparent towards the surface, which is especially seen in moss-peat. Grown in the open air, under full sunlight, it has a yellowish-red colour, becoming browner and darker with depth. Peat derived from the growth of grasses and sedges is also fibrous near the surface, and of a silvery greyish colour, from the colour of the skeletons of the blades of grass of which it is composed ; but all trace of structure is lost at a very small depth, and the peat is earthy while wet, and hard and dense when dry.

---

* For further information on this subject see " Essays on the Natural History and Origin of Peat Moss, by the Rev. Dr. Rennie:" Edinburgh, 1818. "Peat and its Uses, by S. W. Johnson, A.M.:" New York, 1866. " Traité Complet de la Tourbe, par M. Boec :" Paris, 1870.

Many of the unctuous earthy peats found at the oases of the mosses between the Mersey and Ribble, resting on the Grey Clays, appear to have been formed from grasses, while the peat on the slopes of the Fells of Yoredale Grits, where the water is nearly free from lime, is mainly composed of mosses ; as is the case in the soft-water districts of the Lake District of Westmoreland and North Lancashire,—which Prof. S. W. Johnson,* describing similar facts in the United States of America, has shown to be due to the fact that aquatic grasses require much lime for their growth, and therefore cannot thrive in soft waters, becoming choked out by mosses that require very little lime; while in limestone districts the reverse is the case, grasses and sedges choking out the mosses.

The character of the peat, and the sequence of conditions which led to its great development in Lancashire, appear to hold good over a very large area.

The Danish antiquarians classify their peat-moss deposits into three divisions : (1) *Boggy flats* (Engmose), swamps covered with water plants, and traversed by watercourses, with a substratum of peat from 5 to 10 feet in thickness ; (2) *Peat bogs* (Lyngmose or Svampmose), peat of growths of Hypnum and Sphagnum, peat above and water below, 8 to 15 feet in depth ; and *Forest* Moss Pits (Skovmose), occurring in hollows or depressions in the Glacial Clay, sometimes filling them up to a depth of 30 feet, with a fringe of forest trees and branches round the edges.

In the valley of the Clyde Mr. J. Geikie† has shown that the Carse Clays (marine) overlie beds of peat, with trees resting on blue clay overlying the Glacial deposits ; and it is clear that that peat must be older than the 25–30 feet beach, and probably than the 50 feet old sea-margin. And he considers it possible that glaciers still lingered in the upper valleys after the 45-50 beach had begun to be formed, from which the river may have carried much fine silt. In which case the bulk of the buried and submerged peat mosses belongs to a period anterior in date to either of those two raised beaches ; that, in short, the mosses indicate a depression and subsequent elevation of 50 feet and more, since the time that they and the trees which they enclose grew green upon the land. And it is also probable that " the primitive canoe may have floated in the waters of the Clyde when the sea reached, not 25 or 30, but 45 or 50 feet higher than at present."

In the Isle of Man the late Prof. E. Forbes described submerged forests and peat as resting on grey lacustrine clays, filling up hollows in the Boulder Clay, and mentions the occurrence of *Cervus Megaceros* in the lacustrine clays.

Mr. J. Geikie describes the ancient forests as occurring wherever areas of peat mosses occur in Scotland, pines generally being found on the lighter gravelly soils, and oaks in the heavier clays and in the bogs of the lower grounds. At Glenavon, Banffshire, peat mosses with roots of pines occur at a height of nearly 3000 feet above the

---

* See note at bottom of p. 83.
† Great Ice Age, p. 315. Isbister: London, 1874.

sea.* At Lanfine, Ayrshire, Mr. Brown, F.R.S.E., describes an oak found in a peat moss at a height of 500 feet above the sea, that when entire must have contained 534 feet of timber ; while, on the other hand, drowned forests occur all along the coast of Caithness, Aberdeen, Orkneys, Frith of Tay, and the Hebrides, and also on the western coasts of Scotland, as at Oban, where the harbour, 20 fathoms deep, partly rests on peat.

Peat mosses, with submerged forests at their base, fringe the estuaries of all the rivers of Cumberland, and, as described above, the whole length of the Lancashire coast. In Cheshire I found several horizons overlying Scrobicularia clays; and in North Wales the peat beds underlying the alluvium of the Dee extend northwards under the sand hills of the Point of Ayr.

The coasts of Cornwall, Devon, and Somerset, the late Sir H. De la Beche described as fringed with these submerged forests ; of which, and the raised beaches, he wrote, "However numerous,
" from accidental circumstances, they may be, they may happen
" to merely constitute a portion, and it will eventually, in all
" probability, be found a very limited portion, of those which are
" observable in Western Europe, and which show that much dry
" and low ground has been depressed with a growing vegetation
" upon it, and that extensive lines of water have been elevated
" since the era of the existing fauna and flora."†

At several points along the southern coast such traces have been noticed by Sir Henry James and Mr. Godwin-Austen, who describe the occurrence of the oak, elm, chestnut, hazel, and *Pinus sylvestris,* in these submerged forests, and comment on the fact that this tree will not now grow near a sea-coast. This tree is also found in the peat-mosses of the Sussex Weald, and Dartmoor, and is mentioned by the Rev. J. Yates, F.G.S.,‡ amongst the trees occurring in the submerged forests of Merionethshire and Cardiganshire.

The universal presence of these submerged forests around the coasts of Great Britain and Ireland, the Western Isles, Denmark, Holland, and the North of France, when coupled with the fact of land- and fresh-water shells being dredged in deep water, at from 14 to 40 miles from existing land, leaves no possibility of doubt of the continental conditions which must have prevailed immediately after the Glacial Epoch.

The presence of large oaks at great elevations in Britain points to warmer summers than at present ; but the growth of Scotch firs as far south as the South of England *equally points to more severe winters than now obtain;* which prove the extremes of climate to have been more marked through the continental conditions which prevailed in the era immediately preceding the growth of the peat. According to Forchammer, peat is never formed with a higher mean temperature than 45 degrees, while in Lancashire it is now 51 degrees.

---

* Sinclair's Statistical Account of Scotland : Edinburgh New Phil. Jour. vol. xvii. p. 53, 1834.   Cybele Britannica, vol. ii. p. 409.
† Report on Devon and Cornwall, p. 433.
‡ Geol. Soc. Proc., vol. ii. p. 407.

The presence of the various objects of antiquity which have been found at various times in peat mosses of various parts of the country,—as the parcel of coins of Edward IV. mentioned by Dr. Plott* as being found at a depth of 18 feet, from which he calculates the growth of the peat moss at an inch per annum,—are in reality of little use in determining the rate of the growth of peat, from the facility with which objects of any weight will in a few years sink down into a peat moss.

Though the growth of peat to any great extent seems to have ceased in some instances, it appears to have formed with very great rapidity in comparatively modern times; as in the instance related by the Earl of Cromarty, when a plain in the parish of Lochbroom, N.B., which in 1651 was covered with a standing but leafless fir-wood, 15 years afterwards was covered with soft deep green moss, in which in 1699 the country people dug peat.

One cannot but be struck with the extremely small angle of fall from the coasts of Lancashire and Cheshire to the ten-fathom line, it being not more than three and a half feet per mile; and it is easy to understand that the drainage of the whole country west of the great watershed of the Penine Chain, finding its way over these gradual slopes and undulating flats, must have necessarily been much obstructed, and that the obstruction would increase and keep pace with the elevation of the country, which tended to remove the outfall of the rivers further and further from their source.

RECENT ALLUVIUM.

Tidal.—Resting on the peat in the plain of the river Alt, a bed of brown clay or warp occurs, becoming more sandy at the top, where it contains *Cyclas cornea* and other fresh-water shells; but in its lower part, especially in its western area, shells of a small variety of *Scrobicularia piperata* occur, and the fresh-water forms disappear.

The Alt was embanked at an early period. In the Harleian collection of MSS. there is a letter from the justices of Salford to the Lord Lieutenant, asking to be excused from payment of sums of money for the repairs of the banks of the Alt, dated 1590. The whole plain is much subject to floods, the only ground that is free being about 200 acres near the church. In 1779 an Act was passed "for draining, improving, and preserving the low lands of the parishes of Altcar, Sefton, Halsall, and Walton-on-the-Hill," when the floodgates were repaired, the expense being paid by a rate on owners and occupiers, and in 1831 new gates were erected. Previous to that, many parts of a farm would only let for 2s. 6d. an acre.

The peat beneath is split in two at Ince Blundell by a bed of grey clay, resembling that underlying the peat further to the north, as shown in the section, Fig. 20.

---

* History of Staffordshire; and Phil. Trans., vol. xxvii.

Fig. 20.

Section in Alluvium of the River Alt.

Scale 40 ft. to one inch.

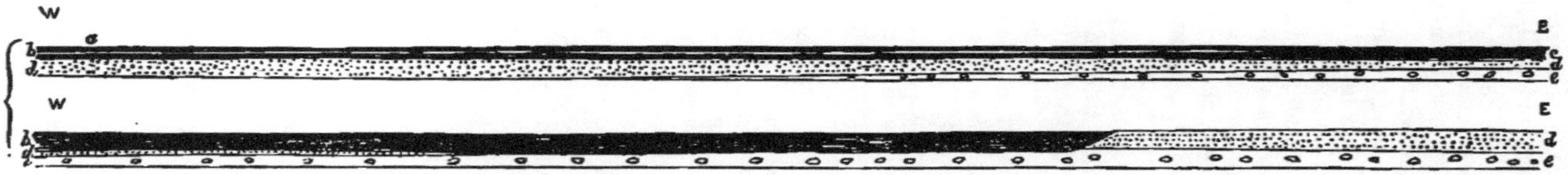

a. Alluvial Warp.   b. Peat.   c. Estuarine Grey Clay.

d. Shirdley Hill Sand.   e. Upper Boulder Clay

This thin bed is probably the representative in time of that described by Messrs. Binney and Talbot on the banks of the same river, a little further west; though it is certain that frequent alternations of fresh-water, obstructed drainage, and marine-estuarine conditions prevailed in the era immediately preceding and succeeding the formation of the peat.

At the Battery on the sandy beach off the coast of Ainsdale and Southport a deposit of dark loamy clay, locally called "Slutch," occurs, with numerous marine shells. It is distant from spring-tide high-water mark 667 yards, and is covered by about two feet of ordinary sand. Large patches of it formerly occurred near Southport, making dangerous quicksands: these have since been dug out and removed at the expense of the town.

Immense quantities of mud, silt, and sand are brought down by the river Ribble from the 380 square miles of Glacial Drift country drained by it and its tributaries, a part of which is carried out seawards. Returning with the tide the sand is deposited on the banks, the mud from its lightness falling last, forms a thin layer on the sand near the shore as the tide recedes, while in the sand banks surrounded by water no mud is observable. The mud being at the surface of the water when the ebb takes place, a wedge of water is removed bodily from the bottom, running out seawards, and carrying with it the principal part of the sand, while the more gradual retreat of the surface allows time for the precipitation of the mud. This takes place every spring-tide, and to a less extent with each ordinary high-tide; an extremely thin leaf-like layer being thrown down, which dips towards the sea, the whole forming a laminated tidal clay reaching a thickness of 12 and even 20 feet. It is found all along the coast, on banks of the estuary of the Ribble from the north of Brow Side House, to Penwortham; and from Freckleton Point to Old Chain House a large tract of it occurs, called Freckleton Marsh, bounded on the north by bluffs formed of the Upper Boulder Clay running by Newton, Clifton, Old and New Lea Hall. The whole of this marsh has been recently reclaimed up to the north wall of the Ribble Navigation Company. In this tract the following section was obtained by a boring of the Preston Farming Company; for the journal of which, and the analysis of the water, I have to thank Mr. Ascroft, of Preston.

	feet.
Sand *with salt water*	24
Clay	12
Sand, *salt water*	4½
Clay	18
Sand, *salt water*	24
Boulder clay	57
Sand, *fresh water*	1
Gravel conglomerate	4
Sand	4
Gravel	4
Clay (not penetrated, probably Keuper marls).	

At Red Bank 2 feet of Boulder Clay, rising above the beach, is capped by

	ft.	in.
Laminated sand	2	0
Pebbles	0	4
Sand	0	3

A considerable area has also been reclaimed on the south side of the Ribble, between Dunkirk and Pipe Houses, chiefly by the late Sir Thomas Hesketh. At the former place the Marsh Clay rests on two feet of peat overlying Boulder Clay.

The Marsh Clay appears on the opposite coast at Brook Bridge and west of Bush, near Freckleton. In the peat at the latter place, lying beneath the tidal clay, horns of red deer were found some years ago.

Between Lea and Howick Marshes the banks of the river are about 9 feet high, and the water about 9 feet in depth at mean tide. On the south side a shoal of gravel 8 feet in height was heaped up on the top of the bank, where I noticed the following section :—

		ft.	in.
Laminated sandy clay :			
First terrace	-	2	0
Second „	- - - -	2	3
Peaty clay and trunks of oaks	-	2	0
Black loamy sand, much laminated, to water level		9	0

The peat surfaces which grow during ebb tides, &c. on these clays are often swamped by fresh-water floods, and by high tides, causing a series of rapidly alternating fresh-water, marine, and land surfaces.

In Ashton, Lea, and Freckleton Marshes, the laminated clay rests on a peaty bed, the undoubted representative of the peat of the Southport Plain. The following is a typical section taken at Boundary Brook, Lea Marsh :—

		feet.
a. Laminated marsh clay	- -	3
b. Peaty clay, with trunks of oak trees	- -	2
c. Black loamy laminated sand, apparently	-	9

Another section in Ashton Marsh, in the north bank of the river, gives—

		feet.
a. Laminated clay	- - - -	5
b. Yellow loam	- - - -	2
c. Grey clay, drying into cubical fragments	-	1
d. Peat	- - - -	2½
e. Yellow clay, with wood	- -	1 (+)

Further west, nearer Freckleton Marsh, the peat layer was found to contain a great number of hazel nuts.

Trunks of trees occur both at the base and at the top of the peaty bed. The former are probably *in sitû;* the latter have evidently been brought down by land floods.

In Preston Marsh the sand *c* is represented by river gravel, which obtains in most of the sections eastward, intervening between the peat and Lower Boulder Clay or Triassic Rocks.

These alluvial beds are seen to rest upon Boulder Clay, all along the shore from Marsh End to a point opposite Pear Tree Bank, the latter apparently resting on a soft red sandstone, with red micaceous shales.

All the alluvium of the small brooks running inland around Longton, as Tarra Carr Gutter, Walmer Bridge, &c., is of a tidal character at its western end, becoming fluviatile on the landward side.

River Wyre.—A large tract of alluvial tidal silt and salt-marsh clay occurs between the River Wyre and the sea between Norbreck and Rossal land-mark, the sand-hills stretching from that point to Fleetwood, resting on this alluvium, which has been described as overlying the peat of Rossal.

This tidal deposit on the south graduates into ordinary brook-alluvium, running up the valleys of the Breck and other depressions in the Poulton-le-Fylde district.

Tidal alluvium occupies a considerable area between the peat mosses and the coast of Morecambe Bay, between Knot End and Pilling and Cockerham, on the seaward margin being more or less covered above spring-tide high-water mark with low sand-hills, and on the land side gradually thinning out upon the peat.

Below high-water mark, in the higher reaches of Pilling and Cockerham Sands, laminated clay is still being thrown down on the surface of the salt-marsh plants ; and this is also the case on the west side of the Wyre, in the great marshes between Cleveleys Station and the railway embankment at Fleetwood.

At Pilling and Cockerham, wells have been sunk through the alluvium to a bed of gravel, and a supply of somewhat brackish water obtained, some of the wells being fitted with Norton's (Abyssinian) pumps.

Water of a similar character was found in several wells on the west side of the Wyre between Cleveleys Station and Cleveleys. In one of these wells, near the Wesleyan Chapel, the Boulder Clay was reached at a depth of $7\frac{1}{2}$ yards, the surface of the ground being only about 14 feet above Ordnance datum-line.

At Flakefleet House, the base of the clay is dark, dense, and full of shells of *Scrobicularia piperata* resting on shingle. I think it very probable that in several sections in this area, the peat is absent ; the shingle underlying the alluvium being of the age of the Preesall shingle. Westward the peat and grey clay rest on Boulder Clay on the coast between Rossal and Rossal land-mark.

Fluviatile Alluvium.

The Ribble.—The sequence of deposits making up the lowest alluvial flat or plain of the Ribble between Preston and the sea is illustrated by the two following sections on the south bank :—

A.	feet.	B.		feet.
Laminated sand -	3	} Loam		6
Yellow clay - -	4			
Grey clay with pebbles -	2			
Peaty beds with hazel nuts	1	{ Peat - - -		1
		{ Grey clay -		3
Gravel - -	3	Gravel -		4
Base not seen.		Red sandstone -		1 (+)

The laminated sand and loam forming the uppermost bed becomes darker and more clayey to the west. In Penwortham Marsh the following sequence occurs :—

	feet.
a. Laminated sandy clay and sand	4
g. Lower Boulder Clay	12
h. Pebble beds (Bunter)	2

In Preston Marsh occurs :—

	feet.
a. Red sandy clay	7
a^2. Grey sandy clay	8
b. Peaty clay	1
f. River-gravel	2
g. Lower Boulder Clay	1 (+)

Bezza Brook. The alluvial flat at the bottom of this small tributary of the Ribble is made of the following beds :—

	feet.
Alluvial sand	4
Gravel	2
Blue sandy loam	2
Red sandstone	(+)

The Darwen alluvium is well seen at Carver's Bridge, Bannister Hall, six or more feet of sand and gravels occurring, the pebbles of which have their long axes pointing in the direction of the stream.

Near Croston the marine clay graduates into a fresh-water alluvium, running from Long Lane. At Bretherton Ees, in the Ees, or Eyes Lane, half a foot of clay rests on peat ; and in Broad Meadow the clay is 3 feet thick on the moss ; so that the whole of the alluvium of the river Lostock, near its junction with the Yarrow, and of the latter river with the Douglas, would appear to rest on peat.

The spring tides flow up the Lostock as far as Little Wood Bridge, Ridley Lane, in Ulnes Walton, so that it is probable that most of the overlying alluvium is more or less of the salt-marsh type; but I did not observe any marine shells in it. The same remark applies to the Yarrow, at Croston, where the tides still flow as far east as Bridge End.

The gravel lying at the base of the lowest alluvium of the valley of the Ribble graduates into sands with marine shells, the equivalents in time of the base of the Shirdley Hill Sand and the Preesall Shingle ; from which it would appear that the re-excavation of the valley of the Ribble was complete before the era of the growth of the great peat beds.

CHAPTER V.

Roman and other Antiquities bearing on the Geological
Changes in South-west Lancashire, and the Agricultural and Industrial Geology of the District.

The traces of a Roman road between Ribchester and Kirkham
are in many places very apparent ; its position being expressed on
the maps of the Ordnance Survey, and a portion of it near Fulwood
Barracks still maintaining the name of "Watling Street." Further
west it is more fragmentary : but its course is well marked, being
known locally as the "Danes Pad,"—pad meaning in the Lancashire
dialect a path or road. The last trace of it is in a field south-east of
Poulton-le-Fylde, near Singleton Carrs, where there is much rounded
gravel scattered over the surface of the peat, which must have
been brought from a considerable distance to raise the road in the
hollow ; such is also the case where the road crosses Dow Brook,
a little east of Kirkham, large stones from the Boulder Clay having
been here collected and used for making an embankment. The level
of the brook is 23 feet above the Ordnance datum-line, or seven feet
above high-water mark, proving that no great change of level has
taken place since Roman times, especially as a pavement of tiles,
which there is strong evidence to show formed part of a Roman bath,
was discovered in an adjacent site, at a similar level, now marked
by the "New England spring."

This Roman road is considered to be the seventh Itin. of Richard
of Cirencester, which he describes as running from York to the
Portus Sistuntiorum, which he believed to be at the Neb or Naze of
Freckleton, in the estuary of the Ribble. This port is described
by Ptolemy as being near the inlet of Morecambe Bay, and was
probably Skippool in the estuary of the Wyre, which river at
that point is three fathoms in depth at high tide, and to which place
a considerable coasting traffic of grain was done, up to the advent
of the railway.[*]

According to Ptolemy the inhabitants of the country between
the lofty ridge (the Yoredale Grit Fells?) and Morecambe Bay
were called *Setantii* or *Segantii*, or "dwellers in waters,"—which
district, on the second invasion of the Romans, was included in the
country of the *Brigantes.*

Between the Roman stations at Carlisle and Warrington, there
was a road, which may still be traced in the Fylde, much of the
present high-road between Preston and Lancaster being on it ; or
perhaps, more correctly, it is the original road kept in repair.

---

[*] Details of the position of the road and other Roman remains are given with
great accuracy by the Rev. W. Thornber, History of Blackpool, 1830, and in various
papers in the Trans. Hist. Soc., Lancashire and Cheshire.

A large number of Roman coins was discovered, some years ago, at Poulton churchyard, one mile distant from Skippool ; the direction of the existing portions of the road aiming at the Wyre at this point, the terminating portion of the road not yet known will be only a few yards from the river, if that direction be maintained.

In Mill Heyfield, near Dow Brook, Mr. Willacy discovered in 1793 a large shield,* dedicated possibly to the river goddess Belisama, the " Minerva Belisma " of the Romans in Britain, and two coins of Adrian. The Rev. W. Thornber also records the discovery of urns, pateræ, burnt bones, and a bone needle, a lachrymatory, a small " druids egg " of light-green glass, and an iron amulet.

In a field near Weeton, called Moor Hey, occurs a cairn of boulders, in which were discovered by Mr. Thornber some half-baked urns; and in cutting a dyke near Martin Mere to the west, he describes the draining of the water as laying bare two skin boots, a skin cap without a seam, and a bronze celt.

Still further west, at Marton vicarage, the Rev. James Cookson discovered a quern, sixteen inches in diameter, and composed of stone which appeared to me to be the Yoredale Grit of Longridge Fell.

Another quern, shown me by Mr. Wheatley Balme, discovered on his property at Loughrigg, Ambleside, appeared to be composed of the same stone. The latter had the peculiarity of the opening in the centre running obliquely to the base, and being at least five degrees out of the perpendicular.

From Weeton Moss, the Rev. Mr. Buck records the discovery of the two oak sides of a sledge and an amulet of white marble.

At Stalmine, near Danes " Pad," a coin (denarius) of Faustinus was found.

At Poulton-le-Fylde, a large number of Roman coins was found many years ago, and, at a later date, one of Domitian, but I failed to obtain any particulars of their destination.

At Fleetwood† a considerable number of coins was found in 1840. The spot in which they were discovered was pointed out to me by Mr. Bond, station master, who was present when the excavation was going on. They consisted, according to the Rev. Mr. Thornber, of 400 denarii of the Emperors Trajan, Adrian, Vespasian, Titus, Domitian, Antoninus, Severus, Caracalla, Sabina, Faustina, &c. Adjoining the spot where the coins were found, close to Rossal landmark, a large paved platform was discovered by the workmen at about eight feet from the surface. As the surface is about 26 feet above the Ordnance datum line, it would appear that the level of this platform is about 18 feet, or some two feet above the highest level of ordinary spring high tides, a 'tolerably clear proof that the country is little higher now than it was in Roman times.

Roman and British remains, including a Roman cooking vessel,

---

* The finder sold it as old brass, for 30s., to a travelling Scotchman, who sold it to C. Towneley, Esq., by whom it was deposited in the British Museum. It is figured by Dr. Whitaker in his " History of Richmondshire," vol. ii. p. 457.

† The site of Fleetwood in ancient times was called "Quaggy Meols," being, I presume, a combination of sand hills and salt marsh. The old name for Layton Hawes was " Kelgrimol."

have been found in the moss near Pilling, where there are the traces of an ancient road, possibly Roman, called "Kate's Pad." On an adjacent hillock, rising above the moss, the Rev. Mr. Bannister found a bronze celt, associated with a quantity of bones of deer.

The Romans had three trajecti near the Wyre, at Aldwith or Shard, where the present bridge is, the ford of Bulk or the higher ford, and the lower which ran from " Mine (Stoney?) End " on the west to the old perch at the mouth of the river.

Near the Roman road below Preston, at Claughton Park, near Garstang, antiquities were discovered in 1822, consisting of an iron spearhead, an axe, glass beads, fibulæ, &c., and an urn of baked clay.

A vast quantity of antiquities has been washed out of the peaty beds lying on the base of the sand dunes of Wirral, including a bronze needle, a bone needle, Roman coins of Nero and of Antoninus, in copper, silver, and gold ; coins struck at Carthage, and early English coins, including some of Ethelred, Canute, William I., &c., and Scotch coins, and a large number of neolithic flint implements.

Dr. Ormerod, in his History of Cheshire,* refers to various old maps and writings showing a stream running from Stanlow Point in the upper estuary of the Mersey to the Dee at Chester ; and argues, therefore, that in Roman times an ancient arm of the sea occupied the valley running along this line, and connected the tidal rivers, the Mersey and the Dee, separating the hundred of Wirral from the mainland, and making it an island;—of which a tradition still remains in the country. He states that the small variation of the level of the country induced Mr. Pennant to make a series of observations which led to the connection of the two rivers by the existing Dee and Mersey Canal.

The summit-level of this canal on the watershed between the two rivers has been shown by Mr. Boult, by evidence obtained from the Ordnance Survey, to be 40·75 feet above Ordnance datum (45 feet above the Old Dock Sill at Liverpool, above which the tide rises 21 feet). He shows that a tide that would cover this watershed would " submerge nearly the whole isthmus, including Celtic settlements and Roman roads."

Mr. Boult in this paper endeavours to prove that the estuary of the Mersey was formerly a fresh-water lake, and that the marshes of Bidston and Wallasey were formerly connected with those of Bootle and Crosby,—that in Roman times the Mersey had no distinct existence, which explains the fact that Ptolemy omits any mention of the river, and appears to include it with the Ribble, Alt, and minor streams in *Æstuarium Belisama,*† and also the possessions of Wulfric Sprott, and the subsequent grant to Roger of Poictiers, *inter ripam et mersham,*—between the river bank and the marsh.

The north-western margin of the bank Mr. Boult believes to have run from Eastham to Speke, the overflow from which escaped

---

* Hist. Ches. vol. ii. p. 187. " The Mersey as known to the Romans: by Joseph Boult, F.R.I.B.A." Proc. Lit. Phil. Soc., Liverpool, No. xxvii., Liverpool, 1873. An examination of this valley proves however it has not been occupied by an arm of the sea, as suggested.—C. E. R.

† Mr. Boult believes " belisama " to stand for submerged sandbanks on the coast.

as a cascade at the Sloyne (*Easlinn* = C. *eas*, a cascade, and *linn* a pool) ; a tract of undulating ground intervening between the marsh and the lake, between Bromborough and Eastham, and Speke and Toxteth on the opposite shore. The sea, after gradually encroaching on the marsh, began to denude the higher ground, and in 1279 broke into the lake, so that the monks of the abbey of Stanlaw had soon to remove to Whalley. The level of the lake, which, before the wearing down of the cascade in the high ground between the marsh and the lake, was probably about 20 feet higher than the Old Dock Sill, became so reduced that it was only two or three feet below the level of high tide; and eventually, when the barrier was destroyed, the tide broke over the whole and added its area to the sea.

List of some of the Stone Weapons found in the North-west of England. (Including list of Mr. Plant, F.G.S., Trans. Man. Geol. Soc., vol. vii. p. 73.)

Hatchet of dark stone, found in peat near Martin Mere. Figured in Leigh's Natural History of Lancashire, 1700.

Gritstone hammer, with circular helve-hole, 12 inches long, at Throstlenest. Figured in Whitaker's History of Manchester, 1771.

Stone hammer at Tabley, Cheshire. Itin. Curios., p. 54.

Stone hatchet from the Lake District, dark slate, 4 inches long. In the Salford Museum.

Stone hatchet found at Flixton, south of Manchester, 1846, 13 inches in length, described in Jour. Arch. Inst., vol. vii., 1850; now in Blackmore Museum, Salisbury;—and by Mr. E. T. Stevens : *Times*, June 1867.

Stone hammer of ironclay stone, at Greenhill Farm, Tatham, near Lancaster; found in 1853 by Mr. T. Hall. In Salford Museum.

A gritstone hammer, from near Darwen. Exhibited to Man. Geol. Soc., 1868, by Mr. Parker.

Two polished stone celts, found in a level of " old moor workings," in a Hematite ore mine. Mr. Jackson, Ulverstone, 1866.

Stone-axe and flint-flake knife, with two other stone implements, from floor of Kirtshead Cave, near Ulverstone. By Messrs. Bolton and Morris, in 1864.

Stone hammer from the soil under floor of a stable at Ouban's Cottage, Ulverstone. By Mr. Wilson, 1868.

Small stone hammer, of dark green colour, highly polished, from gravel of Middleton ; and dark-grey ditto, from valley of the Tame. Exhibited by Mr. Binney, Man. Geol. Soc.

Stone hammer of clay ironstone, from Boulder Clay at Harpurhey. Exhibited at Man. Geol. Soc. by Mr. Devis.

Quoit-shaped implement, 6 inches diameter, from drift 20 feet below the surface, at Staleybridge Railway Station. In possession of Mr. Woolven, station-master, Ashton near Manchester.

Smaller ring of stone, found in Macclesfield gravel in 1866.

Stone hammer and two stone axes, from Clitheroe. Exhibited by Mr. Knowles, Man. Geol. Soc.

Two stone hammers, exhibited by Mr. Horn, from Oldham.

Stone (Lake District hornstone) hatchet, found by side of Loughrigg Tarn, near Ambleside, by Dr. Craddock, of Brasennose, Oxon, and given by him to Mr. Wheatley-Balme, of Loughrigg, 1873.

Agricultural Geology of the District.

The greater part of S.W. Lancashire has probably been brought into an efficient state of cultivation since the beginning of the 17th century. When Roger de Poictou received the whole of the lands between the Mersey and Ribble from Will. II., it only contained (in its six hundreds) 188 manors, valued at 120*l.*, about 13,000*l.* of present money, which tract in 1814 was valued at 2,569,761*l.*

Large portions of the woods and forests would appear to have been preserved, as in a MS. in the Harleian collection of the British Museum, of the time of Edward III., Thomas Molineux, head forester of Simons Wood, and King's parker of Croxteth, R. Worthington, forester of Quernmore, R. Pilkington, keeper of parks at Hyde and Fullwood, Thomas Lord Stanley, parker of Toxteth, and Thomas Richardson, forester of the wood of Mirescough are mentioned.

The secluded character of this tract is also pointed out by the old doggrel, quoted in the county histories:—

" When all England is alofte,
" Safe are they that are in Christis Crofte.
" And where should Christis Crofte be
" But between Ribble and Mersey."

A considerable area of Upper Boulder Clay land in Goosenargh and other parishes is still badly drained, and forms poor permanent pastures, covered with rushes. If it were improved by peat ashes spread in the beginning of November, and again in February, crops of wheat, clover, trefoil, &c. might be obtained, and of barley or oats after it had produced the previous year a crop of turnips. Peat ashes are stated to force barley and oats too forward, producing much coarse straw and little grain. The ashes require to be carefully excluded from light and air, by being kept on dry ground heaped up into a cone, and covered with straw or earth till used.

The Upper Boulder Clay portion of the Fylde was very early brought into cultivation. In the Doomsday Book, the parish of Bispham contained 800 acres (8 carucates) fit for the plough, being more than any other township in the hundred.

In a paper on the Comparative Agriculture of England and Wales, my colleague, Mr. Topley, gives a table showing the percentage of each crop to the total acreage of each county, from which the following results as to Lancashire, the West Riding of Yorkshire, and the average of the whole country, may be found useful.

	Lancashire.	West Riding of Yorkshire.	Mean of England and Wales.
Wheat -	3·4	6·7	9·5
Barley	0·6	3·9	5·4
Oats -	4·3	3·5	4·7
Rye	0·1	0·1	0·2
Beans	0·3	0·9	1·5
Peas -	0·03	0·6	1·0
Total corn crops	8·8	15·7	22·3
Potatoes	3·3	1·7	1·1
Turnips and swedes	0·9	3·6	4·5
Mangold	0·1	0·1	0·8
Carrots, cabbage, kohl, rabi, and rape	0·1	0·1	0·4
Vetches, lucerne, and other green crops	0·1	0·5	0·9
Total green crops	4·6	6·1	7·7

	Lancashire.	West Riding of Yorkshire.	Mean of England and Wales.
Clover, sainfoin, and grasses under rotation - -	4·5	3·4	6·1
Bare fallow - -	0·4	1·1	1·9
Total Arable Land -	18·4	26·6	38·3
Permanent pasture -	40·9	40·1	31·1
Total cultivated land	59·3	66·7	69·4
Uncultivated, towns, &c.	40·7	33·3	30·6
Area of country (in acres) -	1,219,000	1,709,000	37,324,000

The large per-centage of area occupied by potatoes in Lancashire is largely due to the peat flats in the western portion of the county now under consideration; probably from 40 to 60 per cent. of the whole peat area is occupied by these tubers.

In these tables the per-centage of cultivated land, and the area covered with grain crops, is given in reference to the whole area of the county of Lancaster, which consists broadly of three divisions:—lowland peat-plains and alluvial flats; higher plains, and low-sweeping undulations of Glacial Drift; and upland fells composed of lower carboniferous rocks rising from 1,000 to 2,500 feet above the level of the sea. On this upland division, south of the Ribble, which occupies at least 250 square miles out of 1,125 square miles, there is practically no amount of grain grown; nor can the heath-covered slopes of the Fells, which afford subsistence to the mountain sheep, be considered in the light of permanent pasture. So that in reality the per-centage of ground covered with corn and green crops, in such districts as the Fylde and parts of Amounderness, is really four or five higher than that assigned to it in the table. Probably not less than 80 per cent. of the peat lands between the Ribble and Mersey are under cultivation, with the exception of the mosses lying between Croston, Midge Hall and Leyland, which are being gradually cut down, and the exposed surface burnt and laid down for root crops.*

In several mosses near the Wyre, Martin Mere, the Douglas, and the Alt, where floods of fresh water flow over the surface, the quality of the land is invariably improved. This is believed to be partly due to the deposition of a thin layer of loam, but still more to the removal of some included elements in the peat which act injuriously to vegetable growth. The effect of long and continued draining is similar; the richness of the grasses improving in pro-portion as the water flowing away is less and less dark.

From the analysis of various peats given at page 102, it will be seen that the quantity of nitrogen, though somewhat

* The paring and burning of open spongy peat not only affords a cheap manure in the resultant ashes, but effects a mechanical change in the texture of the ground, causing it to be sufficiently dense to be capable of mixing with the marl and other materials which are spread over it after draining and burning.

variable, is still sufficient to render peat that has been acted upon
by the atmosphere valuable as a source of that element to vegetation, especially when spread over and mixed with an ordinary
soil. Peat incorporated with a light sandy soil, under the influence
of moisture and a little air, slowly decomposes, and the nitrogen
assists in the formation of ammonia, from which nitric acid is
produced on the accession of more air.

The quantity of ash produced by the burning of various peats
may be observed in the table at p. 102, and the nature of its constituents in same table ; but the nature of these differs with
the nature of the plants that have produced the varieties of peat.
Much of the ordinary Lancashire peat is made up of the moss
Sphagnum, the ash of which Websky found to contain—

Potash	-	- 17·2	Sulphuric acid	- 6·5
Soda -	-	8·3	Chlorine -	- 6·2
Lime	-	- 11·8	Phosphoric acid -	6·7
Magnesia	-	- 6·7	(Per cent. of ash 2·5)	

All these constituents would not find their way into the peat, as,
on the plant decomposing, portions of the soluble elements would be
carried off by the water, and be used again and again by successive
growths of *Sphagnum.*

Peat ashes spread over the alluvial flats of the Ribble have
been found in some instances of great value, especially when
applied very early in the year, so that the ashes get washed in by
the rain in early spring.

Dr. Angus Smith[*] notices that the water derived from the peat
lands around Manchester, overlying the sandstone or Rough Rock,
though only containing from one to two grains of carbonate of lime
in a gallon, with two grains of peaty organic matter, becomes of a
deep brown colour in warm weather, though perfectly colourless
in winter. Dr. Smith states that in wet, cold, undrained peat-
bogs, the acids of the peat do not become dissolved so as to form
a very deeply coloured solution ; but in warmer or better
drained tracts the soluble matter is much greater, ammonia is
formed by which the acids are dissolved in large quantities, which
ammonia is not formed during cold weather, when grass or other
vegetables do not grow.

The tanning influence of the peat-water is well marked in the
preservation of the skin and hair of men and animals that have
been discovered in peat moss ;[†] especially in the case recorded by
Mr. Stovin, of the discovery of the body of a woman, with antique
sandals, believed to be Roman, in the moss of Arncott, Isle of
Axholme, associated with large quantities of black oak and fir.[‡]

Dr. Smith remarks that caustic lime used to peat land sets the
ammonia free, and makes it available as food for plants ; soda or
other alkalies serving the same purpose.

---

[*] Mem. Lit. Phil. Soc. Man. Second series, vol. viii., 1848, p. 377. "On Water
m Peat and Soil."

[†] For several instances of the discoveries of human bodies in peat, see Phil. Trans.,
vols. xxii., xxvii., and xxxviii., 1734.

[‡] Op. cit., vol. lxiv., 1747.

Peat exposed to the air rapidly passes through a series of changes, but when ploughed into the strong Boulder Clays, it does not decompose, but, retaining its moisture, renders the ground more wet than before its application. Such lands require mixing with some more rapidly fermenting manure.

I have noticed that potatoes are less diseased in the West Lancashire mosses, in years when there is much disease, than in other parts of the county. Potatoes, wanting much potash for tubers, and lime for leaves, find ready food in the drained moss-lands.

The presence of lime causes barley to grow tolerably well, but peat lands are too poor in silicates to grow wheat in rotation with much success. One cubic foot of orthoclase felspar is stated by Liebig to afford sufficient potash to supply an oak copse, covering 26,910 sq. feet, for five years. The oak trees found in the peat of the Lancashire mosses have invariably their roots in the clays beneath. These generally have fragments of felspathic rocks in them, derived from the Lake district, which when decomposed would afford much potash.

The peat tract of "Christis Crofte," as the country between Ribble and Mersey was anciently called, is traversed by long straight roads, whose termination often cannot be seen ; and, if possible, by still straighter sluices or large ditches, locally called dykes, which are cut out of the peat with long narrow spades, the sides being smoothed with an instrument resembling a short scythe placed longways, instead of at right angles to a straight handle. The small dykes are cut so as to fall into the sluices, on which, at different points, are steam-pumping engines to artificially lift the water first to a higher level and then to the sea.

Much of this black land, that now lets at 4l. an acre, a few years ago was only worth 15s., supporting a few half-starved cattle, or being absolutely waste. Since then, peat, locally called turf, has been largely cut for fuel, and the new surface burnt, which, accompanied with thorough draining, produces a rich valuable soil capable of growing white crops for several years in succession, without any diminution of the weight of grain produced. But the main product of this new land is potatoes, which are exported by tons from Ormskirk, for the London, Manchester, and Liverpool markets.

The solitary cottages and farms scattered at long intervals on the moss, though built on large broad flags brought from the edge of the Lancashire coal-field, from the ever yielding nature of the peat beneath, are generally sliding down at one end,—windows, doors, and roof alike making an angle with the surface of the ground. The slope, like that of the permanent bend of the trees, and that of the stubborn and flinty fibres of the marram or starr grass covering the sand hills fringing the peat moss, and intervening like a belt between it and the sea, is towards the E.N.E., the prevalent west-south-west wind influencing trees, the growing crops, and the whole vegetation of West Lancashire, for a distance of at least 20 miles from the sea-coast ; and carrying, during heavy storms, salt water and spray far inland into the Fylde, precipitating it on particular points, and killing or injuring the leaves of the trees on which it falls. In one instance the sea-water was thus carried bodily as far as Blackburn.

Economic Geology of the Superficial Deposits of South-west Lancashire.

The Lower Boulder Clay in the valley of the Mersey, and in the country fringing the coast between the Mersey and the Ribble, is used for the manufacture of bricks and tiles, and the more calcareous portions are dug for "marl," which is applied in improving the moss-lands in the valley of the Ribble; but from its never forming the surface of the ground, and only occurring at the base of deep cliff or valley sections, it is seldom met with in carrying out works and excavations. In a few instances, as near the Wheatsheaf Inn, Preston, where excavations have been made in it, the large boulders occurring so plentifully have either been split up for road metal, or saved for garden rockeries.

The Middle Sand.—The finer sand has been dug largely at Deepdale near Preston, at Kirkham near Leyland, Great Marton, and other places, for building-sand. The beds of fine impermeable loam by which the sand beds are traversed have been found very suitable for use as a brass-casting sand, and have been tried with success at St. Helen's. The water-bearing properties of the Middle Sand are also due to these impermeable beds of loam, which support distinct sheets of water.

The beds of shingle, occurring associated with the sands, at Blackpool only appear in the cliff section, where, by the gradual wasting of the cliff, they afford material for the existing beach. East of Preston also they do not occur in the upper portion of the Middle Drift series, and are only seen in the cliff sections of the Ribble, as at Redscar. At Chorley they appear nearly at the surface, and are worked in a large pit at the north end of the town; the larger pebbles being used for the roads, and the smaller for gravel for paths.

The Upper Boulder Clay is very largely worked for bricks at Blackpool, Preston, Blackburn, and near Croston. Ordinary kilns are used; the bricks obtained are seldom of first-class quality, and rarely free from included pebbles.

"Marl pits" are scattered over the whole Upper Boulder Clay, and occur in almost every field. Some of them must be of great antiquity, and most of them are grassed over, the bottom being filled with water, and used as ponds for cattle. The pits, in fact, are as a rule dug in the side of the hill, so as to serve the double purpose of affording marl, and making drinking places for stock, which, in a springless and streamless area, have to be very numerous.

Over all the ploughed fields in the Boulder Clay area, stones are very plentiful. These are carefully collected in heaps, and used for road-metal by many of the farmers in the Fylde, who give labour and material at those periods of the year when farm labour is not much required, instead of paying highway rates.

All the main roads of the district between the more important towns are paved with large stones six to ten inches in diameter, placed side by side after the Roman pattern. These roads keep in excellent repair for very long periods, though they are exceedingly tiring to drive over. The stones are those from the Boulder Clay, and consist mainly of felstones and granites from the Lake District.

Shirdley Hill Sands.—These have been dug as a building-sand, near Shirdley Hill, near Rufford, and in a sand pit at Holmes, north of Martin Mere. West of St. Helens, sands of this age are dug at Crank, and after being washed and precipitated in narrow pits are used in the glass-works, and for other purposes.

Preesall Hill Gravel.—This bed of shingle has been dug for road-metal at several small pits at the edge of Pilling Moss, and west of Churchtown, Garstang. It contains in some instances fragments of hæmatite.

Estuarine Clays.—Near Formby these have been manufactured into bricks, but when tried at Birkdale they were found to be too sandy. Probably they might be useful to mix with very stiff Boulder Clays.

Peat.—Very large quantities of peat are cut for fuel, in Halsall and other mosses between Liverpool and Burscough, and in all the mosses lying east of Southport, in Rufford, Croston, and Farrington mosses, and north of the Ribble, in Lytham, Rawcliffe, and Pilling mosses. The usual selling price in Preston is 10*s.* a load, which would probably weigh about a ton.[*]

Good peat burns with a clear bright flame, and leaves a light-coloured ash; the inferior quality leaves a heavy reddish ash, and emits a disagreeable smell.

In commencing operations for the cutting of peat a trench is first dug,—the soft, oozy, black consolidated moss being cut out in squares of a foot long, and about three inches thick. These are placed in a row, the edges of each resting on its neighbour, like tiles on a roof. When they are partly dry they are taken up and placed like bricks, with spaces between, in smaller and smaller circles, one over the other, until a dome like an elongated bee-hive, is produced. The side of the trench is cut back until it becomes a bank, which retreats before the peat diggers, until a new surface of the ground, from 5 to 12 feet lower than the original one, comes into existence, the surface of which can be made to part with a large proportion of the water which before it held up like a sponge, by deep narrow ditches sloping towards the main sluices.

As the question of the commercial value of the peat in the Lancashire peat-mosses may become of importance, it may be well to give a few analyses of some foreign and Irish peats for comparison, and some notice of the uses to which peat has been applied.

---

[*] The use of peat for fuel appears to have been very early known. Pliny mentions that the people of Bremen (*Cauchi*) used peat (*lutum*) for wood in cooking. According to Torfæus, the use of peat for fuel was known to the inhabitants of the Orkney and Shetland Isles, by one *Einar*, a Norwegian, who was afterwards called Torf Einar; and from Orkney its use spread to Scotland.

Table of Analyses of various peats, woods, and coals, arranged according to the percentage of carbon they contain.

	Analyst.	C.	H.	O.	N.	Ash.
Peat from Lake in Cashmir -	C. Tookey* -	37·15	4·08	23·48	2·02	33·27
Peat, Ochta, in Eastern Russia -	Woskressensky	39·08	3·78	51·08	—	6·04
Sphagnum, undecomposed -	Websky	49·88	6·54	42·42	1·16	n. s.
Beech Wood, undecomposed (exclusive of ash).	Chevandier -	49·94	6·08	43·02	0·93	1·24
Peat, porous, light-brown, sphagnous - - -		59·86	6·80	42·57	0·77	—
„ Cappoge, in Kildare, Ireland -	Sir R. Kane -	51·05	6·85	39·55	—	2·25
„ Kilbaha, in Clare - - -	„	51·13	6·33	34·48	—	8·06
Oak, decayed wood - - -	Liebig -	53·47	5·16	41·37		—
Peat, porous, red-brown colour -	Jäkel -	53·51	5·90	40·59		—
„ from Dartmoor, Devon -	Vaux - -	54·02	6·21	28·17	2·30	9·73
„ heavy brown - - -	Jäkel -	56·43	5·32	38·25		—
„ of Vulcaire, Abbeville -	Regnault -	57·06	5·63	21·76	—	15·68
„ of Framont, Vosges - -	„ -	67·79	6·11	20·97	—	19·35
„ of Holland - - -	Mulder -	59·37	5·41	35·32	—	14·25
„ Friesland, surface turf -	„ -	59·42	5·87	34·71	—	3·80
„ dark red-brown, well-decomposed.	Websky -	69·47	6·62	31·61	2·51	—
„ black, very dense, hard -	„ -	59·70	5·70	33·04	1·56	—
„ black, heavy, best quality -	„ -	59·71	6·27	32·07	2·59	—
„ of Vulcaire, near Abbeville -	Regnault -	60·40	5·96	33·64	—	5·58
„ Friesland, surface turf -	Mulder -	60·41	5·87	34·02	—	0·91
„ Long, near Abbeville -	Regnault -	60·89	6·21	32·90	—	4·61
„ of Bog of Allen, Ireland -	Dr. Percy -	61·02	5·77	32·40	0·81	7·90
„ Kilbeggan, Westmeath -	Sir R. Kane -	61·04	6·67	30·46	—	1·83
„ Champ-du-Feu, near Framont	Regnault -	61·05	6·45	32·50	—	6·33
„ brown, heavy, best quality -	Websky -	62·64	6·81	29·24	1·41	—
Boghead Coal (Cannel Coal), Scotland	W. A. Miller -	63·10	8·91	7·25		19·78
Lignite, Bovey Tracey, Devonshire -	Vaux - -	66·31	5·62	22·86	0·56	2·37
						4·99
„ Dax, South of France -	Regnault -	69·52	5·59	19·90		—
Parrot Coal, Lesmahago - -	W. A. Miller -	73·44	7·62	11·761		6·034
St. Helen's Coal - - -	Vaux - -	75·80	6·22	10·99	1·92	5·17
Cannel Coal, Wigan - -	„ - -	80·07	5·53	8·08	2·12	2·70
Anthracite, S. Wales - - -	„ - -	90·39	3·28	2·98	0·83	1·61

Where no figures are given the substance has not been determined.

Brandes and Gruner,[†] in an analysis of peat from Pyrmont, found present, besides other constituents, the sulphate of the protoxide of iron, basic persulphate of iron, gypsum, and traces of phosphate of lime. Bergema[‡] in 1825 found in a specimen of peat 0·42, silica 3·8, sulphate of lime 4·5, phosphate of lime 2·7 per cent. L. Oberlin and L. A. Buchner[§] found fibrous moor-peat from Strasburg to have 0·18 of ash. ‖Websky tabulates the following, as the result of 23 analyses of the ashes of peat from the Hartz:—

Potash -	- 0·05 — 3·64	Chlorine -	- ·06 — 6·50
Soda -	- 0·16 — 5·73	Silica (soluble)	- 0·02 — 16·00
Lime -	- 4·50 — 58·38	Carbonic acid	- 2·50 — 30·59
Magnesia -	- 0·04 — 24·39	Phosphoric acid	- 0·25 — 8·00
Alumina -	- 1·14 — 17·30	Residue insoluble	0·99 — 76·56
Sesquioxide of iron	0·88 — 73·33	in acid.	
Sulphuric acid	- 0·70 — 37·40	(Per cent. of ashes 0·57 — 22·07)

* Water 10·40 per cent. (Percy's Metallurgy, vol. i. p. 206.)
† Berz. Jahrb., vii. 206.
‡ Buchner's Report de Pharm., xxi. p. 498.
§ Buchner's Report de Pharm., 1833, xlvi. p. 185; and Leonhard and Bronn, N. Jahrb. d. Mineralogie, 1837, p. 375.
‖ Percy's Metallurgy, vol. i. p. 210.

Two methods have been practised for the conversion of peat into charcoal, the one by exposing it to a smothering heat, as in making charcoal from wood, the other by subjecting it to heat in closed vessels—a kind of distillation.

The first process was used by Lamberville as far back as 1631, but his charcoal was too friable. In the Hartz, Baron Dietrich found that they carbonized peat in large cylindrical vessels, but the latter were injured by volatile matter separated from the peat. The method practised at Villeroi of burning it in kilns was also found to be unprofitable.

The second process is described by Pfeiffer (Histoire de Charbon de Terre et de la Tourbe, &c., 1777) ; and in 1781 Thorin was rewarded by the French Government for an improved iron furnace for making solid charcoal from peat, but the furnaces soon wore out. Later, stone furnaces were used by Blavier.

In the last century peat undried and untreated was used with success at Kilhorn, Wigtonshire, in burning lime in a kiln, by placing layers of chopped peat (pressed down, but with numerous air-holes left) over a layer of limestone.*

Peat is successfully used at Konigsbrunn for the conversion of cast iron into wrought, and on the Bavarian State railways it is largely used for fuel for locomotives, two tons being found to do the amount of work performed by one ton of coal. Charcoal obtained from peat is very valuable for iron smelting, 4 tons of dried peat making one ton of charcoal.

In Sweden, Bavaria, Wurtemburg, and Bohemia peat is used for iron smelting; and Swedish and French horseshoes and wheel-tires smelted with charcoal or peat are found to wear twice as long as those of ordinary manufacture.†

In Italy gas furnaces have been constructed for gas made from charcoal, and gas of similar origin has been used in lighting a village at Westmeath.‡

The Irish Peat Commission of 1872, after visiting the various peat manufactories of Europe, recommend that the peat of Ireland should be cut sufficiently thin to dry in six weeks instead of eight, which causes much loss through heavy rains.

They described *compressed peat*, produced by " Exeter's system " of mechanical force, which is carried out at Kobermoor in Bavaria, at a cost of 12s. a ton, as having been tried at Derrylea, Ireland, in 1868, and turning out a commercial failure.

They describe the following processes of manufacture of dense or condensed peat:—

Rahder's -	Netherlands - cost 10s. 6d.	Much produced.	
Schlickeysen's - -	Prussia cost 6s. 9d.		
Prince Schwartzenberg's	Bohemia - cost 6s. 9d.	Very large briquettes.	
Eichorn's	Bavaria.		
M. Colart's - -	Somme, ⎫ France.		
M. Bocquet's - -	Oureq, ⎬		
Danchell's -	England. ⎭		

* Edinburgh Farmers Magazine.
† " On Peat as a Substitute for Coal. By Ralph Richardson, Writer to the Signet.
‡ English Cyclopœdia.

The last-mentioned system consists of the mixture of peat with clay, for conversion into peat-charcoal for the purifying of sewage waters. The charcoal has, I believe, been used with success in purifying Paris sewage works.

Mr. Danchell states that one ton of clay peat can be produced for 2s. 6d., which will sell for 4s. ; and that four tons of raw peat will produce one ton of charcoal, at a cost of 15s., which will sell for 40s. The difficulty appears to be the drying in a humid atmosphere. One ton of the charcoal is said to be able to absorb two tons of solid sewage matter.*

When the Irish Commissioners finished their labours Messrs. Clayton and Son's machinery for the manufacture of artificial fuel from peat was not completed. The process consists of three stages :—Conveyance, Masticating, and Drying.

Mr. W. Elsam has invented a system of drying sheds, which, with an area of only 250 feet by 100, will dry 60 tons of peat per day during good weather.

Should these operations turn out a commercial success, there would appear to be several places in the Lancashire mosses where the process could be carried out, at points near to railways and large centres of population where a cheap fuel would be invaluable.

Peat dried in air is compact and firm, but any application of sudden artificial heat appears to have the effect of cracking the blocks and causing great waste.

Blown Sand is used at Lytham, Southport, Fleetwood, and Waterloo for building purposes. None of it, I believe, has answered as glass sand. When magnified it is found to be made up of exceedingly small fragments of felspathic rocks, the waste possibly of erratics in the Boulder Clays.

Relation of the Superficial Deposits to Local Water Supply and the Sanitary Condition of the District.

Dr. Leigh,[†] writing in 1700, described the fenny and maritime parts of Lancashire as visited with malignant and intermitting fevers, consumptions, &c., caused by sulphureous saline effluvia, sometimes extremely fetid, especially before a storm ; but there can be no doubt that the immense peat tracts being brought into cultivation must have rendered it much more healthy, so that possibly Dr. Leigh's statement had some foundation beyond the prejudices of the period.

Dr. Plott,[‡] on the other hand, speaks of intermittent fevers never occurring in the neighbourhood of peat mosses.

The following table is given by the Rivers Pollution Commissioners[§] :—

---

* "Peat Engineering and Swamp Filtration Co., Lim.," Red Moss Works, Horwich, Lancashire. "Iron," 8 Feb. 1873. Engineer, 21st Feb. 1873 :—Description of Messrs. H. Clayton and Sons Peat Machinery, Howlett Atlas Works, Harrow Road, W.

† Natural History of Lancashire and Cheshire.

‡ History of Staffordshire.

§ Royal Rivers Pollution Commission. First Report, vol. i. 1870.

AREA AND POPULATION, RIBBLE BASIN.

	Area.	Population.						
	Square Miles.	1801.	1811.	1821.	1831.	1841.	1851.	1861.
Ribble proper :—								
Right Bank -	165¾	28,109	36,369	46,551	55,760	72,615	91,984	106,184
Left Bank -	187¾	25,406	29,651	36,447	42,295	47,547	49,416	56,295
Calder - -	130¾	36,824	45,603	61,782	70,702	80,656	94,008	118,725
Hodder -	103½	3,639	4,143	4,528	4,403	4,006	3,744	3,388
Darwen - -	57	28,044	34,354	47,382	53,691	66,823	79,179	103,247
Douglas - -	171¾	44,471	54,405	66,008	74,342	85,952	94,681	101,337
Total -	816	166,493	204,525	262,698	301,193	357,599	413,012	489,176

The Commissioners comment upon the more rapid increase of population on the Coal Measures than on the Red Sandstone area within the river basins of the Mersey and the Ribble, and on the dense population of the Coal Measure area, leading to increased pollution of streams, through large quantities of water being used, as well as from the introduction of sewage.

Though the occurrence of coal measures in certain tracts of South Lancashire has determined the position of special areas of dense population, the particular localities which may be regarded as the centre or foci of those areas, the town and village, may be considered to owe their origin to the Drift Deposits ; for, just as in the New Red area of Lancashire, the sands of the Middle Drift below the Upper Boulder Clay, by affording a ready supply of drinking water to the earliest settlers in that country, caused them to select such sites as Preston, Lancaster, Kirkham, and nine tenths of all the smaller villages—so the occurrence of these sands led to the original choice of the sites occupied by Wigan, Stockport, and other towns and villages in what is now known as the Lancashire coalfield.

At Croston the wells are sunk in gravel to depths varying from 10 to 40 yards. The lower portion of them, I have no doubt, is in the pebble beds of the New Red Sandstone. The gravel would indicate the Middle Drift, lying below the Upper Boulder Clay. At Ormskirk the Commissioners report 11 feet of marl overlying 7 feet of sand, before the New Red Sandstone was penetrated.

	Towns					
	Unaffected by River Pollution.		Partially affected.			On Polluted Rivers.
	Liverpool.	Walton-on-the-Hill.	Preston.	Chorley.	Wigan.	Manchester.
Annual Average Mortality per 1,000	33·1	20·4	29·3	23·5	32·22	32·2
Area (acres) - -	5,210·0	1,910·0	2,819·0	3,613·0	2,170·0	4,203·0
Population per Acre -	96·0	2·8	33·0	5·0	19·0	86·3
Population - -	500,676·0	—	93,000·0	19,000·0	41,000·0	362,823·0

The late Mr. Armytage, C.E., surveyor to the borough of Preston, gives the density at 300 of population per acre over one eighth of that town.

Leyland, the Commissioners consider a fair type of many other villages in the district. "The liquid contents of the cesspools, &c. rapidly sink into the adjoining shallow wells," through the loose sandy soil. 100,000 lbs. of Leyland water contained 54·40 lbs. of solid impurity, which was only 2 lb. less than the amount found in London sewage after filtration through 15 feet of sand.

The water pumped in this village I found to be derived from the Middle Sands, the water being held by loamy bands. The surface is heavily manured, and consists of market and kitchen gardens.

Contaminated water is pumped from the Blown Sand at Fleetwood, Lytham, Southshore, and Southport; but the drinking water of all the first-mentioned is derived from the Fylde Waterworks, taking their supply from the Yoredale Grit, a few miles from Lancaster. The Southport supply is derived from the New Red Sandstone near Ormskirk.

The water used by the inhabitants of the houses lying scattered over the mosses is very bad, being derived from the peat, and it is exceedingly dark in colour. In the alluvial area between the sea and the River Wyre, north of Shard Bridge, and in that between the Wyre and Pilling Sands, the water is generally brackish and subject to tidal percolation.

CHAPTER VI.

MODERN MARINE DEPOSITS.

The Deposition of Sand and Shingle.

The beach from Bootle immediately north of Liverpool to Southport is entirely composed of sand, having an exceedingly gentle slope seawards In some cases, especially off Birkdale, large areas have a slight landward dip, causing the water to be left standing for a considerable time after the retreat of the tide. At Rimrose Brook and the river Alt deposits of peat are generally seen cropping out from beneath sand; but they do not again occur on the beach until Crossens, north of Southport, is reached; from which point the peat beds of the mouth of the Douglas are seen at several points. At the mouth of the Alt many shells of *Cyprina Islandica, Fusus antiquus,* &c., are thrown up on the beach by the tide, most of which have fragments of yellowish clay adhering to them. They have not the peculiar creamy appearance observable in all the Lancashire Glacial Drift shells, nor are they thickened abnormally as are the latter; so that there is reason to believe that a post-glacial deposit with shells of existing species occurs immediately below low-water mark, but whether older or newer than the peat is uncertain. If referable to the former, the clay is probably of Shirdley Hill Sand age ; if to the latter, it would be of the same general age as the deposit of dark sandy silt, with shells of existing species occurring beneath the sand, off the coast of Ainsdale and Southport further to the north.

At the east end of Lytham, near the windmill and Custom-house, a raised bank of shingle extends inland a short distance. The top of it is considerably above spring-tide high-water mark, probably not less than 11½ feet. It has been dug into at several places, the following being a good representative section :—

		ft.	ins.
a.	Blown Sand - - - -	1	6
b.	Shingle, very large pebbles (storm-beach) -	1	6
c.	Shingle, smaller pebbles, and sand, (*a* and *b*,) thin out landwards - - -	1	10
d.	Small black pebbles, very compact] - -	1	4
e.	Shingle and sand - - - -	5	6
f.	Fine sand, current-bedded, with small pebbles dipping seawards at 10 degrees, thinning landwards to 1 foot -	0	6
		3	6
g.	Fine sand, with thin covering of clay - -	0	6
h.	Large shingle - -	4 to 6	0

In the sands at *f* I noticed shells of the species of *Cardium edule* and *Tellina Balthica.*

H

In the clay bed at the top of q I found the pebbles to consist of the following rocks:—

Granite	- 12
Quartzite	- 4
Porphyry and Breccia (Lake District)	- 28
Volcanic ash and Silurian grits	- 30

At Lytham a slight admixture of clay in the sand between tide-marks enables it to retain peculiarly deep ripple-markings. Good examples of these are seen off Birkdale and other parts of the coast, where the surface traversed by the water agitated by ripples is flat, or but very little inclined, the strike of the furrows running parallel to the direction of the wind waves at the time of the ebbing tide,—the water being sufficiently shallow to allow the impress of the wave to be received by the soft yielding sand, and the bed of the sea beneath being sufficiently level to prevent the water running violently seawards, and obliterating the ripple-mark. This is also found to be the case in the steeper sandy inclines. especially the edges of the sand-banks exposed at low tides.

Between Lytham and Southshore there is a steep bank of shingle beach lying above. neap-tide high-water mark, which protects the coast, and aids the encroachment of the sand-dunes seawards, gradually causing a gain of land, which must have been going on for some length of time, as wherever the base of the sand-dunes is seen they are found to rest on beds of shingle. Between Southshore and Blackpool the beach is also present; but from continual carting away of shingle, which is indiscriminately allowed at all distances further from the land than 60 yards, great denudation of the Boulder Clay slopes takes place.

The extremely low levels of this district render the heights in regard to the Ordnance datum-line of importance. The following table may be useful for reference :—

Above Ordnance Datum Line.

	feet.
Highest spring-tide high-water mark at London Bridge	13·45
Ditto at Prince's Dock, Liverpool	12·65
Trinity high-water mark	12·50
Mean high-water mark, London Bridge	11·23
Neap high-water mark, Prince's Dock, Liverpool	7·25
Mean half-tide level, London Bridge	2·44

Below Ordnance Datum Line.

True mean water-level at Liverpool	0·68
Old Dock Sill, Liverpool	4·75
Lowest low-water mark, London Bridge	8·25
Mersey Tide Gauge Zero	10·75
Lowest low-water mark, Prince's Dock, 4 feet below Mersey Zero	14·75
Thames Tide Gauge Zero	20·00

On the 29th January 1869 a tremendous sea swept over the embankment at Southshore, and tore it and the carriage road up, hurling sand and pebbles over and into the houses, and destroying the sea-wall of the Claremont Park estate. On the 6th of March, with a 21-feet tide, and a N.W. gale, the whole of the embankment was torn up, and deposited in the fields behind, the entire promenade devastated, and thousands of tons of shingle washed up 15 feet on to the road, including boulders several feet in diameter.

An arrangement much resembling ripple-marking is observable in very fine shingle in the bed of the west side of the river Wyre, opposite the site of Fleetwood Docks,—small ridges with a long slope pointing up the river, and a steep slope, a foot to 18 inches in height, towards the sea. These undulations have evidently been formed by the shingle being carried by the ebbing tide up the gradual incline, and over the little escarpment, which thus gradually travels seaward. Here and there slight steep notches facing up stream in the long slope probably a momentary cessation of the movement of the current. In the case of this part of the river, in addition to the matter moved by being held in mechanical suspension, there is some moved along the bottom by friction, varying in quantity and size of material transported with the velocity of the stream.

The surface of the beach at Blackpool, north of the Gwyn, between high and low-water mark, consists of a slope inclined at an angle of ten degrees, composed of sandy Boulder Clay, densely packed with stones and boulders, most of which are scratched, round or sub-angular. The upper portion of this slope from the spring-tide, high-water mark at the base of the cliff to that of neap-tide, is covered with shingle, slightly heaped up in the centre by the action of storms.

An examination of the pebbles composing the beach, gave—

Amygdaloidal ash - - -	1 per cent.
Volcanic Breccia and Trap -	54 „
Hornstone - - -	1 „
Volcanic ash - - -	4 „
Granites· - - -	20 „
Silurian grits - - -	4 „
Carboniferous grits - - -	4 „
„ Limestone -	12 „
	100

At Norbreck I found the beach to consist of :—

Volcanic Amygdaloid - -	4 per cent.
Quartz (vein) -	7 „
Volcanic Breccia and Trap -	9 „
Volcanic ash - -	6 „
Granites - - -	8 „
Silurian grits - -	34 „
Carboniferous Limestone -	17 „
„ Sandstone -	2 „
Permian Sandstone - -	2 „

The rain falling on the shingle and the cliffs and the under-ground drainage of the adjacent country behind, sinks through the shingle, and flows down the clay slope beneath it in definite lines, which it excavates into a series of parallel furrows or grooves about 10 inches deep and 6 inches wide.

Still attached to the crests of many of these ridges occur many stones and erratic pebbles and boulders, (some of them being two feet in diameter,) left isolated by the removal of the clay that originally surrounded them.

H 2

After a time the clay pillar supporting the boulder is completely washed away, and the scour of the flow-tide excavates a hollow around the boulder, the base of which sinks slightly below the adjacent surface. These hollows form oval-shaped pools, the long axis corresponding to the direction of the tide; and the north and north-east side of the boulder accumulates a tail of sand, deposited when the velocity of the flow-tide, (which runs here about S.S.W. to N.N.E.,) is checked.

The slope of the coast from the low-water mark of ordinary tides to that of spring tides is much less, being nearly flat; the Lower Boulder Clay and indurated loam-beds of the Middle Drift are more or less covered by recent accumulations of sand.

Numbers of pebbles and large stones, washed out of the Boulder Clay, collected together on the beach, are locally called "skeers;" some of these off the Rossal coast are called "Lower Ashton" and "Higher Ashton, Blackstone Edge, Ginnel Clout and Patch, Singleton and Oyster Skeers." There is an improbable tradition in this district that a whole village, called Singleton Thorp, was suddenly overwhelmed by the sea, and that the inhabitants migrated in a body to Great Singleton.

I examined the belt between tide marks in front of the Clifton Park Estate, from the North Pier, Blackpool, to a point opposite the Gwyn, after the severe storm of March 1869, and found the terrace of shingle below the cliff to be more heaped up than usual, having a shorter slope seawards; while the sand which usually extends from the ordinary seaward termination of the shingle was entirely swept away. Bright-red and chocolate-coloured Lower Boulder Clay everywhere formed a tolerably level floor down to the low water of the spring-tide of the day, one of the lowest of the year,—here and there dotted with large boulders derived from the Lake District of England and from Criffel in the South of Scotland. As many of these boulders are not seen in ordinary calm weather, and some are nearly 3 feet in height, there must have been not less than 3 or 4 feet of sand removed during these heavy gales.

During the severe frost of the winter of 1870, the sea-water at high-tide freezing every day, and the tide rising to a less height on each day, caused the formation of successive lines of frozen tide-marks down the slope of the beach at Morecambe. When the tide began to rise, after reaching the minimum, these ice-lines were washed away, bearing with them many large stones they had caught up at their base. But nothing was carried away on their surfaces, the sun's heat being sufficient during the day to cause any sand or stones resting on the ice to sink through it, cutting a clean perpendicular hole, at the bottom of which the sand accumulated in a small vertical cone.

The action of the tide in producing small escarpments on soft coast-lines is well exemplified in the marsh-clay of the river Wyre, a little south of Old Rawcliffe. The bed of the river consists of Boulder Clay, the ordinary top water at low-water coming a little above the base of the marsh-clay, which rises in a small cliff, four feet in height (A), formed by the scour of the river at low tides during floods. Above this slopes very gradually a terrace of the clay 9 or 10 yards in width, terminating in a steep or scarp

14 inches high (B), backed by a slope of two yards in width, terminating with a scarp of 8 inches (C), backed by a perfectly level
surface, 4 yards in width, terminating in the last scarp about a foot
in height (D), above which is the surface of the river bank, composed
of the same Marsh Clay; its whole thickness being about 9 feet,
formed by the depositions of tidal mud since the growth of the
peat, which is exposed in the river bank at the ends of the undulations or small hollows in the Boulder Clay. The cliff or scarp (B)
would appear to be formed by the wash of the water at high-tide,
that of (C) by spring-tides, and that of (D) by extraordinarily high
spring-tides, or tides swollen by floods. The river Wyre, wearing
the two sides of its channel unequally at different times, has in
some places entirely denuded away these waste deposits ; while in
others the various tidal lines coalesce into one abrupt cliff, just as
the various lines of shingle on the Blackpool and other beaches
often become one steep "full" or bank, owing to the entire force
of last spring-tide, wearing back the successive lines, and casting
the falling pebbles on to the top of the bank.

Blown Sand.

The whole of the coast line between the rivers Mersey and Ribble,
from Bootle to Crossens, is fringed with sand hills, which in the
neighbourhood of Formby extend inland to a distance of nearly
two miles. They also occur on the opposite side of the estuary of
the Ribble, extending from a little east of Lytham to Southshore,
where the Boulder Clay rises above the surface of the lowest plain.
A third line of sand dunes of small elevation occurs a few miles
to the north of Blackpool, where the Boulder Clay dips below the
alluvial plain lying between the sea at Rossal and the river Wyre.
And a fourth area of blown sand, seldom rising into dunes, skirts
the southern limit of the coast line of the low-lying lands east of
the Wyre, blown from the immense sandy flats of Pilling Sands
and other banks in Morecambe Bay.

The shallower the water, the further will the wave of translation
resulting from the breaker move, and the greater will be the area in
which it can collect matter to throw on shore. The tidal zone
between Liverpool and Southport is broad and composed of sand ;
between the tides the wind has time to dry the surface, and the dried
sand is blown in the direction of the wind seawards or landwards, as
the case may be. With a fresh breeze the sand rises to a height of
about 12 feet from the surface, moving and advancing in a straight
line like a wave. The wind-wave, like the sea-wave, being of unequal
intensity along its length, is able to move a greater quantity of
sand in some portions of its line than in others : thus, when the wind
ceases to blow, or the progress of the sand is stopped by an
obstruction, (as a range of sand-hills or wall), it falls in heaps of
unequal heights, the long axis of which corresponds to the direction
of the wind ; and the direction of the range of the detached billocks,
as a whole, corresponds to a line at right angles to it.

The winds blowing on the Lancashire coast more frequently and
stronger from the sea than from the land, cause the direction of
the sand-hills on the coast, which have been produced in the
manner described above, to be invariably in a W.N.W. direction,

—the steep sides facing that direction, and the sloping side tailing away to the east and north-east.

About 1690 there was a deep-water channel close to the shore at Formby, with a sand bank outside it, which gradually came nearer and nearer. At length it joined the coast, from which sand commenced to blow, so that in a short time the cultivated ground, gardens, orchards, and streets of Formby were entirely covered up; and in 1746 the church had to be taken down, and removed inland to its present situation. The old path known as Church Street still remains, and leads to a modern church built on the site of the older one. But the churchyard contains several tombstones of such dates as 1730 that have since been cleared of sand, which has almost ceased to infringe upon this area, from the exertions of the late Mr. Freshfield, who, by a judicious system of planting and banking, commenced in 1850, stopped the onward progress of the sand.

At Southport and Waterloo the sand-dunes have been gradually carted away to make room for the erection of houses. The uniformity of level, and strictly rectangular character of the line of roads laid out, give the streets of these towns a sameness and uniformity.

The sand hills rising above the general surface, discharge the rain that falls upon them into the sandy plain, which, being originally full of recent shells that have been more or less decomposed by the action of carbonated water,* is sufficiently calcareous to hold a considerable quantity of water. The permanent water-level at Southport being only about two feet from the surface renders it almost impossible for cellars or rooms below the ground floor to be constructed.

The general arrangement of these dunes is a more or less cone-shaped hill, with a gradually sloping tail-spur on the lee side, running parallel to the direction of the heavy westerly gales (about W. 10 N.) The two slopes of this spur are about equal, meeting in a sharp crest, sometimes slightly truncated at the actual top.

The space between two such cones is gradually filled up by the flow of sand down the slopes, forming a col between the cones.

The space between the two tail-spurs is also gradually filled by the action of the E. and especially N.E. wind, which loosens the sand at the apex of the cone, and causes it to flow down the surface slope of the tail-spur, which it does at the rate of a foot a second, starting as a little stream about 3 inches across, and widening to double that distance after traversing perhaps 25 feet.

Such a stream, when it first commences to flow, cuts a groove for the first yard or two where the slope is steepest, and carries the sand removed with it; so that, collecting as it descends, it stands out in strong relief at the bottom of the slope when it has come to rest. At each breath of N.E. wind, another and another streamlet follows its predecessor in the same path, each flow occupying a

---

* Previous to the passing of the Alkali Act in 1863, which forced alkali establishments to condense at least 95 per cent. of the escaping muriatic acid, the rain must for many years have been much more acidulated when the wind blew from Manchester and St. Helen's towards the sand hills,—for previous to the passing of the Act, 16 and even 40 per cent. commonly escaped.

broader space, until, by continual removal of sand, the cones become obliterated, and the space between the two tail-crests filled up.

When cones of sand stand isolated in a plain or slack, the action is somewhat different. The sand blowing from the cone to the tail-spur forms the latter into a new cone at the expense of the old one, the base of which alone remains, a hollow crater, broken towards the windward side, and flanked by a new cone to the leeward.

Many of the dunes are deeply furrowed by the action of N.N.E. winds directed from below, forming a series of hollows and terraces, and, where the action has been extreme, of hollows and ridges.

The sides of the dune facing the W.S.W. generally consist of a series of steep steps inclined at an angle of 50 degrees.

The sides facing W. 10 N. are steep above, but have a gradual sloping talus of loose sand beneath.

The side of the dune facing the N.N.E. is a rounded slope, the top of which becomes furrowed as described.

In some E. and W. dunes, W.S.W. winds have cut furrows 10 inches wide and 5 deep, acting from below upwards, the sand cut away being carried over the ridge, and deposited in a slope on the other side.

At Waterloo, Marine Crescent is built on a yellowish-red compact quartzose sand, without shells, which to the south, at Seaforth, rests upon peat cropping out along the beach. Near Seaforth Hall the sand is traversed by thin seams of red marl, washed probably from the Boulder Clay, containing recent marine shells much broken. Similar red bands occur in four feet of sand overlying the peat, in a section near to the S.W. of Pasture Lane, opposite Water Hey, east of Formby.

Sections showing the thinning out of the blown sand on the peat are well seen at Broad Lane, and in the fields immediately south of it, and at East Pasture Lane, Formby. The thickness of sand is seen to vary much in 50 yards, decreasing from 12 feet to one foot, and alternating with the peat, which in places has grown on a moderate slope of land for a certain distance, and then becomes covered up by sand. From these sections, and many others of a similar character, in other parts of the district, it is certain that when the sand first commenced to blow, it was deposited in fresh water in which peat was forming, the water from the deposition of sand became purer, and fresh-water shells lived and died, and were covered up with sand and fragments of blown marine shells.

At Freshfield, north of Formby, and at several other places between Southport and Liverpool, the sand hills have been levelled and carted away, and the ground reclaimed, the fields being bounded by high banks, locally called " cops," made of a portion of the sand removed, carefully covered and faced with green grazing turf. The banks between Ainsdale windmill and the 16th mile post of the Liverpool and Southport Railway, run N.W., parallel to the strike of the sand dunes.

At Cloven-le-Dale Hill, between Formby and Ainsdale, the sand rises to a height of 83 feet above the mean sea level, while the level of the little farm at its eastern foot is probably not more than 30 feet, giving a height for the dune of 53 feet. Immediately to the north, there is a depression, called Long Slack Gutter, which is covered with water during wet weather, and through it is taken a path to the sea at Long Slack. About half a mile to the south runs a small stream with a definite channel, called Dale Slack Gutter, which has generally more or less water in it though its bed is sand. At its rearward it is lost beneath the line of sand dunes which mark the coast, and is again seen oozing through the sand on the shore.

Broadly this area exhibits a definite line of sand dunes (I.) running parallel to the coast, about 150 yards in width ; then (II.) a parallel belt of very low sand hills, often much broken, depressed, and interrupted by grassy flats and slacks, generally about 60 yards in width ; a broad tract of sand dunes (III.) then sets in, with an average width of half a mile, rising to heights of 50 to 80 feet, and sloping down to the east to a sandy tract (IV.), which very gradually inclines to the peat country inland, on which, at a distance of from 1½ to 2 miles from the sand dunes, it thins out. This inclined surface of sand, though occasionally encroached on by the sand dunes, tends to retreat before the progress of cultivation, the top peat being cut away and used for fuel, leaving an abrupt step of sand-covered peat on the seaward side of the moss.

The incoherent masses of the westward belt of dunes would be of little avail in keeping out the sea, were it not for the matted roots of the sand-reed (*Ammophila arundinacea*), locally called "starr-grass" or "marram," which, protected by an Act of Parliament passed in the time of Queen Elizabeth, making it felony to destroy it, covers much of the West Lancashire desert, and, with the dark-green bands of dwarf willows, relieves the monotony of the continuous yellow glare.

In the small oval plains or "slacks" before referred to, "Bullrushes," "Long," Mayflower, Round, and Dale Slacks, there is in summer a dense carpet of spongy moss mixed with sedges and sprinkled with flowers, many of which are of species usually found on chalk soils, due probably to the presence of calcareous matter in the sand. In winter the carpet of vegetation supports large sheets of standing water, the drainage of the surrounding hills, whence these tracts derive their local name of "Slack," which means in the Lancashire dialect a wet place.

In the Scarisbrick New Road from Southport, the blown sand is seen to gradually thin out eastwards with the slope of the ground. The sand thickens seawards, the banks of each field being composed of peat covered with blown sand, the peat having been dug for fuel.

The manufacture of salt in the 17th century from these sands is thus described by Camden or his editors:—" In many places " near the shore there are great heaps of sand, of which the " inhabitants have an art to make salt after this manner. In " summer time, when the weather is dry, they pare off the upper " part of the sand, and lay it up in great heaps, which, when " they have lain some time, they are put into troughs bored full of " holes at the bottom, and pour water upon it, to make a *lixi-* " *vium* or lye. The water draining through it carries along with " it a salt, which, by changing the sand and making the same " water pass through it again and again, they thicken so that " it will bear an egg ; which done, they boil this impregnated

" water with fierce turf fire till the water being evaporated,
" leaves a white salt."[*]

The sand of North Meols[†] would appear to have commenced to
blow at an earlier period than in the Formby district, for Jameson,[‡]
in his " *Iter Lancastrensi*," 1636, says,—

> " Ormeschurch and ye Meales
> " Are our next journey. We direct no weales
> " Of state to hinder our delight. Ye guize
> " Of those chaffe sands which doe in mountains rise
> " On shore 'tis pleasure to behold, which Hoes
> " Are called in Worold : windie tempest blows
> " Them up in heapes."

The modern town of Southport is on the site of an old fishing
village called South Hawes (Hawes, How, or Hoe, a hill), which,
rising into importance, caused the older and originally larger town of
Meols to receive the prefix " North." The village of Meols is now
generally called Churchtown. A very old path still exists, both
north and south of Southport, called " Church gate," leading to the
hamlet of Birkdale. Near the latter is the site of the "Lost Farm,"
which has been entirely covered up and buried by blown sand.
Fifty years ago part of the building could still be seen, filled in
with sand to a depth of 3 to 4 feet.

The district of Meols would appear to have been early populated,
as in Will. II.'s reign Roger de Poictou gave the monks of Lancaster
the tithes of " Melis."

North of the Ribble.—Capping the cliff of glacial deposits at Uncle
Tom's Cabin, north of Blackpool, there occurs a bed of blown sand,
about 10 feet in thickness. Considerable additions are made to it
during every gale of wind, sand resulting from the waste of the
cliff below, as well as from the sea coast, being constantly blown
to the top. This deposit, which was described in 1842 by
Mr. Binney as the probable equivalent of his forest sand of the
Manchester district, occurs at intervals all along the cliffs to the
north, which gradually diminish in height until they entirely disappear at Angersholme, and a line of sand dunes alone affords a
feeble barrier to the alluvial plain extending between Rossal and
the Wyre.

The gradual thinning away of the glacial deposit, and replace-
ment by sand dunes, is well seen in the following sections:—

Norbreck Cliff, South of Lane to Bispham.

		feet.
Sec. 1.—*a.* Blown Sand	- - -	2
b. Boulder Clay	- - - -	8
Sec. 2.—*a.* Sand (blown)	- - -	4 ⎫
b. Ferruginous gravel	- - -	2 ⎬ Post-Glacial.
c. Loam	- - - -	3 ⎭
d. Boulder Clay, with scratched pebbles	-	4

---

[*] " Magna Britannia et Hibernia Antiqua et Nova," vol. ii. p. 1295. Printed
in the Savoy, London. 1720.

[†] The derivation of the word *Meols* or *Meales* is probably connected with the
Icelandic word "Melar," a "sand heap," used in Iceland for the immeuse dunes
of fine volcanic ashes. North Meols and Raven Meols in Lancashire, Great and
Little Meols, Cheshire, Meales or Males (sand banks) in Norfolk.

[‡] Cheetham, Soc. Edition, p. 4.

Sec. 3. At the above Lane :—

				ft.	ins.	
a.	Blown Sand	- - -		3	9	
	Cemented ferruginous shingle		-	2	0	Post-Glacial
b.	Gravelly sand - -		-	0	3	Deposits.
	Yellow sand -		-	1	8	
c.	Red Loam - -		-	1	0	(+)

Sec. 4. Between Lanes from the Coast to Bispham and Angersholme :—

		ft.	ins.
Blown Sand	- - - - -	10	0
Loam	- - - - -	0	6
Peaty	- - -	0	6
Loam	- - - -	1	0
Gravel	- - -	2	0

Sec. 5. :—

		feet.
Blown Sand	- - -	5
Boulder Clay	- - - -	7

In the last section, the Boulder Clay, which for the last 500 yards has been concealed below the beach, again rises for a short distance, and is again concealed. Though seen at several points on the beach between tide-marks, and forming a knoll at Willcocks, it does not reappear in a cliff-section anywhere south of Morecambe Bay and west of the River Wyre.

Waste of the Sea-coast.—Rossal "Landmark" formerly stood 100 yards further out than it does at present, and was erected on a massive stone base, which, when the sea reached it, was removed inland of the house marked on the one-inch map as Fennys. There is no vestige left of it, though it had been previously twice removed before occupying the site shown in the Ordnance one-inch map of 1848.

Between the landmark and the Wyre at Fleetwood a broader tract of blown sand fringes the coast. The coast line, which consists of blown sand, has been much worn back since it was surveyed for the Ordnance map. This is especially the case at the highest point, called the Mount, a large sand-hill, surmounted by a summer-house, and formerly the centre of a public garden. Between this and the sea formerly ran a road, which has been since entirely swept away by the sea, as has also the seaward slope of the Mount itself; no less than 50 yards having been destroyed since 1846.

At Cleveleys, a farm known as Carr House was deserted at the time of my survey (1869), and the horse-pond behind the house filled with salt water. The coast was formerly protected by sea walls constructed for the late Sir Peter Hesketh Fleetwood, but they are now entirely gone to decay,—far less remaining standing than is destroyed. At ordinary tides the sea is kept out by the formation of sand-hills, now forming to a slight extent on the surface of the Marsh Scrobicularia Clay, which rests on peat, and is seen cropping out on the beach from under the sand between tide marks.

At the base of the narrow strip of blown sand, and low sand dunes, that stretch northwards from these sections to Rossal landmark, occurs a shingly beach, which lies in a sort of trench cut in the alluvial clay resting on the peat. The clay evidently thickens eastwards towards the Wyre, being only two or three feet thick near the sea, and more than 20 feet in some of the wells in the Cleveley plain. But even at the coast the level of the base of the clay, and consequently of the top of the peat, is decidedly below that of high-water mark, so that the alluvial clay is often seen forming the beach below the belt of shingle, which has an average width of 40 yards.

The occurrence of large numbers of shells of *Scrobicularia* in the clay overlying the peat proves this deposit, though thrown down in the ancient estuary of the Wyre, to be a tidal alluvium, formed probably like those still more modern Scrobicularia muds now being quietly deposited on the south banks of the Ribble near Crossens. Though this tidal clay has been found to be very thin along the sea-coast section, yet it is clear that since its deposition a considerable area has been denuded away to the west, though the levels and general relations of sea to land have remained the same;— a circumstance which has a special interest, from the fact of the occurrence of Roman coins at a depth of 8 feet in the tidal alluvium described hereafter.

At the point on which stand the ruins of Cockersand Abbey, founded by Theobald Walter, 5 Richard I., 1193, near the mouth of the Lune, considerable denudation has taken place, for much of the Abbey has fallen into the sea, through the wearing back of the low cliff. This must have taken place in very recent times, as in a Latin charter exhibited a few years since at a chapter of the Rosicrucian Brotherhood of Manchester, dated 30 Hen. VIII., Robert (Abbot of the monastery of Cokersand) confirms, with consent of the convent, the previous grant of the manor of West Houghton, a burgage and lands in Preston, and also common of turbary in Hutton, for 89 years, to Sir Thomes Langton, knt., in consideration of 100 marks and a yearly rent of 50*l.*

Action of Tidal Currents on Lancashire Coast.

In endeavouring to follow the conditions under which the sedimentary deposits are thrown down on the Lancashire coast, Mr. Scott Russell's statements are of importance, as to the necessity of always distinguishing between wave-motion and water-motion—which latter "is an ideal individuality attributed by the " mind of the observer to a process of changes of relative " position or of absolute place, which at no two instants belongs " to the *same* particles in the *same* place."* Thus, floating bodies in the surface of the sea may be seen travelling with the tidal current at Blackpool and Southport in exactly an opposite direction to that of the waves breaking upon the adjacent coast—mounting to the top of the crest, and descending to the bottom of the trough of each successive wave which they meet in their opposing course;—

---

* Reports on Waves. Brit. Assoc., 1842-3.

waves "being the transference of motion without the transference
" of the matter, of form without the substance, of force without
" the agent."*

Those waves which are elevated above the plane of repose are
known as *positive*, those depressed below it as *negative* waves;
while a third class combine the two, as in the wind-waves, each
height of which has a corresponding hollow, like ridge and furrow.
On approaching the shore the positive portion of an oscillating
or wind wave increases in height in regard to the negative portion.
As the depth decreases, the wave diminishes in height, becomes
cycloidal in form, totters and breaks when it reaches a depth equal
to its height above the planes of repose.

Between Southport and Formby, where the coast has a very
gentle incline, when wind-waves run high they necessarily break
at a considerable distance from the sea margin,—the intervening
space, often a mile in breadth, being covered with breakers. Between Blackpool and Rossal the slope is steeper, and the waves
break nearer the shore, with a greater vertical height at the
moment of breaking. After the wave has broken, it continues its course towards the coast as a true wave of translation, carrying in its waters shingle and other materials caught
up from the bottom, and pushed along up the inclined plane of
the sea-bottom, and often thrown on shore above spring-tide
high-water mark, forming a storm-beach which is in no way due to
elevation of the country.

At the Great Ormes Head near Llandudno, and at Heysham Point,
at the mouth of the Lune, where there is comparatively deep
water surrounding rock-bound coasts, the wind-wave breaks close
to the coast, no wave of translation is generated, and shingle
is not accumulated, but carried on by the flow tide.†

The tidal stream strikes the coast at different angles, varying
with the nature of the sea bottom, the source of the current, and
the form of the coast-line against which it is propelled. In the narrow
bays formed by the mouths of the Mersey, Ribble, and Wyre,

---

* Two of Mr. Scott Russell's four wave orders act as direct geological agents; the
" Wave of Translation" as the tidal wave; and the " Oscillating Wave," including
the wind waves, ocean swell, and stream ripples. In the waves of the first order the
whole mass of the water is bodily moved from one place to another, without any
solitary change of particles in a vertical plane,—one enormous relative wave rolling
in along the entire shores of Britain during every tide, carrying with it, or rather
being the vehicle of transmission of the mechanical force which regulates the mode of
deposition of sedimentary matter—J. Scott Russell, F.R.S.: Report of Waves. Brit.
Assoc., 1842–43.

† The deeper the water near a rocky cliff, the greater will be the action of breaking
upon it. Thus, at points where there is a great tidal scour preventing the lodgment
of shingle at the base of cliffs with deep water outside, as on the coasts of the
Western Islands of Scotland and the Atlantic coast of Ireland, the waves strike the
coast with a force, calculated by Mr. Stephenson at 6,083 lbs., or about three tons to
the foot, at Skerryvore Rock, the average pressure in winter being 2,086 lbs., the
average summer being only 611 lbs., wearing the rocks into hollows and caverns, and
exerting a power of denudation increasing with the steepness of the angle of slope
of the tidal zone. This angle decreases at the base of the zone, and wave-denudation
is therefore at a minimum at low-water mark, increasing to a maximum at high-
water mark. At the Bell Rock lighthouse, where the wave pressure is sometimes
3,013 lbs. on the square foot, stones measuring 30 cubic feet and weighing 100 tons
are lifted from deep water and thrown up on the rock—being called by the light-
house keepers " sea travellers."

the flow tide reaches that point on the coast first, which is immediately opposite the deepest water channel of the entrance of the bay; while wind-waves running parallel to the entrance break where the water suddenly shallows, and propel small semi-circular waves of translation, which accommodate themselves to the shape of the bay, reaching every portion at the same moment, as may be seen on the coast of Llandudno Bay. But if the direction of the crest of the wind-waves is oblique to the trend of the bay, then the end of the wave will be truncated by the coast, and successively pass over every portion of the bay, commencing at the windward end. In this movement of translation nearly all the pebbles and other material are caught up and deposited at the leeward end or side of the bay, which is well seen between Morecambe and Hest Bank.

In this way the prevalent westerly direction of the wind of the coast has an important secondary influence on the deposit of sand and shingle, by determining the direction of the crest of the waves, which run at right angles to the direction of the lately prevailing wind. Should the coast be shallow, the direction of the wind-wave materially affects the line the induced wave of translation will take, as between the Mersey and the Ribble; and still more so, should, from the steepness of the incline of the coast between tide-marks, the high-wind-wave be able to break sufficiently close to the shore to throw its weight upon rocks or cliffs, and denude, throw down, and waste them away; which is only the case on the Lancashire coast at very high spring-tides between Blackpool and Norbreck. But this action is totally distinct to that longitudinal denudation produced by the edges of tidal currents running along a coast line, gradually wearing it back, and carrying with them the fallen material; pressing the heavier portion along the sea-bottom until it is stopped either by a projecting headland or an artificial breakwater, and depositing the finer sediment at the sea-bottom at a distance from the point from which it was taken.

Around most of the shoals of Morecambe Bay and the mouths of the Ribble, Mersey, and Dee, where the motion of the ebb is obstructed in its line of retreat, it exerts a slight denuding power, catching up some of the sand deposited, and, when its velocity is checked, redepositing it near the shore; but the remainder as well as all the sediment remaining in the sea gathered up by the flood before the turn, is carried by it far out to sea, and deposited in deep water, when the velocity is checked. Only such materials are deposited near the shore as are between the sea-margin and the line of breaking waves,* especially when the tidal current has been split into a primary offshore current and a secondary inshore current, the shoals occurring between the two. Mr. Cromwell Varley, F.R.S., states that he has only known of one instance of a telegraph cable being shifted by storms or currents at a greater depth than 40 fathoms.

The flow tide enters the Irish Sea by two routes, one from the north passing between Rathlin and the Mull of Cantire,

---

* Lieut. C. H. Davis, U.S. Navy, "On the Law of the Deposit of the Flood Tide, its Dynamical Action and Office." Smithsonian Contributions to Knowledge. Washington. 1852.

the other from the south running between Carnsore Point and Pembroke, the two currrents meeting on the English coast in Morecambe Bay. The ebb runs back along the same lines, with the exception of pressing rather more on the Irish coast.

The tides of the Irish sea, as pointed out by Captain Beechey, R.N., F.R.S.,* "partake of the nature of river tides in having their " ebb longer than their flood, except those of Tuskar and Holyhead, " which are the reverse." At Bardsey it rises 5h. 24m., and falls 6h. 52m.; at Peel it rises 6.0, and falls 6.15 ; at Fleetwood it rises 5.46, and falls 6.39. It is also found that the upper half of the tidal wave rises and falls more rapidly than the lower half, and that the whole of the ebb stream of the eastern portion of the Irish Sea runs into the Bristol Channel, where it forms the incoming or flow tide of the northern portion, while the ebb tide of that Channel helps to form the flood-tide of the Irish Sea. The southern portion of the Bristol Channel receives its flow from the offing and the English Channel.

These channels, possibly, mark the old lines of river and glacier drainage, into which the rivers Mersey, Dee, and Ribble were tributary before the Glacial Epoch. The deposition of the various Boulder Drift beds must have filled in these depressions to a great extent, and it is quite possible that some of the more basin-like hollows are due rather to the infilling of the end of a sloping trough than to the formation of a rock-basin by land ice.

Captain Beechey states that the tidal stream in the English Channel is 265 miles long, and in the Irish sea 262 miles long, and that both enter from the south-west, and that both flow onwards until stopped by a counter-stream. In the English Channel he gives the rate of progress of the tide-wave at 50 miles an hour, in the Irish at 52, from Holyhead to end of tide 78, from Dieppe to end of tide 75. In estuaries the velocity of the current is diminished by the shallowing of the water, increasing where the banks are steep, the channel narrow, and obstructions removed. In regard to the relation between the velocity of a free tide-wave and the depth of water in which it flows, the following observations give useful data for finding the rate of the tidal current on the Lancashire coast at any given point, the depth being obtained from the Admiralty charts.

Depth of water, in feet.	Velocity of free tide wave per second, in feet.	Length of free tide wave, in miles.	Space described by free tide wave per hour, in miles.
1	5·67	47·94	3·86
4	11·34	95·89	7·73
10	17·93	151·62	12·28
60	43·93	371·38	29·95
100	56·71	479·46	38·66

In the Irish Sea from St. David's Head to Morecambe Bay, the direction of the transport of shingle governed by that of the flood

* Phil. Trans., 1848.

tide is in a general south-west and north-east direction, and from the Mull of Cantire to Morecambe in a general north-west and south-east ; but in the broad estuaries of the Dee and Mersey, the Ribble, and Solway Firth, there is a division of the flood current, especially at the half flood, which has caused the deposition of central shoals and sand banks, the two portions hugging the opposite shores of the estuary, with dry sand between, and not coalescing until the tide has sufficiently risen to cover the banks.

In the estuary of the Ribble, a flood-current runs past Lytham inwards towards the river only a few minutes later than that running by Southport, while the main portion of the current runs past the entrance of the estuary in a north-east direction, or at right angles to that running inland at Lytham. This may account for the fact of the occurrence of a shingle beach between South Shore and Lytham, derived from the wasting away of the Blackpool Cliffs further to the north, the pebbles of which are also carried by the ordinary flood-tide into Morecambe Bay as far as the Wyre, which cuts off their easterly extension.

The pebbles travelling east along the coast of North Wales, cut off by the river Dee, cause the north coast of Wirrall to be almost pebble-less. The ground above high-water mark is here low, and covered with sand dunes, and there being no cliffs of Boulder Clay to be denuded, there are consequently no pebbles or boulders to be obtained. The clay, however, occurs between ordinary and spring-tide low-water marks, but between these limits the sea appears to have little power to denude; thus, on the flats of Boulder Clay at Morecambe, slightly embedded stones, covered with fine glacial striations, not only maintain their position month after month, but retain their striæ unworn ; and I am informed by Prof. Ramsay, F.R.S., that he had previously observed similar facts on the coast of Anglesea.

The power of small streams to arrest the extension and on-ward transport of shingle is often well marked, the direction and form of the shingle-bank at its termination being pri-marily due to the particular manner and angle at which the river or stream breaches the coast, rather than to the angle at which the flood-tide impinges upon it. The abrupt termination of the large shingle-bank between Fleetwood and Rossal landmark, by the scour of the river Wyre at low tide, is a good example of this action on a larger scale.

Near the Lighthouse west of Lytham, water has accumulated in slacks amongst the sand dunes, and forms a channel, or small brook, which runs out in the direction of the flood-tide ; a shingle hook has formed beyond it, followed by a series of shingle hooks. The flow of the brook cutting off the movement of the shingle formed the first hook ; this curved ridge of pebbles joined the shore on the side of the flood-tide and brook; in process of time another hook was added to the latter, and so on in succession, until the force of the brook could no longer carry forward the pebbles that fall from above, and percolated through the shingle bank. This action continuing, and the pebbles being no longer carried forward, the additional hooks of shingle commence to approach the shore, and the curve of the whole nearly became an arc joined to the land at both ends ; but that on the ebb side was generally kept open, owing to the hooks of shingle, after the maximum curve is reached, becoming smaller and smaller, from the flood-current no longer impinging on that portion of the shore best suited for the transport of shingle. The flats behind the shingle-banks become a salt-marsh alluvial plain ; many of these are often entirely reclaimed from the sea, and covered with blowing and blown sands.

The action of the small watercourses breaching the coast between Freckleton and Southshore near Blackpool is comparatively unimportant. East of Lytham, where small streams run in a simila direction to that in which shingle is being transported, a long narrow-spit of beach has formed, with a fresh or brackish-water channel between it and the land. Where the streams face the direction of the flow, they either directly force a passage through the shingle ; or if not sufficiently powerful to breach it, percolate through the beach, and have no tendency to flow behind the shingle bank, which closely hugs the shore.

The flood-tide appears to cause a general transport of all material which travels mainly between tide-marks, (or, more strictly, between spring-tide high-water and neap-tide low-water marks,) the greater portion of the heavy material being arrested in its progress by projecting headlands. Deposits of shingle occur in bays on the side opposite to that in which the flood-tide entered, the sizes gradually diminishing flow-wards, fine sand invariably occurring at the opposite end.

Projecting headlands, unlike the breaks formed by tidal rivers, have only the power to temporarily and partially arrest the flow-ward progress of the shingle ; all that escapes round the headland is carried to the lee end of the next bay, and sometimes on to shoals forming in the middle of the next bay.

A portion of that deposited is every now and then carried out to sea by waves of translation generated by the breaking of storm wind-waves, but is for the most part brought back to its old position by the action of the tidal flow during the succeeding calms ; which phenomena I have twice observed to take place in the Chesil beach in Dorset. Viewing the whole bay from Anglesea on the one hand, and Black Coombe in Cumberland on the other, the absence of any great accumulations of shingle would be expected.

The power of the Mersey to bear back and arrest the movement of sediment in regard to its action on the deposition of matter brought down by it from the land is interesting. This generally consists of fine angular sand and impalpable mud, which Admiral Denham, R.N.,[*] found to amount to 29 cubic inches per cubic yard of water during the flood-tide, and 33 cubic inches during the ebb, or 4 cubic inches in excess of the flood ; from which he calculated that 48,065 cubic yards of silt are annually detained and deposited on the banks outside the Narrows during each tide, excepting that portion which the succeeding ebb disturbs and carries further.

The velocity of the flood-tide in the Narrows is from 1 to 6¾ miles an hour, running .5 hours and 20 minutes, that of the ebb being from ¾ of a mile to 7 miles an hour, running

---

out for 6 hours and 30 minutes. The greatest velocity of the flow he found to be at the third hour, that of the ebb being at the second; the greatest impetus of the former occurring after that hour, that of the latter being at the third hour before, or, in other words, two hours before and two hours after the completion of the flood-tide. He found the waters to be most turbid at the second hour of flow, and the second, third, and fourth hour of the ebb, or, in fact, commencing one hour before and after the periods of greatest impetus and greatest velocity, the current being found to be most turbid at a depth of 30 feet.

The excess of silt carried through the Narrows, and deposited in the first tidal area, Admiral Denham estimates at 35 million and odd cubic yards per annum, equalling a layer of mud 21 inches thick ; but this is partially denuded and carried into the second tidal area and into the sea, where the residue is still further disturbed. The total deposit in the mouth of the Mersey is about 11½ million cubic yards a year, which is not spread out in sheets, but deposited in spits, knolls, and banks, precisely resembling those met with, at various levels, in Western Lancashire, of Middle Glacial Age.

Admiral Evans, conservator of the Mersey, stated in 1843 that " the extension of the Victoria Bar is occasioned by a greater quantity of detritus being held in suspension by the ebb than by the flood-tide, which causes the point of deposit to be continually extending outwards to where the stream of ebb is exhausted . . . . The excess of matter held in solution by the ebb near the flood in the Mersey is in great measure " due to the emptying of mud flats in the centre of the river, just before high-water, of materials collected daily by steam dredges in the Liverpool docks, which in 1843 amounted to 200,000, and in 1873 to probably not less than 600,000 tons. Since this report was made, the mud-boats are discharged at the first quarter ebb.

Mr. Binney* states that the estuary of the Mersey is mainly kept open by the ebb tide, and the back waters of the Mersey, Weaver, and other streams ; and that the contraction by embankments of the Mersey, by diminishing the quantity of the water entering at the flood, has diminished the scour of the ebb.

At the mouths of the Mersey, Ribble, and in Morecambe Bay, these banks undergo extensive denudation during the ebbing tide. Where straight channels intervene, the tidal current, like a straight river, wastes the sand on both edges, making an angle of waste steeper than the angle of repose, causing the little clifflets to fall in, and the channels to widen, the action being great in proportion to the velocity of the current ; this, diminishing as the tide ebbs and water falls, causes the bottom of the banks to be less denuded than that portion lying towards the top. The action of breakers and the tides tends to flatten the tops of the bank, and prevents them raising their crests above a line a little below neap-tide high-water mark.

Where a curved channel runs between two banks, that bounded by the outer curve is gradually worn back and back, while matter

---

* Proc. Lit. Phil. Soc. Man., Dec. 30, 1873.

I

is deposited upon the inner (outward curve in the sand bank), until at last the former is entirely worn away and the latter occupies its place, having travelled in the direction of the outward or convex side of the tidal channel;—just as the convex curve of a river wears a cliff or bluff back and back, dragging after it the concave curve, which is covered with alluvium.

In addition to the wearing away of the sides of sand-banks and shoals by the ebbing tide, their entire surface suffers waste from the running off in air, of the water left on them from their crests to the sea. On landing on one of these, all the various stages of valley-making, as would be experienced by a country whose undulating surfaces of deposition and plains of marine denudation were fresh from the sea, may be seen exhibited in miniature. The depth of the valley is regulated by the height of its source and its outfall. The latter becomes lower and lower with the receding tide, and the groove becomes deeper and deeper. It flows, perhaps, over a convex curve of deposition swelling out in the centre. It cuts a chord to this curve, often following the lines of shrinkage produced by evaporation, with deep banks of sand; while above and below, where the slope is less curved, it flows almost vertically at the surface. When it can denude no lower, the streamlet begins to curve, to swing from side to side, and produces the sides of the deep sand-gorge; it wears them back and back; an alluvial plain comes into existence, with a river running obliquely across it, with a cliff on one side, while a rounded bluff, no longer kept vertical by removal of matter from below, exhibits the angle of repose of sand upon the other side.

The various denuding actions going on during the ebbing tide would well account for the excess of matter in the ebb-water over the flood-water found by Admiral Denham ; but it by no means follows that that matter is deposited during the ebb, and I think it probable that the excess in the ebb barely represents the matter deposited by the flow before it reached Liverpool and was gauged. Admiral Denham found it to be most turbid at the second hour, probably because every hour after that it deposited more and more material, while the return flow laden with sand from the sea would receive river water with a fresh supply of matter from the land, which, with a portion of that just thrown down by the previous flow and stirred up by the ebb, would be carried seawards, gathering additional matter every hour, from the wasting of banks. This would account for the waters of the Mersey being more turbid at the second hour of the flow, and from the second to the fourth hour of the ebb, than at any other time.

The denudation of the sandy foreshores by fresh water, and the retreat of salt water during low tide, is well seen in the sand below the outcrop of the peat at Cleveleys, between Blackpool and Fleetwood. Where a considerable quantity of water issues from the junction of the peat with the grey clay beneath, from each point of emergence it spreads in a fan-like shape, cutting for itself a series of sinuous channels, the inosculation of their various lines of hollow much resembling that exhibited by the mounds and shoals of the sand-banks of the estuaries of the Mersey and Ribble, and the curving arrangement of the sands and shingle beds of Middle Glacial age.

The water which issues from the grey clay is probably the over-flow of the sheet of water which is found in borings and wells in the marsh clay over the whole of the low country between Bispham and Fleetwood, which is invariably brackish, as the sea runs up the ditches at high tide, and charges the clay on either side.

The cliffs formed of Glacial Drift, the alternate wetting and drying causes the surface to crumble away rapidly. It is only here and there, however, that marine action has much direct influence over the waste of the cliffs; more often their bases are slightly above ordinary high-water mark, and are beset with land-springs, which undermine their foundations and cause landslips, the fallen matter from which is carried away by the sea, in the direction of the flood-tide, and spread out on the littoral zone. These landslips generally occur where permeable strata, like the gravel and sand of the *Middle Glacial Drift*, rest on an impermeable one like the *Lower Boulder Clay*.

In the Ribble I have observed that turbid fresh water at low tide runs over the salt water in the estuary a less and less distance, in proportion to the greater quantity of matter held in it in mechanical suspension. But during very heavy floods this distance is increased by the high velocity of the river, and the sea is only brackish between Lytham and Southport; but when this water—the muddy fresh above, and the salt below—reaches the open seas at the horns of the estuary, the velocity is checked, and the sand is for the most part precipitated, forming the Salters, Crusaders, and other large banks. The westward or seaward edges of these are cut off by the denuding action of the ebbing tide, which exerts a similar influence on the seaward edges of the banks of Morecambe Bay, bringing with it in suspension southwards the sand that it has cut away. This I have seen travelling in cloudy masses of globular form, with clear water between, ever changing shape like the sheets of cumuli driven by a fresh breeze across a blue sky. The sand which is not immediately precipitated, on the river reaching the open sea is probably carried a considerable distance, for it would sink with exceeding slowness in the denser salter water beneath. In some cases the pent-back river-water laden with débris from the land, plus the salt flood-tide water returning with the ebb, has a greater specific gravity than the ordinary sea-water outside the estuary; in which case the former, with its included sediment, flows under the clear sea-water, until the friction accumulated by the head of pent-up waters behind is spent, when the motion ceases, and the matter is deposited without discolouring the water of the adjacent coasts.

APPENDIX.

This Appendix has been revised by Mr. Etheridge, F.R.S., Palæontologist to the Geological Survey. It is compiled from the following sources :—

The Northern and Southern range of the species is taken from Mr. J. Gwyn Jeffreys's British Conchology, which has been used as an authority for the names and synonyms.

The list of shells, in column III., is drawn up from my own notes of their occurrence in the Lower Boulder Clay of Lancashire.

Column V., Blackpool Middle Sands:

 1, gives the shells mentioned by the Rev. Wm. Thornber, in his "History of Blackpool;"

 2, those described by Mr. Binney, F.R.S., Mem. Lit. Phil. Soc. Man., vol. x., second series, 1851–2;

 3, those by Mr. Darbishire, F.G.S., Geol. Mag., vol. ii., p. 298;

 4, those collected by myself.

The shells in columns VI. and VII. (with the exception of three in the latter column, collected by Miss Ffarington) are from the list given by Mr. Darbishire in the Q. J. G. S., vol. xxx., p. 38, (1874).

The shells in column VIII. were collected by myself.

The Crag columns are taken from the table given by Prof. Prestwich, in his paper on the Crags, in the Q. J. G. S., vol. xxvii., p. 115, (1871).

Those of Scotland from Prof. Geikie's paper on the Scotch Glacial Deposits in the Trans. Geol. Soc., Glasgow.

Those of Yorkshire from Mr. S. V. Wood's, jun., paper in the Q. J. G. S., vol. xxvi., p. 92, (1870) ; and from Mr. J. Gwyn Jeffreys's on the so-called Bridlington Crag. Report of the Brit. Assoc. 1874, p. 83, (marked J.)

The Cheshire columns are from Mr. Reade's paper in the Q. J. G. S., vol. xxx., p. 27, (1874) ; and Mr. Mackintosh, in the Q. J. G. S., vol. xxviii., p. 388, (1872); and Mr. Darbishire, in the Geol. Mag., vol. ii., p. 298 ; as is also the Moel Tryfan list.

I have also to thank Prof. T. Rupert Jones, F.R.S., for revising the list of Foraminifera. p. 98.

128

APPENDIX.

SPECIES OCCURRING IN THE LANCASHIRE GLACIAL DRIFT. Names of the Species are omitted which (though occurring in the Glacial Deposits of adjacent districts) are not met with in the Glacial Deposits of Lancashire.	Northern Species.	Southern Species.	Lower Boulder Clay. 1. Preston. 2. Blackpool. 3. Scarisbrick.	Liverpool District - 1. Mr. Morton. 2. Mr. M. Reade. 3. Mr. I. Roberts. Linacre.	Blackpool { 1. Rev. Thornber. 2. Mr. Binney. 3. Mr. Darbishire. 4. Mr. De Rance.	Middle Sands and Gravels. 1. Garstang. 2. Preston. 3. Ribble Valley.	1. Chorley. 2. Leyland. 3. „ (Miss Ffarington).	Upper Boulder Clay. 1. Garstang. 2. Blackpool. 3. Preston.
MOLLUSCA.								
1. Ostrea edulis, *Linn.* -	×	×	2.	1. 2. 3.	3.	2. 3.	3.	2. 3.
2. Pecten opercularis, *Linn.*	×	×		2. 3.	.	2. 3.	3.	2.
3. Mytilus edulis, *Linn.* -	×	×	1. 2.			2.	1.	3.
4. „ modiolus, *Linn.* -	×			2.			3.	
5. Nucula, sp. -	.	.	.	.	4.	2.	2.	.
6. Leda pernula, *Müller* -	.	.		2.			.	
7. Pectunculus glycimeris, *Linn.*	<	<		2.		2. 3.	2. 3.	
8. Cardium aculeatum, *Linn.*	×	×			3.		.	
9. „ edule, *Linn.* -	×	×	1. 2. 3.	1. 2.	4.	1. 2. 3.	1. 2. 3.	1. 2. 3.
10. „ echinatum, *Linn.*	×	×		2. 3.		.	1. 3.	1. 2. 3.
11. „ fasciatum, *Mont.*	×	×						
12. „ Norvegicum, *Spengler*	×						1. 2. 3.	
13. „ tuberculatum, *Linn.* -	×	×		2.		1. 2. 3.	1. 2. 3.	2. 3.
14. Cyprina Islandica, *Linn.*	∨	.		1. 2. 3.	3. 4.	1. 2. 3.	1. 2. 3.	
15. Astarte borealis, *Chemnitz* (=A. arctica, *Gray.*)	×	.		2.		1. 2. 3.	1. 2. 3.	1. 3.
16. „ crebricostata, *Forbes*	.	.						
17. „ elliptica, *Brown*	.	.		2.		3.	3.	
18. „ compressa, *Montagu*	×	.		2.				
19. „ sulcata, *Da Costa*	×	×	-	2.	3. 4.		2. 3.	
20. Venus casina, *Linn.* -	×	×					2. 3.	
21. „ chione, *Linn.* -	×	×		2.	4.	2.	2. 3.	2.
22. „ exoleta, *Linn.* -	×	×		2.		2.	2. 3.	
23. „ gallina (= striatula), *Don*	×	×		2			2. 3.	
24. „ lincta, *Pult.* -	×	×		2.		2.		
25. Tapes virginius, *Linn.* -	×	×		2.		2.		
26. Tellina Balthica, *Linn.* - (= T. solidula, *Pult.*)	×	×	1. 2. 3.		4.	1. 2. 3.	2. 3.	1. 2. 3.
27. „ pusilla, *Phillipi* - (= T. calcarea, *Chemnitz.* = T. proxima, *Brown.*)	×	×						
28. Psammobia Ferröensis, *Chemn.*	×	×	2.	2.	4.	2.	2. 3.	2.
29. Donax vittatus, *Da Costa* (= D. anatinus, *Linn.*)	×	×	.	2.		2.	.	
30. Mactra glauca, *Gmelin.* -	.	.						
31. „ solida, *Linn.* -	×	×		2.		2.	2. 3.	
31a. „ var. elliptica, *Brown*	×	×						
32. „ stultorum, *Penn.*	×	×						
33. „ subtruncata, *Da Costa*	×	×						
34. Lutraria elliptica, *Lam.* -	×	×				2. 3.	3.	
35. Scrobicularia piperata, *Gmelin* (= S. plana, *Da Costa.*)	×	×		2.				
36. Solen ensis, *Linn.*	×	×	.					
37. „ siliqua, *Linn.*	×	×						
38. Corbula gibba, *Olivi* -	×	×						
39. Mya arenaria, *Linn.* -	×	×		2.				
40. „ truncata, *Linn.* -	×	×		2.	4.			
41. Panopæa plicata, *Mort.* -	×	×						
42. Saxicava rugosa, *Linn.* -	×	×	1. 2.	2.				
43. „ Norvegica, *Spengl.* -	×	.		2.				

APPENDIX.

	CRAG. (Prof. Prestwich, F.R.S.)				SCOTLAND. (Prof. Geikie, F.R.S.)				YORKSHIRE. (Mr. S. V. Wood, jun.)			CHESHIRE.			N. WALES.				
	Norwich Crag.	Red Crag.	Coralline Crag.	Belgium Crag.	Boulder Clay.	Stratfield Beds.	Clyde Beds.	Brick Earth.	Lower Glacial.	Middle Glacial.	Upper Glacial (Bridlington Crag).	1. Birkenhead } Mr. M. Reade. 2. R. Dee 3. " Mr. R. Mackintosh.	Warrington.	Macclesfield:— 1. Older Deposit } Mr. Darbishire. 2. Newer " 3. Mr. Prestwich's Patch.	Coast of Flintshire, Denbighshire, and Carnarvonshire — 4. Mr. De Rance.	Moel Tryfan, Carnarvonshire. } Mr. Darbishire.	1. Shirdley Hill Sand, and 2. Presall Shingle.	Sand Dunes of Lancashire Coast.	Recent Lancashire Sea Coast, Crosby, Formby, Southport, Lytham, Blackpool.
1	×	×	.	.	×	×	.	.	.	×	.	.	.	1.	4.	V.R.	1.2.	×	×
2	×	×	×	×	×	×	.	.	.	×	.	.	×	1.	4.	R.	1.2.	×	×
3	×	×	×	×	×	.	×	.	×	×	×	1.	.	1.3.	4.	F.	1.2.	×	×
4	×	×	×	×	×	.	×	.	.	.	×	.	.	.	.	F.	.	×	×
5	.	.	.	.	.	.	.	.	.	.	.	.	.	.	.	.	.	.	.
6	.	.	.	.	×	×	.	.	.	.	×	3.	.	.	.	R.	.	.	.
7	×	×	×	×	.	.	.	.	.	×	J	.	.	1.	.	V.R.	.	.	.
8	.	.	.	.	.	×	.	.	.	.	.	.	.	?	.	.	.	.	.
9	×	×	×	×	×	.	×	.	×	×	×	2.3.	.	1.2.3.	4.	C.	1.2.	×	×
10	×	×	×	×	×	.	×	.	×	×	×	2.3.	.	1.	.	R.	1.2.	×	×
11	×	×	×	×	×	.	×	.	.	×	.	.	.	1.	4.	F.	.	.	×
12	.	×	.	.	×	×	.	.	.	×	.	.	.	1.	4.	E.	.	.	×
13	.	.	.	.	.	.	.	.	.	×	.	.	.	1.	4.	.	.	.	×
14	×	×	×	×	×	×	.	.	×	×	×	.	.	1.	.	C.	.	×	×
15	×	.	.	.	×	×	×	.	×	×	×	1.2.	×	.	4.	C.	2.	×	×
16	.	.	.	.	.	×	.	.	.	×	×	.	.	1.	.	V.R.	.	.	.
17	×	.	.	.	×	×	×	.	×	×	×	.	×?	1.	4.	F.	.	.	.
18	×	×	.	.	×	×	×	.	×	×	×	.	×?	.	4.	C.	.	.	.
19	×	×	.	.	.	×	.	×	.	×	×	3.	×	.	.	C.	.	.	.
20	.	×	×	×	.	.	.	.	.	.	.	.	.	.	.	V.R.	.	.	.
21	.	×	×	×	.	.	.	.	.	.	.	.	.	.	.	.	.	×	×
22	.	×	×	×	.	.	.	.	.	.	.	.	.	.	.	V.R.	.	×	.
23	.	.	.	×	.	×	.	.	.	.	.	.	.	.	.	V.R.	.	.	×
24	×	×	×	×	×	.	.	.	.	.	.	.	.	.	.	.	.	.	.
25	×	×	×	×	.	×	.	.	.	.	.	.	.	.	.	V.R.	.	.	.
26	×	.	.	.	×	×	.	.	×	×	×	1.2.	×	.	4.	R.	1.2.	×	×
27	.	.	.	.	×	×	×	.	.	.	J	.	.	.	.	.	.	.	.
28	.	.	.	.	.	×	.	.	.	.	.	2.	×	.	.	.	.	.	×
29	×	×	.	.	.	×	.	.	×	.	J	.	.	.	.	V.R.	.	×	×
30	×	×	.	×	.	×	.	.	.	.	J	3.	×	.	.	.	1.2.	×	×
31	×	×	×	×	.	×	.	.	.	?	J	.	.	.	.	R.	.	×	×
31a	×	×	×	×	.	×	.	.	.	.	.	.	.	.	.	V.R.	.	×	×
32	×	×	.	.	.	×	.	.	.	×	.	.	.	.	.	.	.	×	×
33	×	.	.	.	.	×	.	.	.	×	.	.	.	.	.	.	.	×	×
34	.	×	×	×	.	×	.	.	.	.	.	.	.	.	.	.	.	×	×
35	.	.	.	.	.	.	×	×	×	×	.	2.3.	.	.	.	.	.	×	×
36	.	×	×	×	.	.	×	.	.	.	.	.	.	.	.	.	.	×	×
37	×	×	.	×	.	.	.	.	.	.	.	.	.	.	.	.	.	×	×
38	×	×	×	×	.	.	.	.	×	×	J	.	.	.	.	V.R.	.	.	.
39	×	×	.	×	×	×	.	.	×	×	×	1.2.	×	1.	4.	E.	.	×	×
40	×	×	×	×	.	×	.	.	×	?	×	1.2.	×	1.2	.	.	.	×	×
41	.	.	.	×	.	.	.	.	.	.	.	.	.	.	.	.	.	×	×
42	×	×	×	×	.	×	.	.	×	×	×	.	.	.	.	R.	.	×	×
43	.	.	.	.	.	×	.	.	.	.	.	.	.	.	.	.	.	.	.

SPECIES OCCURRING N THE LANCASHIRE GLACIAL DRIFT. Names of the Species are omitted which (though occurring in the Glacial Deposits of adjacent districts) are not met with in the Glacial Deposits of Lancashire.	Northern Species.	Southern Species.	LANCASHIRE.					
			Lower Boulder Clay.		Middle Sands and Gravels.			Upper Boulder Clay.
			1. Preston. 2. Blackpool. 3. Scarisbrick.	Liverpool 1. Mr. Morton. District. 2. Mr. M. Reade. Linacre - 3. Mr. I. Roberts.	Blackpool {1. Rev. Thornber. 2. Mr. Binney. 3. Mr. Darbishire. 4. Mr. De Rance.	1. Garstang. 2. Preston. 3. Ribble Valley.	1. Chorley. 2. Leyland. 3. (Miss Ffarington).	1. Garstang. 2. Blackpool. 3. Preston.
44. Pholas candida, *Linn.*	×	×						
45. „ crispata, *Linn.*	×	×	1. 2.	2.				2.
46. „ dactylus, *Linn.*	×	×						•
47. Dentalium Abyssorum, *Sars.*	×	×						
48. „ entalis, *Linn.* = D. striatum, *J. Smith*	×	×	2.	2.		1. 2. 3.		2.
49. „ tarentinum, *Lam.*	×	×		2.				
50. Patella vulgata, *Linn.*	×	×			2. 3. 4.			
51. Fissurella reticulata, *Don*								
52. Trochus cinerarius, *Linn.*	×	×			4.			
53. Littorina rudis, *Don*	×	×			2. 3. 4.			2.
54. „ obtusata, *Linn.* (= litoralis.)	×	×			2. 3. 4.			•
55. „ litorea, *Linn.*	×	?		1. 2. 3.	4.	1. 2. 3.		•
56. Lacuna vincta, *Mont.*								
57. Cæcum mammillatum, *Wood.*								
58. Turritella terebra, *Linn.*			1. 2. 3.	1. 2. 3.	4.	1. 2. 3.		2.`
59. Scalaria Grœnlandica								
60. Natica Alderi, *Fl.* (= nitida, *Don.*)								
61. „ catena, *Da Costa* (= monilifera, *F. & H.*)	×	×			3.	1. 3.		
62. „ clausa, *Brod.*	×	×						
63. „ Grœnlandica, *Beck.*	×			2.				
64. „ heliocides, *Johns.*	×							
65. Aporrhais pes-pelicani, *Linn.*	×	×		2. 3.	2. 3. 4.	3.	1. 2.	
66. Trichotropis borealis, *Brod.*	×	^						
67. Purpura lapillus, *Linn.*	×	×		1. 2. 3.	3. 4.	1. 2. 3.	1. 2.	2.
68. Buccinum undatum, *Linn.*	×		2.	1. 2. 3.	2. 3. 4.	2. 3.	1. 2.	
69. Murex erinaceus, *Linn.*	×	×	2.	1. 2.	2. 3. 4.	3.		
70. Trophon clathratus, *Linn.* (= scalariformis, *Gld.*)					3. 4.	2. 3.	1. 2.	
71. „ var. Gunneri, *Loven.*								
72. „ truncatus, *Strom.* (= T. Bamffius, *Mont.*)	×	×		2. 3.				
73. „ Barvicensis, *Johnstone*	×							
74. Fusus antiquus, *Linn.*	×	×		2.	3. 4.	1. 2. 3.	1. 2.	
75. „ ear. contrarius, *Linn.*	×							
76. „ gracilis, *Loven.*	×							
77. „ Islandicus, *Chem.*	×			3.		3.		
78. „ propinquus, *Alder.*	×							
79. Nassa reticulata, *Linn.*	×	×	2.	1. 2. 3.	2. 3. 4.	1. 2. 3.	1. 2.	
80. „ incrassata, *Müller*	×	×	2.	1. 2.				
81. Pleurotoma rufa, *Mont.*	×			2. 3.	3.			
82. „ nebula, *Mont.*					3.			
83. „ pyramidalis, *Strom.*					3.			
84. „ turricula, *Mont.*	×			2.	3.			
85. Cypræa Europæa, *Mont.*					3.			
86. Balanus Hameri, *Asc.*								
87. „ crenatus, *Brug.*								
88. „ porcatus, *Da Costa*								
89. Cliona, sp. in bivalves					3. 4.			
90. „ sp. in Turritellæ					3. 4.			

	CRAG. Prof. Prestwich, F.R.S.				SCOTLAND. Prof. Geikie, F.R.S.				YORKSHIRE. Mr. S. V. Wood, jun.			CHESHIRE.			N. WALES.				
	Norwich Crag.	Red Crag.	Coralline Crag.	Belgium Crag.	Boulder Clay.	Stratfield Beds.	Clyde Beds.	Brick Earth.	Lower Glacial.	Middle Glacial.	Upper Glacial (Bridlington Crag).	1. Birkenhead } Mr. M. Reade. 2. R. Dee 3. Mr. R. Mackintosh.	Warrington.	Macclesfield:— 1. Older Deposit } Mr. Darbishire. 2. Newer 3. Mr. Prestwich's Patch.	4. Mr. De Rance. Coast of Flintshire, Denbighshire, and Carnarvonshire.	Moel Tryfan, Carnarvonshire. } Mr. Darbishire.	1. Shirdley Hill Sand, and 2. Pressall Shingle.	Sand Dunes of Lancashire Coast.	Recent Lancashire Sea Coast, Crosby, Formby, Southport, Lytham, Blackpool.
44	·	·	·	·	·	·	×	·	·	·	·	·	·	2.	·	·	·	×	×
45	×	·	×	·	·	×	·	·	×	×	×	·	·	1.	·	·	·	×	×
46	·	×	×	·	·	×	·	·	·	·	·	·	·	·	·	·	·	·	·
47	·	·	·	·	×	×	·	·	·	·	×	·	·	1.	·	·	·	·	·
48	·	·	·	·	×	×	·	·	·	×	J	·	×	1.	·	V.R.	·	×	×
49	·	·	·	·	·	·	·	·	·	×	×	·	·	·	·	·	·	·	·
50	×	×	·	·	×	×	×	·	·	·	·	·	·	2.	·	·	·	·	·
51	·	·	·	·	·	×	×	·	·	·	·	·	·	2.	·	V.R.	·	·	·
52	·	×	·	·	·	×	·	×	·	·	·	·	·	2.	4.	V.R.	·	·	·
53	×	·	·	·	·	×	×	·	×	×	J	·	·	2.	·	V.R.	·	×	·
54	·	·	·	·	·	×	×	·	·	·	·	·	·	2.	·	·	·	·	·
55	×	×	·	·	·	×	×	·	×	×	×	3.	×	2.	·	F.	·	×	×
56	·	·	·	·	·	×	·	·	·	·	·	·	·	·	·	V.R.	·	·	·
57	·	×	×	·	·	·	·	·	·	·	·	·	·	·	·	·	·	·	·
58	×	×	·	·	×	×	×	×	·	×	×	1. 2. 3.	×	1. 2. 3.	4.	A.	1.2	×	×
59	×	×	·	×	·	×	·	·	·	·	J	·	·	·	·	·	·	·	·
60	·	×	·	·	×	×	·	·	·	·	·	·	·	2.	·	·	·	·	·
61	×	×	·	×	·	×	·	·	×	×	·	·	·	1.	4.	V.R.	·	×	×
62	×	×	·	·	·	×	×	·	×	×	×	·	·	·	·	V.R.	·	·	·
63	×	×	·	·	·	×	·	·	·	·	×	·	·	·	·	·	·	·	·
64	·	·	·	·	·	·	·	·	·	·	J	·	·	·	·	·	·	·	·
65	×	×	×	×	×	×	·	·	·	·	·	·	·	1.	·	V.R.	·	×	×
66	·	·	·	·	·	A	·	·	·	·	×	·	·	·	·	V.R.	·	·	·
67	×	×	·	×	×	×	×	×	×	×	×	2. 3.	×	1.	·	F.	·	×	×
68	×	×	×	×	×	×	·	·	×	×	·	3.	×	1.	4.	·	·	×	×
69	×	×	×	×	·	×	·	·	·	·	·	·	·	1. 2.	·	B.	·	×	×
70	×	×	·	×	×	×	·	·	·	·	×	·	·	1.	·	F.	·	·	·
71	×	·	·	·	·	·	·	·	·	·	×	·	·	·	·	F.	·	·	·
72	·	·	·	·	·	·	×	·	·	·	×	·	·	·	·	·	·	×	×
73	·	×	·	·	·	×	·	·	·	·	·	·	·	·	·	V.R.	·	·	·
74	×	×	·	×	·	×	·	·	·	·	×	·	×	1.	4.	C.	·	×	×
75	·	·	·	·	·	·	·	·	·	·	×	·	·	1.	·	·	·	×	·
76	×	×	×	×	·	×	·	·	·	·	×	·	·	·	·	V.R.	·	×	·
77	·	·	·	·	·	×	·	·	·	·	×	·	·	·	·	·	·	·	·
78	·	·	·	·	·	·	·	·	·	·	×	·	·	·	·	·	·	·	·
79	·	·	·	·	·	·	·	·	·	·	·	3.	×	1.	4.	R.	·	×	×
80	×	×	×	×	×	×	·	·	·	×	×	·	·	1.	·	V.R.	·	×	×
81	×	×	·	·	·	×	·	·	·	·	·	·	·	1.	·	V.R.	\	·	·
82	·	·	·	·	×	×	·	·	·	·	·	·	·	·	·	V.R.	·	·	·
83	×	×	·	·	·	×	·	·	·	×	×	·	·	1.	·	V.R.	·	·	·
84	×	×	·	×	·	·	·	·	·	×	×	·	·	1.	·	F.	·	·	·
85	×	×	×	×	·	·	·	·	·	·	·	·	·	1.	·	·	·	·	·
86	·	·	·	·	·	×	×	·	·	·	·	·	·	1.	·	·	·	·	·
87	·	·	·	·	·	×	·	·	·	·	·	·	·	·	·	·	·	·	·
88	·	·	·	·	×	·	×	·	·	·	·	·	·	·	·	·	·	·	·
89	·	·	·	·	·	·	·	·	·	·	·	·	·	1.	·	·	·	·	·
90	·	·	·	·	·	·	·	·	·	·	·	·	·	1.	·	V.R.	·	·	·

—	Lower Boulder Clay.	Middle Sands.	Upper Boulder Clay.	West Lancashire Estuarine Clay.	Recent on Lancashire Coast, Professor Williamson.
RHIZOPODA.					
FORAMINIFERA.					
Biloculina ringens, *Lamk.* -	×	.	×		
Quinqueloculina seminulum, *Linn.*	×	.	×		
„ Ferussaci, *D'Orb.* -	×	.	×		
Lagena sulcata, *W. & J.* -	×	.	×		
„ globosa, *Mont.* -	×	.	×		
„ marginata, *Mont.* -	×	.	×		
„ squamosa, *Mont.* -	×	.	×		
„ vulgaris *var.* striata -	.	.	×		
Nodosaria radicula, *Linn.* -	×	.	.	.	×
„ pyrula, *D'Orb.* -	×	.	.	.	×
Nonionina asterizans, *F. & M.* -	×				
„ depressula, *W. & J.* -	×	.	×		
„ faba, *F. & M.* -	.	.	.	×	
„ scapha, *F. & M.* -	.	.	.	×	
„ umbilicatula, *Will.* -	.	.	.	×	×
Polystomella crispa, *Linn.* -	×	.	×		
„ striato-punctata, *F. & M.* -	×	.	×	×	×
Planorbulina vulgaris, *D'Orb.* -	.	.	.	×	
Polymorphina compressa, *D'Orb.*	×	.	.	.	×
„ lactea, *W. & J.* -	.	.	×	×	×
Bulimina pupoides, *D'Orb.*	×	.	×		
Discorbina rosacea, *D'Orb.* -	×	.	×	×	
„ mammilla, *Will.*	.	.	.	×	
„ vesicularis, *D'Orb.* -	.	.	.		
Truncatulina lobulata, *Walker* -	×	.	×		
Rotalia Beccarii, *Linn.* -	×	.	×		
CRUSTACEA.					
(OSTRACODA.)					
Cythere villosa, *Sars* -	.	.	×		
„ antiquata, *Baird* -	.	.	×		
„ tuberculata, *Sars* -	.	.	×		
„ Jonesii, *Baird* -	.	.	×		
„ dunelmensis, *Norman* -	.	.	×		
„ tenera, *Brady* -	.	.	×		
Cytheridea punctillata, *Brady* -	.	.	×		
Cytheropteron nodosum -	.	.	×		
Eucythere argus -	.	.	×		
Loxoconcha tamarindus, *Jones*	.	.	×		
„ impressa	.	.	×		
Paradoxostoma arcuatum, *Brady* -	.	.	×		
„ flexuosum, *Brady* -	.	.	×		
„ ensiforme, *Brady* -	.	.	×		

Of 60 species of Mollusca occurring in the Lancashire Glacial Drift—

- 35 species occur in the Norwich Clay.
- 36 „ „ Red Clay.
- 18 „ „ Coralline Clay.
- 27 „ „ Belgium Clay.
- 28 „ „ Scotch Boulder Clay
- 39 „ „ „ Stratfield Beds.
- 17 „ „ „ Clyde Beds.
- 16 „ „ Yorkshire Lower Glacial.
- 26 „ „ Yorkshire Middle Glacial.
- 31 „ „ Upper Glacial.
- 38 „ „ Welsh Moel Tryfan Beds.

INDEX OF PLACES AND PERSONS.

References which do not strictly relate to South and West Lancashire are printed in brackets.—The figures refer to the pages.

LIST OF GEOLOGICAL MAPS, SECTIONS, AND PUBLICATIONS OF THE GEOLOGICAL SURVEY OF THE UNITED KINGDOM.

THE Maps are those of the Ordnance Survey, geologically coloured by the Geological Survey of Great Britain and Ireland under the Superintendence of Prof. A. C. RAMSAY, LL.D., F.R.S., &c., Director-General. The various Formations are traced and coloured in all their Subdivisions.

ENGLAND AND WALES.—(Scale one-inch to a mile.)

Maps, Nos. 3 to 41, 44, 64, price 8s. 6d. each, with the exceptions of 2, 10, 21, 24, 27, 28, 29, 32, 38, 39. 58, 4s. each. Sheets divided into four quarters, 42, 43, 45, 46, 52, 53, 54, 55, 56, 57, (59 N E, SE), 60, 61, 62, 63, 71, 72, 73, 74, 75, (76 N S), (77 N), 78, 79, 80, 81, 82, 88, 80, 105 (87 NE, SE, SW), (90 SE, NE), (91 SW, NW, 93 SW, NW), (98 NE, SE, SW), (109 SE). Price 3s. Except (57 NW), 76 (N), (77 NE). Price 1s. 6d.

SCOTLAND.—Maps 2, 3, 7, 14, 15, 22, 24, 31, 32, 33, 34, 40, 41, 6s. each. Maps 1, 13, 4s.

IRELAND.—Maps 21, 23, 29, 36, 37, 47, 48, 49, 50, 59, 60, 61, 70, 71, 72, 74, 75, 78 to 93, and from 95 to 205, price 3s. each, with the exception of 38, 50 72, 82, 122, 131, 140, 150, 159, 160, 170, 180, 181, 182, 189, 190, 196, 197, 202, 203, 204, 205, price 1s. 6d. each.

HORIZONTAL SECTIONS, *Illustrative of the Geological Maps.*
1 to 120, England, price 5s. each. 1 to 5, Scotland, price 5s. each. 1 to 24, Ireland, price 5s. each.

VERTICAL SECTIONS, *Illustrative of Horizontal Sections and Maps.*
1 to 62, England, price 3s. 6d. each. 1, Ireland, price 3s. 6d. 1 to 6, Scotland, price 3s. 6d.

Memoirs of the Geological Survey and of the Museum of Practical Geology.

REPORT on CORNWALL, DEVON, and WEST SOMERSET. By Sir H. T. DE LA BECHE, F.R.S., &c. 8vo. 14s.
FIGURES and DESCRIPTIONS of the PALÆOZOIC FOSSILS in the above Counties. By PROFESSOR PHILLIPS, F.R.S. 8vo. (Out of print.)
THE MEMOIRS of the GEOLOGICAL SURVEY of GREAT BRITAIN, and of the MUSEUM of ECONOMIC GEOLOGY of LONDON. 8vo. Vol. I. 21s.; Vol. II. (in 2 Parts), 42s.
The GEOLOGY of NORTH WALES. By PROFESSOR RAMSAY, LL.D. With an Appendix, by J. W. SALTER, A.L.S. Price 13s. boards. (Vol. III., Memoirs, &c.) (Out of print.)
The GEOLOGY of the LONDON BASIN. Part I. The Chalk and the Eocene Beds of the Southern and Western Tracks. By W. WHITAKER, B.A. (Parts by H. W. BRISTOW, F.R.S., and T. McK. HUGHES, M.A.) Price 13s. boards. Vol. IV.
BRITISH ORGANIC REMAINS. Decades I. to XIII., with 10 Plates each. MONOGRAPH No. 1. On the Genus Pterygotus. By PROFESSOR HUXLEY, F.R.S., and J. W. SALTER, F.G.S. Royal 4to. 4s. 6d.: or royal 8vo. 2s. 6d. each Decade. MONOGRAPH No. 2. On the Structure of Belemnitidae. By PROFESSOR HUXLEY, LL.D., &c. 2s. 6d.
RECORDS of the SCHOOL OF MINES and of SCIENCE applied to the ARTS. Vol. I., in four Parts.
CATALOGUE of SPECIMENS in the Museum of Practical Geology, illustrative of the Composition and Manufacture of British Pottery and Porcelain. By Sir HENRY DE LA BECHE, and TRENHAM REEKS, Curator. 8vo. 155 woodcuts. 2nd Edition, by TRENHAM REEKS and F. W. RUDLER. Price 1s. 6d. in wrapper; 2s. in boards.
A DESCRIPTIVE GUIDE to the MUSEUM of PRACTICAL GEOLOGY, with Notices of the Geological Survey of the United Kingdom, the School of Mines, and the Mining Record Office. By ROBERT HUNT, F.R.S., and F. W. RUDLER. Price 6d. (3rd Edition.)
A DESCRIPTIVE CATALOGUE of the ROCK SPECIMENS in the MUSEUM of PRACTICAL GEOLOGY. By A. C. RAMSAY, F.R.S., H. W. BRISTOW, F.R.S., H. BAUERMAN, and A. GEIKIE, F.G.S. Price 1s. (3rd Edit.)
On the TERTIARY FLUVIO-MARINE FORMATION of the ISLE OF WIGHT. By EDWARD FORBES, F.R.S. Illustrated with a Map and Plates of Fossils, Sections, &c. Price 5s.
On the GEOLOGY of the COUNTRY around CHELTENHAM. Illustrating Sheet 44. By E. HULL, A.B. Price 2s. 6d.
On the GEOLOGY of PARTS of WILTSHIRE and GLOUCESTERSHIRE (Sheet 34). By A. C. RAMSAY, F.R.S., F.G.S., W. T. AVELINE, F.G.S., and EDWARD HULL, B.A., F.G.S. Price 8d.
On the GEOLOGY of the SOUTH STAFFORDSHIRE COAL-FIELD. By J. B. JUKES, M.A., F.R.S. (3rd Edit.) 3s. 6d.
On the GEOLOGY of the WARWICKSHIRE COAL-FIELD. By H. H. HOWELL, F.G.S. 1s. 6d.
On the GEOLOGY of the COUNTRY around WOODSTOCK. Illustrating Sheet 45 S.W. By E. HULL, A.B. 1s.
On the GEOLOGY of the COUNTRY around PRESCOT, LANCASHIRE. By EDWARD HULL, A.B., F.G.S. (2nd Edition.) Illustrating Quarter Sheet, No. 80 N W. Price 8d.
On the GEOLOGY of PART of LEICESTERSHIRE. By W. TALBOT AVELINE, F.G.S., and H. H. HOWELL, F.G.S. Illustrating Quarter Sheet, No. 63 SE. Price 8d.
On the GEOLOGY of PART of NORTHAMPTONSHIRE. Illustrating Sheet 53 S.E. By W. T. AVELINE, F.G.S., and RICHARD TRENCH, B.A., F.G.S. Price 8d.
On the GEOLOGY of the ASHBY-DE-LA-ZOUCH COAL-FIELD. By EDWARD HULL, A.B., F.G.S. Illustrating Sheets 63 N.W. and 71 S.W. Price 3s.
On the GEOLOGY of PARTS of OXFORDSHIRE and BERKSHIRE. By E. HULL, A.B., and W. WHITAKER, B.A. Illustrating Sheet 18. Price 3s. (Out of print.)
On the GEOLOGY of PARTS of NORTHAMPTONSHIRE and WARWICKSHIRE. By W. T. AVELINE, F.G.S. Illustrating Quarter Sheet 53 NE. 8d.
On the GEOLOGY of the COUNTRY around WIGAN. By EDWARD HULL, A.B., F.G.S. Illustrating Sheet 80 S.W. on the One-inch Scale, and Sheets 84, 85, 92, 93, 100, 101 on the Six-inch Scale, Lancashire. (2nd Edition.) Price 1s.
On the GEOLOGY of TRINIDAD (West Indian Surveys). By G. P. WALL and J. G. SAWKINS, F.G.S., with Maps and Sections. 12s.
On the GEOLOGY of JAMAICA (West Indian Surveys). By J. G. SAWKINS, &c. With Maps & Sections. 8vo. 1871. Price 9s.
COUNTRY around ALTRINCHAM, CHESHIRE. By E. HULL, B.A. Illustrating 80 NE. Price 8d.
GEOLOGY of PARTS of NOTTINGHAMSHIRE and DERBYSHIRE. By W. T. AVELINE, F.G.S. Illustrating 82 SE. Price 8d.
COUNTRY around NOTTINGHAM. By W. T. AVELINE, F.G.S. Illustrating 71 NE. Price 8d.
The GEOLOGY of PARTS of NOTTINGHAMSHIRE, YORKSHIRE, and DERBYSHIRE. Illustrating Sheet 82 NE. By W. TALBOT AVELINE, F.G.S. Price 8d.
The GEOLOGY of SOUTH BERKSHIRE and NORTH HAMPSHIRE. Illustrating Sheet 12. By H. W. BRISTOW and W. WHITAKER. Price 3s.
The GEOLOGY of the ISLE OF WIGHT, from the WEALDEN FORMATION to the HEMPSTEAD BEDS inclusive, with Illustrations, and a List of the Fossils. Illustrating Sheet 10. By H. W. BRISTOW, F.R.S. Price 6s.
The GEOLOGY of EDINBURGH. Illustrating Sheet 32 (Scotland). Price 4s. By H. H. HOWELL and A. GEIKIE.
The GEOLOGY of the COUNTRY around BOLTON, LANCASHIRE. By E. HULL, B.A. Illustrating Sheet 89 S.E. Price 2s.
The GEOLOGY of BERWICK. Illustrating Sheet 34 (Scotland). 1 inch. By A. GEIKIE. Price 2s.
The GEOLOGY of the COUNTRY around OLDHAM. By E. HULL, B.A. Illustrating 88 SW. Price 2s.
The GEOLOGY of PARTS of MIDDLESEX, &c. Illustrating Sheet 7. By W. WHITAKER, B.A. Price 2s.
The GEOLOGY of the COUNTRY around BANBURY, WOODSTOCK and BUCKINGHAM. Sheet 45. By A. H. GREEN, M.A. Price 2s.
The GEOLOGY of the COUNTRY between FOLKESTONE and RYE. (Sheet 4.) By J. DREW, F.G.S. Price 1s.
The GEOLOGY of EAST LOTHIAN, &c. (Maps 30, 34, 41, Scot.) By H. H. HOWELL, F.G.S., A. GEIKIE, F.R.S., and J. YOUNG, M.D. With an Appendix on the Fossils by J. W. SALTER, A.L.S.
The GEOLOGY of part of the YORKSHIRE COAL-FIELD (88 S.E.) By A. H. GREEN, M.A. J. R. DAKYNS, M.A., and J. C. WARD, F.G.S. Oct. 1869. 1s.
The GEOLOGY of the COUNTRY between LIVERPOOL and SOUTHPORT (90 SE.) By C. E. DE RANCE, F.G.S. Oct. 1869. 3d.
The GEOLOGY of the COUNTRY around SOUTHPORT, LYTHAM, and SOUTH SHORE. By C. E. DE RANCE, F.G.S.
The GEOLOGY of the CARBONIFEROUS ROCKS NORTH and EAST of LEEDS, and the PERMIAN and TRIASSIC ROCKS about TADCASTER. By W. T. AVELINE, F.G.S., A. H. GREEN, M.A., J. R. DAKYNS, M.A., J. C. WARD, F.G.S., and R. RUSSELL. 6d.
The GEOLOGY of the NEIGHBOURHOOD of KIRKBY LONSDALE and KENDAL. By W. T. AVELINE, F.G.S., T. McK. HUGHES, M.A., F.S.A., and R. H. TIDDEMAN, B.A. Price 2s.
The GEOLOGY of the NEIGHBOURHOOD of KENDAL, WINDERMERE, SEDBERGH, and TEBAY. By W. T. AVELINE, F.G.S., and T. McK. HUGHES, M.A., F.S.A. Price 1s. 6d.
The GEOLOGY of the NEIGHBOURHOOD of LONDON. By W. WHITAKER, B.A. Price 1s.

THE COAL-FIELDS OF THE UNITED KINGDOM ARE ILLUSTRATED BY THE FOLLOWING PUBLISHED MAPS OF THE GEOLOGICAL SURVEY.

COAL-FIELDS OF UNITED KINGDOM.
(Illustrated by the following Maps.)

Anglesey, 78 (SW).
Bristol and Somerset, 19, 35.
Coalbrook Dale, 61 (NE & SE).
Clee Hill, 55 (NE, NW).
Denbighshire, 74 (NE & SE), 79 (SE).
Derby and Yorkshire, 71 (NW, NE, & SE), 82 (NW & SW),
    81 (NE), 87 (NE, SE), 88 (SE).
Flintshire, 79 (NE & SE).
Forest of Dean, 43 (SE & SW).
Forest of Wyre, 51 (SE), 55 (NE).
*Lancashire, 80 (NW), 81 (NW), 89 (SE,NE, NW, & SW), 88
    (SW). (For corresponding six-inch Maps, see detailed list.)
*Leicestershire, 71 (SW), 63 (NW).
Newcastle, 105 (NE & SE).
*North Staffordshire, 72 (NW), 72 (SW), 73 (NE), 80 (SE),
    81 (SW).
*South Staffordshire, 54 (NW), 62 (SW).
Shrewsbury, 60 (NE), 61 (NW & SW).
*South Wales, 36, 37, 38, 40, 41, 42 (SE, SW).
*Warwickshire, 62 (NE & SE), 63 (NW & SW), 54 (NE), 58
    (NW).
Yorkshire, 88, 87 (SW), 93 (SW).

SCOTLAND.
*Edinburgh, 32, 33.   *Haddington, 32, 33.
Fife and Kinross, 40, 41.

IRELAND.
*Kanturk, 174, 175.   *Castlecomer, 128, 137.
*Killenaule (Tipperary), 146.
(For Sections illustrating these Maps, see detailed list.)
* With descriptive Memoir.

GEOLOGICAL MAPS OF ENGLAND AND SCOTLAND.
Scale, six inches to a mile.
The Coalfields of Lancashire, Northumberland, Cumberland,
Westmorland, Durham, Yorkshire, Edinburghshire, Haddington, Fifeshire, Renfrewshire, Dunbartonshire, Dumfriesshire, Lanarkshire, Stirlingshire, and Ayrshire are
being surveyed on a scale of six inches to a mile. Price 6s.

Lancashire.
47. Clitheroe.
48. Colne, Twiston Moor.
49. Laneshaw Bridge. Horiz. Sect. 62, partly illustrates
55. Whalley.   this sheet.
56. Haggate.   6s.   Horiz. Sect. 62, 88.
57. Winewall.
61. Preston.
63. Balderstone, &c.
63. Accrington.
64. Burnley.
65. Stiperden Moor. 4s.
69. Layland.
70. Blackburn, &c.
71. Haslingden.
72. Oliviger, Bacup, &c.
75. Todmorden. 4s.
77. Chorley.
78. Bolton-le-Moors.
79. Entwistle.
80. Tottington.
81. Wardle. 6s.   .   -   Horiz. Sect. 66. Illustrates
84. Ormskirk, St. John's, &c.   the sheet.
85. Standish, &c.
86. Adlington, Horwick, &c. -   "   68.   "
87. Bolton-le-Moors -   •   "   67.   "
88. Bury Heywood   •   -   "   68.   "
89. Rochdale, &c.   "   66.   "
92. Bickerstaffe, Skelmersdale.
93. Wigan, Up Holland, &c. •   "   68.   "
94. West Houghton, Hindley,
     Atherton -   •   "   67.   "
95. Radcliffe, Peel Swinton, &c.   "   66-67. "
96. Middleton, Prestwich, &c.   "   68.   "
97. Oldham, &c.   •   "   64.   "
101. Knowsley, Rainford, &c.   "   67-68. "
102. Billinge, Ashton, &c. .   "   68.   "
102. Leigh, Lowton .   •   "   67.   "
103. Ashley, Eccles •   -   "   66.   "
104. Manchester, Salford, &c. -   "   64-65. "
105. Ashton-under-Lyne   "   64-65. "
106. Liverpool, &c. .   "   68.   "
107. Prescott, Huyton, &c.   "   68.   "
108. St. Helen's, Burton Wood   "   67.   "
109. Warwick, &c. 6s.
111. Cheedale, part of Stockport, &c.
112. Stockport, &c. 4s.
115. Part of Liverpool, &c. 4s.

Durham.
Scale, six inches to a mile.

Sheet.
1. Ryton. 4s.
2. Gateshead. 4s.
3. Jarrow. 4s.
4. S. Shields. 4s.
5. Greenside. 4s.
6. Winlaton.
7. Washington. 4s.
8. Sunderland.
9. ——— 4s.
10. Edmond Byers. 4s.
11. Ebchester.
12. Lantoydy.
13. Chester-le-Street. 6s.
14. Chester-le-Street.
16. Hunstanworth.
17. Waskerley.
18. Muggleswick.
19. Lanchester. 6s. Vertical
        Section, 39.
20. Hetton-le-Hole.
25. Wolsingham.
26. Brancepeth.
32. White Kirkley.
33. Hamsterley.
34. Sunny Brow.
41. Cockfield.
42. Bishop Auckland.

Northumberland.
Scale, six inches to a mile.

47. Coquet Island. 4s.
50. Druridge Bay, &c.
63. Netherwitton.
65. Newbiggin. 4s.
68. Bellingham.
60. Redesdale.
72. Bedlington.
73. Blyth. 4s.
77. Swinburn.
78. Lngoe. 6s.
80. Cramlington.
81. Earsdon.
84. Newborough.
85. Chollerton.
86. Matfen.
87. Heddon-on-the-Wall.
88. Long Benton.
89. Tynemouth.
92. Haltwhistle.
95. Corbridge.
96. Horsley. 4s.
97. Newcastle-on-Tyne. 4s.
98. Walker. 4s.
103. Allendale Town.
105. Newlands.
107. Allendale.
108. Blanchland.
109. Shotleyfield.
110. ———
111. Allenheads.

Yorkshire.
100. Limley.
184. Kelbrook.
201. Bingley.
204. Aberford.
216. Bradford.
217. Calverley.
218. Leeds.
219. Kippax.
231. Halifax.
232. Birstal.
233. East Ardsley.
234. Castleford.
246. Huddersfield.
260. Honley.
272. Holmfirth.
278. Penistone.
274. Barnsley.
275. Darfield.
276. Brodsworth.
281. Langsell.
282. Wortley.
283. Wath upon Dearne.
284. Conisborough.
287. Low Bradford.
288. Ecclesfield.
289. Rotherham.
290. Braithwell.
293. Hallam Moors. 4s.
295. Handsworth.
296. Laughton-eu-le-Morthen
209. ———
300. Harthill.

SCOTLAND.
Scale, six inches to a mile.

Edinburghshire.
2. Edinburgh, &c.
3. Portobello, Mussel-
     burgh, &c.
6. Gilmerton, Burdie
     House, &c.
7. Dalkeith, &c.
8. Preston Hall. 4s.
12. Penicuick, Coalfields of
        Lasswade, &c.
13. Temple, &c.
14. Pathead. 4s.
17. Brunston Colliery, &c.
18. Howgate.

Haddingtonshire.
Six inches to a mile.
8. Prestonpans, &c. Price 4s.
9. Tranent, Gladsmuir, &c. Price 6s.
13. Elphinstone, &c. Price 4s.
14. Ormiston, East Salton, &c.

Fifeshire.
Six inches to a mile.
24. Markinch, &c.
25. Scoonie, &c.
30. Beath, &c.
31. Auchterderran. 4s.
32. Dysart, &c.
33. Buckhaven.
35. Dunfermline.
36. Kinghorn.
37. Kinghorn. 4s.

Ayrshire.
Six inches to one mile.
19. Newmilns.
26. Glenbuck. 4s.
27. Monkton, &c.
28. Tarbolton, &c.
30. Aird's Moss.
31. Muirkirk. 4s.
33. Ayr, &c.
34. Coylton.
38. Grieve Hill.
40. Chiltree.
41. Dalleagier.
42. New Cumnock.
46. Dalmellington.
47. Benbeock.
50. Daily.
53. Glenmoat.

MINERAL STATISTICS
Embracing the produce of Tin, Copper, Lead, Silver, Zinc, Iron, Coals, and other Minerals. By ROBERT HUNT F.R.S.
Keeper of Mining Records. From 1853 to 1857, inclusive, 1s. 6d. each. 1858, Part I., 1s. 6d.; Part II., 5s. 1859, 1s. 6d.
1860, 8s. 6d., 1861, 2s.; and Appendix, 1s. 1862, 2s. 6d. 1863, 2s. 6d. 1864, 2s. 6d. 1865, 2s. 5d. 1866 to 1875, 2s. each.

THE IRON ORES OF GREAT BRITAIN.
Part I. The IRON ORES of the North and North Midland Counties of England (*Out of print*). Part II. The IRON
ORES of South Staffordshire. Price 1s. Part III. The IRON ORES of South Wales. Price 1s. 3d. Part IV. The
IRON ORES of the Shropshire Coal-field and of North Staffordshire. 1s. 3d.